PRAISE FOR

# please don't come back from the moon

"Much of the emotional heft of this witty and well-wrought novel lies in its ability to see the heroism of these damaged families struggling with gritty circumstances. Satisfyingly, some of these characters do better than survive; they—like Bakopoulos—pull off a triumph."—*O, The Oprah Magazine*

"Endearing…A tale that, despite the boys' empty longing, is full of hope." —*People*

"A combination of different ingredients, including raw literary talent and a sprinkling of magical realism, forms the kind of story that I suspect people will be talking about in book clubs and sharing with neighbors…Strange and beautiful…We watch [Michael Smolij] grow up over the span of a few hundred fast-turning and often brilliantly accomplished pages…A bildungsroman that is also clever, unusual and exciting." —*The Washington Post*

"Bakopoulos [has] considerable talent for capturing young-male ennui." —*Entertainment Weekly*

"Bakopoulos's debut shows him to be a steady hand at drawing subtle magic from simple means…[His] story excels at getting us to root for and against leaving, building up a tension that is not resolved until the story's heartbreaking climax (and lingers, even then)…*Please Don't Come Back from*

*the Moon* is sure-footed even as its characters stagger beneath the weight of their grief. Bakopoulos has rendered a world that is enchanting without being suspect... This is a novel sharp with the lime and oxide dust from which the invisible steps to the moon are poured. When you set it aside, it will continue to tug at you with its own quiet force."
—*Minneapolis Star-Tribune*

"Families, heartbreak, political and social comedy—there is little that Dean Bakopoulos doesn't grasp in an articulate, wittily perceptive, and soulful way, before he hands it back to the reader as literary art. *Please Don't Come Back from the Moon* is an original and brilliant first work of fiction."
—Lorrie Moore, author of *Birds of America*

"It would also be a mistake to pin down the precise meaning of this memorable novel's paternal exodus. Sociological statement? Personal nightmare? Bakopoulos is juggling both at once, and that gives *Please Don't Come Back from the Moon* much of its gentle, persuasive power." —*Los Angeles Times*

"[Bakopoulos's] surreal premise cuts to the quick of the desolation felt by deserted families." —*The Seattle Times*

"A beautifully smart, comic, and moving narrative about the fathers who disappear and the sons who take their place, *Please Don't Come Back from the Moon* is somehow both realistic and visionary. Its eerie take on the working lives of men and women is like nothing else I've ever read. In this novel Dean Bakopoulos shows us what keeps us on earth, and how, finally, those burdens also tempt us to float away; he also shows us how speculative fiction can co-exist with the grit of daily life. This is a wonderful book."

—Charles Baxter, author of *The Feast of Love*

"Melancholy, surreal and funny all at once."

—*Milwaukee Journal Sentinel*

"Richly imagined... *Please Don't Come Back from the Moon* is such a persuasive mixture of realism and the supernatural that you will want to believe in its fantastical premise just as much as the characters do."

—*Ruminator*

"Well-told... [Bakopoulos's] picture of confused, aimless young men in a forgotten corner of prosperous America is haunting."

—*The Economist*

"Haunting, sorrowful, and full of humanity, this beautiful novel is an elegy to loss itself. It will stay with me for a long time." —Ann Packer, author of *The Dive from Clausen's Pier*

"Intensely written... This is a graceful first book."

—*Hartford Courant*

"Moving... Bakopoulos knows about the hidden fears that motivate men to do unspeakable things, about the forces that drive them away from sad places like Maple Rock, Mich. But most of all, as a young author from a family much like the one in his book, he knows how to describe it all with genuine grace and simplicity... Part of the beauty in this book is that it can be read in so many different ways. It could be an allegory for the industrial decline of the northeastern United States. It could be a character study in abandonment or a street-spoken musing on the heart-breaking results of a fatherless post-adolescence. It is in fact all these things, which is quite an accomplishment, not only for a first novel, but any book at all." —*The Buffalo News*

"Captivating…Bakopoulos…keeps the reader enthralled."
—*The Capital Times* (Madison)

"An unflinching look at young adulthood, with enough optimism to give readers hope." —*Wisconsin State Journal*

"Marvelous…Bakopoulos doesn't make a single wrong move, seamlessly integrating the magic-realism elements into the rest. A dazzling debut that's both earthy and anguished as hope battles despair, with heartbreak always just below the surface." —*Kirkus Reviews* (starred)

"*Please Don't Come Back from the Moon* is a pitch-perfect debut by a fine young novelist. Dean Bakopoulos makes his indelible mark on the coming-of-age novel."
—Robert Olen Butler, Pulitzer Prize–winning author of *A Good Scent from a Strange Mountain*

"Soft-hearted yet tough-minded, this book somehow manages to fuse those opposites: yearning and scorn. In prose both careful and corrosive, Dean Bakopoulos invites the reader into a cityscape of dreams and harsh reality; we meet both a boy and generation lost and found."
—Nicholas Delbanco, author of *The Vagabonds*

please don't come back
from the moon

# DEAN BAKOPOULOS

# please don't come back
# from the moon

A HARVEST BOOK
HARCOURT, INC.
Orlando   Austin   New York   San Diego   Toronto   London

Requests for permission to make copies of any part of the work
should be mailed to the following address: Permissions Department,
Harcourt, Inc., 6277 Sea Harbor Drive, Orlando, Florida 32887-6777.

www.HarcourtBooks.com

The Library of Congress has cataloged the hardcover edition as follows:
Bakopoulos, Dean.
Please don't come back from the moon/Dean Bakopoulos.
p.  cm.
1. Single-parent families—Fiction.  2. Working class families—Fiction.
3. Fatherless families—Fiction.  4. Runaway husbands—Fiction.
5. Teenage boys—Fiction.  6. Michigan—Fiction.  I. Title.
PS3602.A593P56  2005
813'.6—dc22  2004011237
ISBN-13: 978-0-15-101135-3  ISBN-10: 0-15-101135-4
ISBN-13: 978-0-15-603167-7 (pbk.)  ISBN-10: 0-15-603167-1 (pbk.)

Text set in Janson MT
Designed by Linda Lockowitz

Printed in the United States of America

First  Harvest edition 2006
A  C  E  G  I  K  J  H  F  D  B

*For Amanda*
*and*
*in memory of Gregory Smolij (1916–2000)*

*We all drink from a leaking cup.*

—WILLIAM MATTHEWS, "Memory"

The title of this novel comes from a composition
by jazz great Charles Mingus.

# contents

## please don't come back
## from the moon

WHEN I WAS SIXTEEN, my father went to the moon. He was not the first man from Maple Rock to go there; he only followed the others on what seemed to be an inevitable trail. My uncle John was the first to leave.

The last time we saw John, we were in the parking lot of the Black Lantern, the bar on Warren Avenue where my father and his friends did their drinking. I was there with John's wife, my aunt Maria, and their son, Nick. It was the first day of June, just before midnight. I suppose I should remember if the moon was in the sky that night, but I honestly can't recall. The moon was not yet important. The bar owner, a big Greek named Spiros, had simply called my aunt and said she should come and take John home. Nick and I had been hanging around watching a movie, and she made us come with her.

When we got there, a half circle of men stood in the parking lot, all of them wearing grease-stained work shirts or rumpled dress shirts and loose ties. In the middle of the circle was John, standing with his shirt off in a weary boxer's stance. He was soaked in sweat and his face seemed to be darkened with bruises or dirt. He had not been home for a few nights.

My father, too, was there. Across the crowded lot, I saw him under a streetlamp, still wearing his tie, two or three pens in his pocket. He looked green in the weak and forced light, as if he might be sick.

Across from John was an enormous man, red-haired and fat-faced. He was wearing coveralls and his skin was dark with grime. He had a crescent wrench in his hand.

My uncle reached into his pocket, and then I must have turned to look at my father again, because the next thing I knew the crowd was screaming and laughing and John had on a pair of brass knuckles. The red-haired guy was on the pavement. He had wet himself. People started to scatter.

My uncle, in the chaos, disappeared. By the time the police came, he and his truck were gone.

"Does anybody know who the assailant was?" an officer yelled at the crowd, which was jeering at him.

Just as my aunt was reaching out to the officer, about to wave her hand and say something—I don't know what— a woman wearing a red halter top and black cutoffs came forward. She was barefoot, and some men whistled at her as she walked in front of the mob. She turned to the crowd and flipped them off, then turned back to the officer and said, "I know him. He's my boyfriend."

My aunt Maria walked away. We followed, because we had been waiting for a way to retreat without cowardice.

We were too young to join in the fight but too old to flee from it.

FOR A FEW WEEKS that summer, Nick and I positioned ourselves around the city and waited to run into my uncle. We went to the Black Lantern for lunch and sat for three hours, picking at a plate of nachos, looking at the face of every man who came into the bar. We sat outside the mall and drank frozen orange drinks most of the evening, watching girls and waiting for John to walk by eating an ice-cream cone, a shiner darkening each eye. We rode our bikes around the parking lots of motels, strip bars, and movie theaters, looking for his rusted Ford truck, the one with "Kozak's Sun & Snow: Quality Pool Maintenance, Lawn Care, and Snow Removal" hand lettered on each door.

Uncle John didn't come home. The speculation was that he'd gone off to hide somewhere, maybe Canada, perhaps because he thought he had killed the fat red-haired man in the parking lot. But he hadn't. That man simply got a row of stitches and went on his way.

It was a few weeks later that Walker Van Dyke's father left for a fishing trip, muttering something about killing the President, and didn't come back. J. J. Dempsey's dad, who had worked at the night-light factory, tried to rob the Ukrainian Credit Union the week after the factory went down. He left town directly afterward. Michael Pappas' father, Gus, owner of the recently bankrupted Gus's Coney Island Restaurant, left too.

Our neighbor and my father's best friend, a pipe fitter named Norm Nelson, whose son Jimmy was about my age, also vanished. His Corvette, which his wife had been trying to get him to sell since he'd been laid off, was found wrapped around a tree in Hines Park. Norm was nowhere to be found. There was no blood in the car—it was as if he'd vaporized out of the driver's seat and floated away just as the car wrecked. My father went over and showed Mrs. Nelson how to start the lawn mower, change a fuse, set the thermostat. I went with him, and Mrs. Nelson kept looking at me and laughing, saying, "Isn't it silly, Michael, that a grown woman like me doesn't know how to do a goddamn thing?"

By August, as Detroit stewed in a steamy layer of ash and grit so toxic that breathing made you feel stoned or delirious, many of my friends' fathers had disappeared, and as we played baseball or hung out at the bike racks near Wonderland Mall, all of a sudden, some kid would blurt out, "My dad's gone."

Some men left in the traditional fashion, slipping out at night, a note left behind. Sonya Stecko, my sometime girlfriend, said her father wrote a rambling sixteen-page letter before he left, in which he affirmed that he loved her, her mother, and her siblings, and in which he offered advice about marriage, money, and other subjects. It was as if he planned to miss the next thirty years of her life.

Some men left in broad daylight, giving goodbye kisses to their children in the driveway as their wives watched from behind the curtains, furious and brokenhearted. We watched Sharon Mills give her father a kiss goodbye as her mother threw pots and pans at his truck.

Peter Stolowitz's father owned Sol's Shoes on Six Mile Road. One day he left the store unattended, the front door propped wide open with a rock. Across the front windows he had lettered FREE SHOES in huge strokes of brown latex paint. He'd taken all the cash from the register and the safe and left a note: "I'm going to the moon," it said. "I took the cash."

Everyone in town went and helped themselves to a new pair of sneakers. We opened the boxes in the stockroom like it was Christmas, tossing lids aside, tearing out white tissue paper. Some people left their old shoes behind: a formidable pile of castaway footwear grew by the fire exit. Old men took home shiny wingtips, young women took high-heeled sandals. Nick and I helped ourselves to some Converse high-tops.

I was friends with Peter Stolowitz. I stood there in my new shoes as he walked into his father's store, holding his mother's arm. She wailed and he wept. "All that we worked for," his mother sobbed. "All that I worked for."

Peter glared at Nick and me. I pointed to the FREE SHOES sign and shrugged. The gleam of the white sneakers was too much to resist. I left with the shoes.

After that, other men began using Mr. Stolowitz's line. "We're going to the moon," they'd say, walking away from us. "I'll be on the moon," they'd say, their eyes staring through us.

ALL OF THE DISAPPEARED men were from Maple Rock, a working-class suburb tacked onto the southwest side of Detroit. Our little neighborhood was made up of Poles,

Ukrainians, Greeks, Italians, and other ethnic groups that came from Europe after the Second World War. The disappeared all knew each other, from church or the Black Lantern or bowling league. Our fathers did not golf. They did not wear pressed khakis or docksiders. They knew how to throw punches, and they did throw punches when a situation called for it.

Most of them had facial hair, beards, or at least a mustache. Most of them were not raised by English-speaking parents. Some of them had been in Vietnam, but few of them ever mentioned it. They liked to fish and hunt and left the city for long weekends in Michigan's vast and sandy north. Many of them were out of work.

The factories seemed to vaporize in Michigan, big factories, small factories. With the factories gone, engineers, sales reps, and marketing specialists lost their jobs too. Newly unemployed men hung around their children's schools, working as crossing guards and cafeteria monitors, chaperoning field trips and driving buses. I could remember Ronald Reagan appearing on television when I was very young, saying, "We face an economic calamity of epic proportions." By 1990, we still hadn't recovered in Maple Rock.

George Callas had been a factory rat. After he was downsized, he became our health teacher. Most of the time, Mr. Callas would talk about lifting weights (a good thing) or smoking (a bad thing). One time, he showed us a film about domestic violence that featured a lot of unfocused shots of women in shadows, looking out of rain-streaked windows while Roberta Flack sang "Killing Me Softly."

Mr. Callas, a darkly handsome, powerful-looking man, cried through the whole thing. When the film ended and the lights flipped on, he hid his face and told us we could leave early.

By far the most disturbing disappearance was that of our parish priest, Father Walter Gorski of St. John's Ukrainian Catholic Church. He was last seen late on a Saturday night, in his clerical collar and black smock, buying a carton of cigarettes, a case of beer, and three hot dogs at a 7-Eleven on Middlebelt Road.

We arrived for Mass the next morning, sat straight-backed in our pews, prayer books ready, the choir standing at attention, waiting for the altar doors to open, for the smell of incense to fill the sanctuary, for Father Walt to emerge in his robes.

We sat for fifteen minutes. No one moved. No one said anything. Finally, it was my aunt Maria who cried out, "No, God! Not him too!"

The next morning, the archbishop had the police looking for Father Walt. Cops skulked around the neighborhood looking for clues, but this was old hat for them already, looking for men who would not be found. A few cops had even disappeared that summer—Slim Kowalski, Jim Owesko, Big Teddy Lukens.

We heard that a clerk at 7-Eleven told police that Father Walt had offered him a ride.

"I don't even know where you're going, Father," the clerk had said.

"The moon," Father Walt had said, leaning in closer and winking. "You know, the moon."

AFTER FATHER WALT'S disappearance, we stopped going to church. Another priest was brought in to replace Walt, but my mother said she no longer wanted to sit through Mass every Sunday morning. If all these men could simply go free, could let go of their social and cultural obligations, then why couldn't she?

So instead, on Sunday mornings my mother would play her violin. My mother may have been the most educated and cultured woman in Maple Rock. Very few of the women in our neighborhood had been to college. My mother had a B.A., spoke three languages, had studied Russian literature and Latin and music. As a young woman, she had played in orchestras around the city. She had also played backup at Motown studios on some marginal albums of that era. One Sunday morning my mother played "Eleanor Rigby" and "The Great Pretender" while my father sat at the kitchen table, tearing apart the newspaper, tears streaming down his face.

My mother stopped playing and tilted her head at my dad.

"I need a job, Eva," he said. "I lost mine."

My father had been a draftsman, and his job was considered a good secure one.

My father said he'd been out of work for three weeks, and instead of going to work, he'd been spending time at the Black Lantern or the bowling alley or the mall.

The admission seemed odd from him, because he was a slight man, known more for reading science-fiction novels and watching nature documentaries on PBS than for drinking and bowling. My father was always more refined than his friends in Maple Rock. He did not waste his time drinking one-dollar taps, throwing a sixteen-pound ball down a wooden lane. He did not fit in well with his peers. Most of the time he looked the way I had seen him that night outside the bar—shaky and green, nervous, like he might be sick.

After my father made his announcement, he took his newspaper and went into the bathroom, and my mother began to play her violin again. I did not yet realize the tears in his eyes were not for what had happened to him but for what would eventually happen.

My little brother, Kolya, was in the room. He was nine years old, and his belly hung over his belt as if he were a man in his fifties. He looked very somber all the time and was not prone to talking. He stood, always, with his hands in his pockets.

I looked at him that morning to see if he had any idea what was going on, to see if the idea of unemployment and marital discord had any effect on his small brain. It did. His face was shadowed with sadness, and his eyes appeared so far-away and pensive that it seemed like he could see the future better than any of us adults. He stood, hands in pockets, looking at me, his blond hair sticking up like matted straw.

THE VERY LAST MEN LEFT, it seemed, out of a sense of duty. For a while, you'd see them in their garages on Saturdays, puttering with old car engines, dragging old toilets to the curb. Some of them still had work; their lives were following a plan and a purpose, and their horizons, if not bright, were certainly visible. Still, it was almost as if by hanging around, they were obstructing the natural order of things. They were like robins that wander stupidly through the snow in January.

And so they disappeared.

Later my mother said that all men have it in them, the capacity to leave behind, at a moment's notice, the world they know. My mother said that the last men left because they felt they had to, because they had to prove they were capable of acting on that buried impulse as well as any other man. My mother said she'd like to take me to a doctor and have my synapses reconfigured, lest someday the abandonment impulse would fire up inside of me and then I too would be gone.

Did I think my father was immune? My father was only human. How could he not leave?

My father was in the driveway when I came riding up on my bicycle. Nobody else was home. It was a Saturday, and my mother and brother were out shopping. He was loading a few duffel bags and a box into the trunk of his Oldsmobile. He wore a blue Oxford shirt tucked into faded jeans, and he was red-faced and puffy-eyed.

"Dad," I said, standing at the edge of the sidewalk, "where are you going?"

He stared back at me, squinting and tight-lipped, as if my head had suddenly burst into a ball of fire and the brilliant light was blinding him, as if my voice were the voice coming from a burning bush.

He drove away at a crawl. His speedometer must've not even reached ten miles per hour. Every few seconds I could see him glance in his rearview mirror and then avert his eyes quickly, as if my head were still behind him, burning and flaring up into the sky.

I stood alone in the driveway, throwing sycamore pellets down the wide, empty street. They sailed over the concrete and then bounced and landed, exploding into fluff like crashing birds.

When my mother and brother came home from shopping, I said nothing.

At dinner, my mother set out meat loaf, mashed potatoes, and gravy. She called my father. "Roman! Dinner!"

He didn't come. Kolya and I sat and watched each other, waiting. Kolya seemed to know the score. He didn't look worried or confused, just sad. My mother went to the fridge and took out a bowl of tossed salad, a bottle of Italian dressing, and a jar of pickles.

"Roman!" she called. "Dinner, honey!"

She went back to the counter, got the salt and pepper shakers. She went to the fridge and brought out some butter and some slices of Wonder bread; she called again. When he still didn't come she went to the fridge and got mustard and ketchup, some leftover macaroni and cheese, some lunch meat that she arranged on a paper plate. She called again. She brought to the table a jar of beets, some olives, a bottle of vinegar, and a jar of mayonnaise. "Roman, come on, honey! Dinner!"

Her voice trailed around the house and floated up the stairs where nobody was waiting to hear it. She brought out honey, marshmallows, and chocolate sauce.

She smiled. "For dessert," she said.

Kolya and I started eating. The meat loaf was getting cold.

Mom kept setting out food until everything in the fridge and freezer and pantry was on the table.

I sat between a bag of frozen corn and a box of crackers. Kolya shoved aside a can of sliced peaches and drank from his glass of milk. He put a bag of frozen peas on his head and we both laughed, and then felt bad for laughing.

My mother left the kitchen and opened the door to the garage where my dad's car was missing. She looked at me hard, for fifteen or twenty seconds, then I nodded, and she left the room instantly. Kolya started to put the food back where it belonged and I sat still and listened to our mother play her violin—"Norwegian Wood" and "I Am a Rock" and "Penny Lane."

BY SEPTEMBER, the heat began to give a little bit, and the summer wilted and yielded to a far-off breeze and jet streams and cold fronts. Broke and bored and without better options, my friends and I went back to school for our senior year. My mother was so pleased that I was going voluntarily that she took me to Wonderland Mall and bought me some new clothes with a Penney's charge card. In a pair of stiff, clean Levi's and new brown hiking boots, I wandered through the halls with Nick and Tom Slowinski, noting what was new and what was the same. Maple Rock High had launched a "Success for All" campaign ("Sex for All" became the too-easy nickname) which, as far as I could tell, meant only that we started school a week earlier than most other public schools, and that our hallways were decorated with a few murals urging us to REACH FOR THE STARS and DREAM THE IMPOSSIBLE DREAM.

A guidance counselor or someone must have decided that the school's color scheme could help relieve the gloom of economic recession and the widespread abdication of fatherhood, because during our sad and muggy summer break, somebody had painted the hallways and classrooms a deep canary yellow. Under the fluorescent lights, the new color scheme turned our faces muted and soft. We looked jaundiced and puffy, like alcoholics. With the buzz of the lights, the teachers' rolling monotones, and the smells of Lysol and stale coffee that pervaded every room, school felt more like a drying-out facility than a place of education. It was appropriate. Nick and Tom and I would drink beer in the janitor's room in the basement. Sometimes Big Tim the janitor, who was only a few years older than us, would come in and drink too. He said, "Why should I care if you guys go to class? Then you go to college and become the kind of assholes I have to spend the rest of my life working for."

ON A COLD AIMLESS autumn afternoon, Nick and I skipped class and drove out to a mall in Novi to get a gift at Victoria's Secret for one of his girlfriends. I was envious of him, having girlfriends at that level of sophistication.

At the mall, I made Nick go into the lingerie store alone and I went over to the drugstore to look at baseball cards. I wandered up and down the rows of toiletries and stopped near a display of razors. There stood a life-size cardboard cutout of a man with a towel wrapped around him, his face covered in shaving cream, the razor about to touch his cheek.

When Nick found me, I was smelling a bottle of Old Spice and tears were in my eyes. Nick asked me what I was doing. I shrugged, and smelled the Old Spice a little more. Nick stood there, a white gift bag stuffed with tissue paper in his right hand.

"Are you crying?" he said.

"No," I said, my nose still hovering over the bottle of Old Spice that smelled like my father.

"You're crying," he said.

I handed the bottle to Nick. "Try it."

He took the bottle and put it under his nose. He inhaled slowly and deeply, then he recapped the bottle and set it back on the shelf. He walked up and down the aisle, found a bottle of Brut, and inhaled. He closed his eyes, dropped his head, and inhaled again.

The manager kicked us out. "This isn't a 'free smell' store," he said.


WITH ALL THE MEN GONE, we boys became men. Suddenly, the week of my seventeenth birthday, in the endless gray dampness of a Michigan autumn, I became an adult male. Nick and I drove to the Black Lantern and ordered vodka shots, and then beer after beer. Around us in the bar, everyone was drinking illegally. Spiros shrugged as he made thirteen-year-old Billy Markovich a vodka martini. "Nobody else is here to drink," he said. "I need to make a living, don't I? If you have money, you drink."

Billy nearly gagged on his olive, but he knocked the drink back and motioned for another.

Other boys of thirteen and fourteen howled wildly, glasses raised, bottoms up. The television was switched from ESPN to MTV. We made lewd comments about the women in the music videos.

We took after-school jobs to help our mothers pay bills. You could find us gutting abandoned houses, cutting lawns, pumping gas, flipping burgers. After work we'd come back to the Black Lantern. Vodka, our fathers' drink of choice, coursed through our veins and through our minds and hearts and finally down to our pubescent cocks, which were alive and on fire. Every sixteen- and seventeen-year-old male in Maple Rock was a commodity that year, and we lost our virginity like it was spare change. I had sex with Mrs. Gagliardi, a large-breasted, dark-eyed Avon Lady in her early thirties, who came to the Black Lantern one Saturday evening, drunk, and led me up Warren Avenue to her house. In the morning, she had me get dressed immediately and leave. She didn't want to see me in the daylight, and because I was young and unskilled in these areas of the heart and flesh, I was hurt by her coldness.

Nick, always more precocious and confident than me, was having sex with half the women who worked at the Kroger where he was a stock boy. His redheaded manager, Sue Parsons, was the best, he said. He said there were rainbows in his eyes when he came. He said he didn't care if the fathers ever returned from the moon.

Older women didn't seem to have the same consistent interest in me, but many nights I did go over to see Sonya

Stecko, and we made out in her basement for hours. I pulled off her sweatshirt and she undid the zipper of my jeans, knowing that there was nobody who'd come tearing down the stairs, wanting to kill me for what I was doing with his daughter.

Walking home from Sonya's one night, I saw Nick sprawled out on the front lawn of Tanya Jaworski's house.

He had a puffy eye and blood all over the front of his shirt. He said he thought his nose was broken.

I said, "Is Tanya's father back?"

He said, "No. Her mother did this."

And believe me, it was true: if we became men, our mothers did too. They took jobs. Those who already had jobs took second jobs. Sometimes a few of the mothers came to the Black Lantern and drank with us. They arm-wrestled and hollered and broke bottles for emphasis when making speeches. They were working ten, twelve, sixteen hours a day. Once the police even brought my mother home. I stood there in the living room, appalled, as they told me to get her some aspirin and put her to bed. My mother yelled, "Fucking fascists." The cops simply nodded and said good night. They were thinking, I imagine, what I was thinking. These strong women were doing the best they could. So what if they acted a little out of character, if sometimes they let their responsibilities slide? Their husbands were on the moon. Who could deny them some happiness?

My mother worked two jobs. Days, she taught music at St. John's grade school, and three nights a week she cleaned offices in Plymouth, one of the suburbs to the north where men could still be found on Saturday afternoons, mowing lawns, washing cars, fixing bikes. Meanwhile, our house was in chaos. Kolya and I tried to keep up with the laundry and dishes, but we failed. My mother would come home tired, and soon her face was blank and void of worry thanks to a few beers. On her bed would be a pile of clean laundry I had not had time to put away. She'd crawl into towels and underwear and sleep the sleep of the hardworking under heaps of clean linen, smelling of fabric softener. The next morning, she'd try to get some housework done, but she could do little more than drink half a pot of coffee, shower, get dressed, and drive off to work.

THAT DOESN'T MEAN that we gave up hope that our fathers would return. Nick had the idea that he knew where some, if not all, of them had gone—Camp Kiev, an old hunting cabin on forty acres up near Cadillac where his father, and many of our fathers, went a few times a year.

Kyle Hartley was pretty much sober, and he owned an old Dodge work van that had room for almost a dozen of us to cram in the back. My mother was working that night and Kolya was with me, smiling like God's grace itself. I let him have a can of beer as we sat in the back, balancing on paint cans and crates and toolboxes. When we hit the interstate, we yelled and sang and roared, whiskey fires in our bellies. We made Kolya dance. We boasted of the women we planned to sleep with, the jobs we were going to get in places like Texas and Alaska, the houses and cars we were going to buy someday.

Near Midland, people started to fall asleep and it got quiet. Kyle kept driving, Nick in the front seat egging him on, whispering how he knew this was the place—the only place—all those men would have gone.

"What will we do when we find them?" Kyle said.

"Kick the shit out of them," Nick said. "And then drag their asses back home so they can take care of everybody the way they're supposed to, the cocksuckers."

I stayed awake, sitting on an overturned five-gallon bucket, picturing a sandy lot on a small lake, a lot covered with a rainbow assortment of small tents where our fathers slept under the stars, the sounds of nature lulling them into dreamless sleep. And now—this is stupid—I started to tell Kolya about it: Oh yeah, Kolya, they fish for their supper there, they wear deerskins and make fires for heat. Oh yeah, they have a nice time, and at sunset they sing all the Ukrainian songs, the ones Grandpa used to sing to us. Man, Kolya's eyes were about to fall out of his head. He kept standing on his tiptoes to see out the window. It was too dark to see, though, so I kept up the stories about this place we were going to be at by morning.

Kolya laughed so hard he nearly wet himself. I turned a coffee can over and emptied out the nuts and bolts, then let him pee in it. He thought peeing in the can was hilarious, and I saw a joy in his face I hadn't seen for a long, long time. Of course, he was nine, and he'd had a whole can of beer. But I didn't see that. I just saw myself as the best big brother in the world.

It was almost dawn when we arrived at the cabin. Nick hadn't remembered the directions perfectly, and we drove down a number of wrong roads, curvy tree-lined gravel roads with small animals darting across them. Kolya fell asleep.

The driveway to the cabin was rough and narrow. Those of us in the back of the van half stood, looking out the windshield. The sun was close enough to the horizon now that even coming down the driveway we had enough light to see nobody was there.

Somebody suggested that we might as well get out and swim in the lake for a while, but nobody else wanted to do that. It was late October and cold, a strain of winter hung tight in the sky, ready to snap through with ice and wind. We turned around and went back home. Kolya slept through the whole thing, curled up on my down hunting vest like a cat. I didn't wake him until we got home, and then I told him it was all a dream.

NICK AND I HAD NOT been going to school much that fall. We did this partly because we wanted to spend our time working and making money, but mostly because, by missing first period, we could begin drinking in the mornings at the Black Lantern. I was shaving daily and had the first markings of a serious stubble. Nick didn't shave much yet, but his curly hair had grown long and frizzy; he chain-smoked Winstons like a movie star.

We ate bacon and eggs every morning and scarfed down fast food for dinner. We put on weight. Our faces grew fat and square. We kept ball-peen hammers and thick chains under the seats of our cars in case there was trouble. Once, I watched Nick take a hammer to a man's face.

Then, in late November, Nick and I and some friends went back up north to Camp Kiev to hunt deer. We figured, having gone to all the trouble of finding it in the first place, we could at least take it over and make it a hideaway of our own. We loaded our cars with coolers and guns and blaze-orange hats and coats. We were all smoking and drinking coffee. Our mothers watched us get in and drive away. We knew what they were worrying about, and we knew that the week we were gone, they would stand staring at the moon, wondering if we'd disappear too.

I had always been a good shot, though my father was one of the few men in Maple Rock who did not hunt. I learned how to hunt from Uncle John, who'd been manic in his pursuit of venison for the winter. I had shot bucks before, though I was in no mood to do it that season. Nick, however, was on fire with determination.

The first two days, he sat in the woods for ten hours or more. He'd come back to camp after dark, dehydrated and empty-handed.

On the third day, we were walking back to camp around noon when we heard a shot. Then a buck came tearing across the path and seeing us, froze. Nick lifted his gun. The buck was easily an eight-point, maybe ten. I didn't want Nick to kill it. I almost yelled to scare the buck away, and I should have.

Nick lifted his gun and fired two shots. The buck staggered and fell.

I do not know how to explain what he did next, but it hangs in my memory as something sad and hopeless and sick. Seeing the buck fall, Nick let out a howl as shrill and eerie as the call of a wounded coyote. He ran down the path to the deer. He spit on it and kicked at its back legs. Then he dropped to his knees, yelling and screaming and began to punch at the deer with his fists. Blood covered his knuckles. "You're mine, you bitch," he yelled. He yelled and yelled it, over and over. Like his father, Nick had large hands, and as he punched the deer, you could hear tendons and bones snapping, and the dull thud of flesh pounding flesh echoed off the trees. It must have carried for miles.

I watched his war celebration for a while from down the path. Then I lifted my gun, took the safety off, and aimed it at Nick's head. I yelled "Hey!" but he ignored me. I yelled three more times and he ignored me. Finally, I shot the gun straight into the air. Nick fell on the ground.

"What the fuck?" he said.

"Get up and leave that buck alone. Quit fucking around. I mean it. Now, or I'll blow your goddamn head off."

Nick had his father's temper. I could see his heart was swelling with the violence of his father, and I could tell that he did not know where it was coming from or what he should do with it. We were angry and young and full of adrenaline and booze and there were firearms in our hands.

Nick stood up and brushed himself off and dropped his hands to his sides.

"Okay," he said. "Help me drag this fucker back to camp."

The anger was what was becoming of us. Don't think for a moment that because we were good, strong boys we could handle all of this: we couldn't. We almost killed ourselves with rage. We would grow up trampling over things, tearing things down, and people would look at us and wonder why we had such violence in our hearts.

Nick and I dragged the buck through the woods. Behind us, the carcass crunched through leaves and snapped sticks. Nick was fighting tears, his hands shaking.

"I feel sick," he said, his voice breaking. "My heart's going a mile a minute."

When we came home from deer hunting, the buck tied to our roof, we smelled of sweat and the woods and blood, and our mothers cupped our faces in their cool hands and kissed us and cried from joy. For a moment, we were all boys again.

DID WE MISS THEM? We did.

I know the women missed their husbands, but we, the boys, we missed our fathers.

At night, we looked off in the distance for a set of headlights that might signal that one of the disappeared was home. I sometimes imagined that several buses would pull into the parking lot of the Kmart and our fathers would stream out of the doors with baseball caps and pennants, like they'd been away at a game somewhere. Sometimes I imagined aliens would land in spacecrafts and release the men, like the hostage situations you'd see on the news. Our fathers would come down the ramp with their hands on their heads, tears on their unshaven and greasy faces.

Inexplicably, I felt a war was coming on, and for many nights I had dreams that I died in battle. I dreamed of mountains that crumbled and rivers that flooded. My dreams were apocalyptic and savage. I began to fear that I was a prophet and that I would soon be called upon to speak. I waited for God's voice.

By Christmas it was clear that we were not going to see our fathers anytime soon. We roasted turkeys and learned how to carve them alone. Ours ended up in ugly chunks, like a carcass ripped apart by dogs. My mother had become a vegetarian, and Kolya was spending Christmas at Disney World with his friend's family—a richer, larger, father-still-there family that had moved from Maple Rock to Northville. So I was the only one there to eat the bird. I ate turkey for a week, and still there was some I had to throw away.

One night in January, a blizzard dumping snow on metro Detroit, I fought a Serbian guy in the parking lot of the Black Lantern, a guy who said he was nailing Sonya Stecko. He broke a glass bottle across my back, cracking a rib and knocking the wind out of my lungs. Things went black and then things got clear and started spinning in a lovely fog. Finally, when he hit me with another bottle, this time across the back of my head, I passed out. The bottle didn't break.

Nick woke me up in the empty lot. He said, "Thank God you have a soft head."

He helped me off the ground. Back inside the bar's restroom, I dusted myself off and cleaned my face.

When I came out, Spiros had poured me a tall glass of beer. I drank the beer and checked my jaw. Spiros, who seemed more and more senile each week, said, "Honestly, Roman, you and John, you get worse each week. I worry about you, drinking so much, fighting, swearing."

In his old mind we had become our fathers. Nick and I didn't correct him. We grinned at each other and drank our beers. I felt fine. I was going to be okay. Please understand—I missed my father, but I was having one of those moments when I didn't want him to come back home. I would survive many things without him and I was capable of doing things on my own.

FOR THE MOST PART, we pictured our fathers sad and alone. We could see them riding in flea-ridden freight cars on bumpy tracks. We could see them struggling to make campfires on a beach as the wind whipped off the ocean and sand stung their faces. We saw them in anonymous cities, dwarfed by skyscrapers, trying to get together enough spare change for a hot dog or a bowl of soup. We saw them climbing desert mountains, muscles tearing and burning with fatigue, tongues swollen with thirst.

True, as much as these desolate images appealed to us, we also pictured our fathers happy. We imagined them with castles and pools and huge wooden tables of food and beer. We imagined them lounging nude in hot tubs and saunas with women half their age, women we'd never seen before, women who maybe were already on the moon when our fathers arrived. We imagined the climate of the moon to be temperate, and we imagined our fathers singing songs in praise of the lives they had there. We sensed that there was music on the moon. Sometimes, we imagined, a man—one of our fathers—would glance down at the earth and feel a vague memory and the sting of loss, but we knew that such moments would be rare. As we grew older and the men stayed away, such images of happiness became stronger and seemed more realistic. We saw our fathers in a paradise. We could not escape these images and certainly we could not escape the truth—men had disappeared, and their sad lives became happy ones.

Sometimes, when we drank too much and such thoughts angered us in the parking lot of the Black Lantern, we threw stones and bottles at the moon, and we imagined that we were tearing the hearts from our chests, sending them hurtling through heaven where our fathers could see them and know this: we, their sons, were below them, bleeding.

# some memories of my father

I MISSED MY FATHER'S cheese sandwiches, the way most nights around nine o'clock he'd go to the fridge, take out two slices of Wonder bread and two pieces of individually wrapped American cheese, and make a sandwich. The process by which he did this was nearly surgical and it yielded a perfect sandwich, square and neat, nothing falling out from the sides. He never left a crumb on the counter. He simply put the perfect sandwich on a clean plate, set a pickle down beside it, and returned to the television, where he was watching, no doubt, PBS or the evening news. Such methodical operations my father sometimes had, and I missed them. I missed the smell of his breakfast in the morning (one poached egg, dark rye toast, Nescafé). I missed the way he folded his newspaper, leaving it, finally, at day's end, open to the crossword puzzle (which he always seemed able to finish, every slot, using a green felt-tip pen). I missed the slippers at his bedside, the smell of cigarette smoke hanging in the bathroom, the cracking of his knuckles, the precise way he folded towels.

Yes, it's true that I missed my father, but in a larger sense, I missed all the fathers. I'd drive into other neighborhoods, neighborhoods with names like Quail Ridge and Oak Hills where people could not even imagine the mass exodus we had experienced, and I'd watch the fathers washing cars or practicing golf swings. In these neighborhoods, fathers could be seen strolling up and down driveways, monitoring the progress of the landscapers and deck-builders and sprinkler-system-installers. Neighborhoods like this could have been a million miles away from us.

What I missed most was the collective drone of our fathers' lives, their big and clumsy presence. I even missed their cussing and their labored breathing from too many cigarettes. I missed the roar of the sick engines inside the hoods of the hobby cars that would never run quite right. I missed their beer and coffee breath, missed their cheap aftershave that stunk up the church on Sunday mornings. I missed the cranking of their power tools on Saturday afternoons, and the roar of their voices while watching the Lions play on television. I even missed the yelling, the arguments gone over the edge, the occasional sound of a fist going through the door.

Still, in truth, I could remember very little about my father. Already, in a matter of less than a year, his image had grown vague and hazy. I listed the few memories I had in a notebook, afraid they might leave me:

I am three years old, my father is smoking and sweating, swearing at some sort of machine, while I sit on a concrete floor, banging an old coffee can with a screwdriver.

I am four. My father and I are stacking firewood at the side of the house. A hornet swirls around my head and lands on the small log that I am holding. My father says nothing, puts his hand out. I give him the log. The hornet doesn't budge. My father takes his pocketknife, flips it open with one hand, and sticks the blade into the hornet, pinning it to the wood. I hear an anemic buzz and the hornet falls to the grass in two pieces.

Five years old. We are at a wedding. It is late. Ambulances have arrived. Somebody has had a heart attack. Some adult, a mustached man with floppy gray hair, pours beers on my head. I start to cry. My father grabs the beer-pourer by his necktie and throws him to the floor.

When I am six, my father lives in the basement for a week. He sleeps on the couch, does not shave, never goes to work. Sometimes my mother and I hear him vomiting in the bathroom down there. My mother says he is sick. We sometimes hear him crying, loud sobs. I am not allowed to go downstairs. He stays there for another week, a third week. My mother goes downstairs only after I am in bed, and they yell at each other so that I can't sleep. One night there is the crash of a broken mirror and the sound of a hole being kicked into the wood paneling. In the morning, my father joins us for breakfast and, clean-shaven, returns to work.

When I am seven, my father disappears for a weekend. Eventually, my mother calls the police, who find him hitch-hiking on I-75. My mother asks: Where were you going? My father says: Maybe Florida?

When I am eight, my father announces that he is breaking the Good Friday fast, and that he doesn't want any god-damn fish, what he wants is kielbasa and ham. He rips into our Easter meats and sits at the table, drinking beer and eating pork. My mother yells at him; she tries to call the priest on the telephone but he doesn't answer. My father inhales the smoky smell of kielbasa and offers me a piece. I take it, eat it, then eat several more. My mother yells for me to stop. My mother begs me, but my father laughs and so I laugh with him. Later, my father leaves the house, and it's me and my mother in the kitchen. She is trying to salvage what's left of the meat for basket blessing the next afternoon. She says I've done a horrible, sinful thing. In my room that night, I stay up as late as I can, crying and saying the Rosary, begging the Virgin Mary to ask Jesus to forgive me, although, because it is Good Friday, I am not sure if Jesus is available.

When I am nine, my father announces that we are moving to Arizona, and he and my mother stay up all night fighting. My mother says, "What do you hope is different for us in goddamn Tucson, Roman?" And my father says, "Everything." But by morning, my father no longer mentions Arizona, and we never move or discuss it again.

When I am ten, my father kisses a woman at an office party. He confesses this to my mother, moves out for a week, and then comes back home, bearing two large pizzas and a jug of root beer.

When I am eleven, my father gets a ticket for drunk driving. My mother threatens to leave him.

When I am twelve, my father grows a beard and mustache and begins to work in the garden, bird-watch, and listen to opera. He quits drinking for six months and buys a family pass to the Detroit Symphony Orchestra.

When I am thirteen, while we're eating cheeseburgers at a White Castle, my father tells me that I should prepare myself for disappointment. "This is the way our lives turn out, Mikey," he says. "Disappointing."

When I am fourteen, my father and I drive to Florida after his uncle Five dies. We think we are set to inherit nearly half a million, but instead, we find that Uncle Five has spent all his money on his widow, a thirty-one-year-old waitress who won't let us in the house. On the way home, my father says, "This is what I mean by disappointment."

These were my fragments of my father. I could remember only his many phases, his fleeting obsessions, and his periodic bouts with depression. I'm not saying there was no happiness in my childhood. No, I remember my father as a loving, bighearted man capable of hitting low points that lasted for weeks. I remember him often looking confused and broken, as if he'd just woken up from a long sleep plagued by sad dreams. Still, although I tried and I tried, I couldn't retrieve a single extended memory: there was no camping trip that we took alone, no long talk in which he offered me advice, no fishing from a metal rowboat, just us guys, our lines in the water and the sun barely starting to rise. And this is one of the things that I was afraid of: that my father was gone for good and that my memories of him weren't clear and lasting. Perhaps my memory was just bad. My memories of my childhood were pleasant ones, mostly. But they were dim, and my father was a shadow in them all.

Now only one thing remains:

When I was sixteen, my father went to the moon.

## summer 1992

IT WASN'T UNTIL the next summer that we sifted through the chaos of our lives looking for order. The women in Maple Rock were holding yard sales—"memory sales" they called them—joking and furious at the same time. Our mothers, your wives, made signs with poster paints on the lids of pizza boxes—MEMORY SALE: EVERYTHING MUST GO! People came from all over the city to try on your old coats and pants, to buy up your old tools, your bikes, your bowling balls. They even bought your half cans of latex paint and your opened bottles of Goo Gone. What was left went to Goodwill, as if you were dead relatives we barely knew.

And then there was the warmth of that summer, long endless days with a burning omnipresent sun, and the women in Maple Rock began to crave something: newness. They fell in love with all things new—new cars, new jeans, new haircuts. They took on new loves, new jobs, new facial expressions, new joys and sorrows, new personalities. Our mothers consulted with lawyers and filed divorce-by-abandonment papers, eager to wipe their slates clean.

All things new; it was overwhelming.

I was over at Tom's place during one of the many yard sales and his mother offered me Mr. Slowinski's old Carhartt jacket. I tried it on, and it fit perfectly. I had just been through a cold winter with a thin coat, and so I accepted it. "Thanks, Mrs. S," I said.

Just then, Tom came out on the front lawn.

"What the fuck are you wearing?" he said. He was barefoot and shirtless and looked even smaller than he was, as if he were sinking into the crabgrass patches on the lawn.

"Tommy," Mrs. S said.

"A jacket," I said.

"That's my fucking jacket," he said.

"Thomas," Mrs. S said, "it's way too big for you."

"It's not," he said.

It was. Mr. Slowinski was nearly six feet tall. The jacket fit me perfectly, but I was six inches taller than Tom.

"Try it on," I said, and Tom stormed off.

When I found him, he was talking my mom into giving him my father's old drafting pencils. I let him take them all. The metal pencil box was sticking out of his back pocket as he walked away, as if he'd been collared and tagged by some zoologist.

I WAS STILL DATING Sonya Stecko, and she was spending the summer getting ready to go to college in Ann Arbor. She had worked hard in high school, pulled off a 4.0 GPA, and scored highest in Maple Rock High on the ACTs. She had a list of recommended reading for freshmen, some list they had sent her for the Honors College, full of novels and history books and poems, and every Monday morning we'd go over to the library in Livonia, which was ten times bigger and cleaner than the library in Maple Rock, and she'd check out more books.

We were sitting there in the library one morning. I was reading magazines, and she was reading *The Odyssey*. She had her long brown hair pulled back in a loose ponytail, and she twirled her hair around one hand as she read. She caught me looking at her. Her eyes were bluer than mine, and with the mix of daylight coming through skylights and the fluorescent glow of the library, they looked like tiny round mirrors submerged in water.

She said, "You really should read this. You'd like it."

"What's it about?" I said.

"It's about Odysseus, who wants to get home to his family, but he can't, he's kind of being held prisoner on this island. So his son goes and looks for him."

"It's good?" I said.

"It's a classic," she said.

"So? Big fucking deal. I know it's a classic. Is it good?" I said.

"You won't understand it, on second thought."

"Maybe I'll read it when you're done."

Sonya looked back down at her book. I flipped through my copy of *Rolling Stone* again.

"When you go to college," I said, "will you have a roommate?"

"I don't know yet," she said. "Hold on a minute. I'm almost done with this chapter."

I WAS TRYING TO check out a few books on the sly—*Huckleberry Finn, Walden, Moby Dick*—just some stuff I knew I was supposed to read if I wanted to be anybody in life, the kind of stuff I figured Sonya might read in college. The librarian was a chatty old lady who had to provide a running commentary as her shaky hands scanned each book and stamped it with a due date.

"This is a very impressive reading list," she said. "You're an ambitious young man."

"Yes, ma'am."

"You know, Jack London used to read dozens of books every week. He never had a formal education."

"Really," I said. "I didn't know that, ma'am."

I had then—and still have—a tendency to be overly polite in places like libraries, bookstores, or art galleries. I've always felt, for some reason or another, that somebody would eventually come after me in a place like that, and inform me that I wasn't welcome.

"Thank you for telling me that, ma'am," I said. "Maybe I will read one of his novels next."

"What does your father do?" she asked.

It was the kind of question only an old lady would ask. I ran through the options in my mind. My father lives in a small cabin near Escanaba where he handcrafts stringed instruments and snowshoes. My father is employed by the federal government and drives a Lincoln from city to city, inspecting institutions for fraud and general incompetence. My father went to Nashville to make a country music album which is due to hit stores in January. My father disappeared into a thin mist one morning while walking along the rocky shores of the North Atlantic. These are all lies I have told at some point in my life. Even now, at the age of thirty, I tell people these kinds of lies when they ask about my father. But back then, I was seized by honesty.

"My father," I said, "is on the moon."

"How's that?" she said. She adjusted her hearing aid while sliding my stack of books across the counter. I took the books and walked away.

"Those are due in three weeks," she called after me.

WHEN SONYA WAS DONE with *The Odyssey*, she checked it out again and gave it to me. For a week, it sat on my nightstand. Finally, one night when she was out with her mother in Ann Arbor (they were "exploring the city") I opened the book.

My mother saw me reading it. She'd come downstairs to get a load of laundry from the dryer, and she said, "Are you reading Homer?"

"Yeah," I said. I sat up in bed, a little embarrassed. I don't know why. I felt like she'd caught me flipping through a copy of *Hustler*.

"Great," she said and went into the laundry room.

When she came out again, she was holding a white basket full of dark clothes. She sat on the edge of my bed without setting down the laundry. She was resting it on her knees.

"Have you thought about going to college?" she said. "Sonya seems pretty excited about it."

"I don't know," I said.

"You should think about applying for colleges early," she said. "For scholarships and all that."

"I know that, Mom. Goddamn, I'm just trying to read a book, not become some professor."

She set down the basket and started folding the clothes while she talked. "What do you think you want to be, Michael?"

"I don't know," I said. And she waited, not saying a word, just folding my clean clothes. I knew I had to say something. "A writer, I guess."

I don't know why I said that. But my mother's face had lit up and she was smiling at me.

"Really?" she said. "A writer?"

"Yeah," I said. "Really."

It had just occurred to me, but suddenly it sounded right. It was what I wanted to do.

My mother handed me a stack of folded jeans and sweatshirts, my socks and underwear resting on top of them. They were still warm from the dryer.

"Wonderful," she said. "I think that's wonderful. That's the dream you're chasing. We all have one."

"What's yours?" I asked.

"Mine?" she said. "Right now, I'm just trying to get this house cleaned up."

In fact, the whole house was already clean. Once it had been cluttered with the debris of nineteen years of marriage, but it seemed like a new place that summer. We'd had at least three yard sales by then. The attic and basement were almost empty, the closets spare, the rooms—free of the extra couches, armchairs, and end tables we once owned—were airy and open. My mother had painted the walls white. She had pulled up all the carpeting to reveal hardwood floors that she swept and mopped until the oak planks reflected the light from the windows. She never used the air-conditioning anymore, and instead kept the windows open, day and night. A breeze moved constantly through our home. My mother lit candles in every room, like she was trying to get rid of some primitive scent, a territorial marking that no longer had meaning.

STILL, WE DID REMEMBER the coats you wore, the musty smell of the cars you drove, the brands of cigarettes you smoked.

We remembered how your voices sounded, singing in the back of St. John's Church, low and monotone, but reverent and aching with confession and regret. We remembered how you sometimes laughed, loudly and suddenly, while we were down the hallway in our bedrooms, trying to sleep.

We remembered how some nights, we'd find you alone at the kitchen table in your pajamas, drinking, and your faces were haunted and lost.

We remembered how you walked with a mix of arrogance and caution, and how sometimes your shoulders would slump and your hands would plunge deep into your pockets.

We remembered when you gave us dollar bills or watched baseball games with us or let us hold the garbage bag open while you raked in the grass clippings.

We had these memories of you: What memories did you have of us?

SONYA WAS WORRIED about getting pregnant, and she wouldn't have sex with me anymore after she graduated.

"This is a harsh thing you're doing, Sonya," I would say, when we were in bed, almost naked, and she told me to back off.

"What?" she asked. "Do you want to spend your whole life in Maple Rock, raising a bunch of brats, working at some fucking stupid job, in a factory or whatever? You'll leave me just when parenthood is starting to get tough, and then what, Michael?"

That pretty much killed the mood every time, and deep down, I knew it was risky for her future. She was smart. She had plans.

So when Sonya finally broke up with me at the end of July, I wasn't too surprised. Now she was worried that even being around me might somehow affect her future.

Did I blame her for thinking such things?

"No, I guess not," I said.

She said she would always remember me as her first lover. Wasn't that enough?

"It's something," I said.

She said you just don't go off to college with a boyfriend back at home. It's limiting. Didn't I think so too?

"I guess I do," I said.

I could hear her mother's voice coming from somewhere inside of her. We were in Sonya's bedroom, and there was a framed picture of her father as a young man on the dresser. Then there was a picture of me in my prom tux. There was a picture of her dead cat Hal. It was the middle of the day, and it was hot in the house. Her room was filled with sunlight. I still remember that room as being perpetually full of sunlight.

"You'll be in Ann Arbor. That's, like, forty miles away. I could see you every day," I said.

"Exactly. Wouldn't that be—honestly, now—the worst thing for both of us?"

"How the fuck is your mom going to afford college anyway?" I said.

"Loans, Michael," Sonya said. "Student loans."

"What do you mean?"

"You can get loans for going to school," she said.

"From who?" I said.

"The government, Michael. What is wrong with you? How come you don't know anything, Michael?"

"How come everybody else calls me Mikey, but now you always call me Michael?" I said.

"It's more appropriate," she said. "Wishful thinking, maybe? Maybe you'll grow up if I call you by a grown man's name."

"Your dad's name was Jimmy," I snarled, or tried to snarl, but my lips were shaking too much and it sounded more like a slurp or a sniffle.

"My point exactly. You should go now."

Her hair caught the sunlight and cast a weblike shadow on her cheek.

"I want to go down on you," I said. "One last time."

I knew it was what she liked best.

"Honestly, Michael, I don't know what goes through your head," she said. "You've got to be kidding, right? You're fucking putting me on."

"I'm serious. It's all I can think about. I can taste it sometimes just from thinking about it. I need to do it one last time."

She flopped down on her bed and looked up at the ceiling and sighed a few times. I stood there looking at her exposed navel, getting hard. She undid her jeans, and said, "Kneel down."

I did.

"Don't expect me to do it for you," she said.

"Fine."

I pulled her jeans down, and slid her ankles out of them.

"This is so fucked up," she said.

"Do you want me to stop?" I said.

"No," she said.

I pulled off her white socks, which was the hardest thing to do. My hands shook. She was lying back on her bed in a pair of white underwear. She always liked this, she used to want to do this every day, twice a day. It was why she could do without fucking. She liked oral sex better. She left her T-shirt on, and said, "Close the door and pull down the shades."

I did what she said. When I got back on my knees in front of her, she said, "My mom will be home in an hour."

"Will we need that long?" I said. I saw her almost smile, but it wasn't the same worked-up, ecstatic kind of smile I was used to getting from her. Her smile was tentative, and we were both awkward and afraid of what would happen next.

SONYA LEFT MAPLE ROCK on Labor Day weekend.

At nine in the morning, I showed up at her house with Nick, and we helped her and her mother load the minivan with Sonya's stuff—clothes and books, mostly. They also packed some new stuff they'd just gone out and bought with a Sears charge card—a mini-fridge, a microwave, a small television, a bike.

I wondered aloud if they needed me to drive to Ann Arbor with them, and help them move all of that stuff into the dormitory. Nobody said anything, and when it was time to head off, Sonya kissed me and Nick on the cheek, both of us in the exact same way, and left us there. We watched the van pull out of the driveway and down the street and out of Maple Rock.

"Should we get drunk?" Nick asked.

"Why?" I said.

"Cause Sonya's leaving," he said.

"So?"

"So, dude, she was really hot and she was your girl-friend and I liked looking at her, and now she's gonna be mounting some fucking frat boy from West Bloomfield who is pre-med or something."

"Why do you think you know so much?" I said. "Fuck you."

"Do you want to get drunk or not?"

"No."

"Fine. Suit yourself," he said, and walked away while giving me the middle finger. "You're one miserable bastard, Mikey," he said.

And he was completely right.

A FEW WEEKS LATER, my mother came down into the basement while I was reading *The Odyssey*. It was way overdue already, but it was checked out on Sonya's card and I didn't care. I was reading three or four hours a night.

"Still working on Homer?" my mother asked.

"Yes," I said. "It's slow going."

"Have you talked to Sonya lately?"

"No. Not really."

"Her mother gave me her address. I ran into her at the store."

"So?"

"So, if you're gonna be a writer, you should learn to write good letters. You should always know how to write letters to a woman."

"Whatever," I said. But my mother left a slip of paper on the bed. I tried to go back to Homer, but everything was ruined. Fuck letters, I thought.

I drove to Ann Arbor that night and asked at a gas station for directions to Alice Lloyd Hall. The dorm wasn't as nice as I expected. The floors in the entranceway were yellowed and dull, the windows were all dirty, and a mass of silver mailboxes on one wall made the place feel like a warehouse. I wandered around until I found the third floor, and then wandered around even more until I found room 313. It was the same room number as our area code in Maple Rock. It was easy to remember, so I didn't have to look at the crumpled-up piece of paper in my pocket.

There was a sign on the door that said SUNNY. There was a dry-erase board with a rainbow on it, and a black marker hanging from a black string. Somebody had written "Hey, Foxy" and somebody else had written "Theo came by. Call me." I knocked softly on the door. I heard a slapping noise and turned to my left. A tall guy with a hairless, pale chest was walking down the hall in a towel and flip-flops, and he stopped at the room across from Sonya's and went inside. "I don't think Sunny is here right now," he said.

"Oh," I said. I had imagined her living with all girls, but here was this half-naked man, who lived right there.

After he'd closed the door—his sign said SWEET JIMMY— I picked up the pen and tried to think of something to write on my ex-girlfriend's door. It was a feeling of wordlessness a would-be writer should not have. I wanted to write something nice, something that would make her sorry that she had missed me. Instead I wrote "Your name is Sonya not Sunny." I walked down the hall slowly, hoping that maybe Sonya would come around the corner and find me, but she didn't.

A FEW DAYS LATER, Bill Clinton swung through the area to make a campaign appearance in Detroit, and he stopped in Maple Rock at the Polish-American Hall. He talked about the bright futures of communities like ours, the communities that built America, the union-made communities. He praised our strength and our resilience. He talked of being raised by a single mother, and he talked of his simple beginnings, beginnings of both grace and grit.

He looked at us with his eyes twinkling and his face brightening with blood.

"There are some things that my hometown—Hope, Arkansas—and your hometown of Maple Rock have in common," he said.

He bit his lip; he made a fist.

Then he pointed his thumb at each and every one of us and said, "You are the future of our great nation. The future of this great nation is in the hands of the people who do the nation's work, who pay the nation's bills, who live in the nation's neighborhoods. You should be proud of what you do. I am proud of what you do. America is proud of what you do."

We exploded in cheers. We were still young and we believed in things. Somebody from the back of the room yelled, "We don't do shit!" But, really, what can you expect in Maple Rock? We just tried to drown out bastards like him with our cheering. We waved our Clinton-Gore banners, and pinned new buttons to our parkas and coats. Bill Clinton ate pierogies and kielbasa with us, he shook our hands, and he played his saxophone with Pauly's Polka Princes when they performed their famous polka version of "Born in the U.S.A."

When Bill Clinton smiled from the stage, we could see our mothers swooning, their cheeks bathed in the flashes of camera light. Later, after he'd won the admiration of our mothers, after he'd won all of their votes, Bill Clinton would do things he couldn't ever take back. He would break our mothers' hearts, and they would not be able to forgive him.

WE WERE DEEP INTO the yellow and melancholy days of autumn and Sunny spent the crisp, dragging afternoons in Ann Arbor, wandering across the Diag with her arms full of books. I could picture her, clearly and accurately, I thought, in her jeans and a thick, hooded Michigan sweatshirt, stopping to talk to some East Coast guy from her philosophy class. They would go to a café and order black coffee in giant bowl-shaped mugs, and he would say something like, "Tell me about the place that you're from," and she would say, "It's nowhere."

Meanwhile, Nick and I rambled, bored and sulking, through our post-high-school lives. We took part-time jobs at car washes and oil-change shops, then came home and watched cable and lifted weights in the basement. We went down to the Black Lantern, where Spiros was still willing to serve us. Sometimes he called us by the names of our fathers; we didn't correct him. We sat at his bar, listened to his stories, smoked cigarettes, and complained about the lack of interesting nightlife in Maple Rock.

To pass the long, aimless nights, we came up with a game we called Auto Theft. We'd round up about a dozen guys and then split into teams of two. We'd drive around the richer suburbs late at night, and we'd steal lawn ornaments, street signs, hubcaps, whatever we could. We stole a bench from the middle school, the mascot from the high school. We stashed all of these things in a wooded drainage area behind the football field. Eventually the police found our stash, and hauled ceramic deer and wooden sheep out of the woods in wheelbarrows.

This made the *Maple Rock Observer*. COPS FIND CACHE OF STOLEN GOODS IN LOCAL WOODS the headline read. We all secretly hoped you would read the Crime Watch and know that it was your sons who were responsible for the petty thievery. We imagined you'd come home to save us before we progressed as criminals.

But you stayed away.

We progressed as criminals.

We threw a smoke bomb in a crowded Taco Bell because the manager had tossed us out the night before.

We tied a Porta Potti to Kyle Hartley's van and dragged it down Eight Mile Road. In the morning the street was slick with a stream of blue chemicals and sewage.

We destroyed a car with baseball bats.

We "kidnapped" a married father of four, a chemistry teacher who allegedly propositioned one of Nick's girlfriends. We held him, blindfolded and hands tied, at gunpoint until we deemed him sufficiently scared. "Are you scared shitless yet, Mr. Haller?" we said. This went on for five or six hours. Just before dawn, we left him in Rotary Park, still blindfolded. He never told the police, as far as we knew, which meant the allegations against him were likely correct. This was our idea of justice.

Our anger was dangerous.

But we ignored it, laughing like drunks do when they punch their fists through windows and are surprised by the spurting blood.

Eventually there would be arrests, I imagined. Our records would be spotty, our pasts would be checkered. It seemed glamorous. We longed to be captured so we could wear our convictions like badges of honor, the way an amateur boxer wears a split lip.

We were still young, heading toward eighteen and nineteen. It was easy for many people to write us off at that point, to assume that our futures were set irrevocably toward longing and sadness, or worse. Our old teachers, our neighbors, our ex-girlfriends, even some of our mothers, I think, began to believe we were without hope. And if you had been with us then, you might have said the same thing. You might have said we were lost young men too, without goals or courage or aim.

But God, our hopes were high, our visions were glorious and moving. I bet if you could have stepped inside of our squirrelly heads for one minute and seen the impossible futures we were already imagining, well, then your heart would break. You'd weep.

# the calming effect
# of jelly doughnuts

Nick and I couldn't sleep. We were up all night, driving around Detroit in his old Pontiac, smoking bud with the windows down, red-faced from the cold. It was February, and Michigan Avenue was empty. We were looking for an auto parts salesman named Burt Nelson, who, somebody had just told me, had slapped my mother in the face earlier that evening outside the Black Lantern.

"We'll kill him," I said.

"Be careful what you wish for," Nick said. "We could kill him, if you want."

"Hell yes, I want to kill him," I said. "He hit my mother."

"I've got a gun in my backpack," Nick said.

"Bullshit," I said.

"I do."

"Let's see it," I said.

"My backpack's in the trunk."

"You don't have a gun."

"I do. I carry one now, for work."

"What kind?"

"A .38 Special."

What did I know about handguns. I shrugged. "That's a good one?" I asked.

"Well," he said, "it's more than enough to do the job."

Nick worked the night shift at a doughnut shop on Michigan Avenue. On his nights off, he had trouble sleeping and I often got stuck staying up with him. The doughnut place was in a rough stretch of city, and sitting behind a cash register all night would have made anyone a little skittish. A lot of night clerks around Detroit carried guns, I guessed. Three Brothers Donutz was nestled between a topless bar and an abandoned pharmacy known as The Shop, where a three-hundred-pound ghost-pale man named Dough, whose father was the retired pharmacist who once owned the building, sold drugs each night from midnight to dawn.

"Have you ever used it?"

"Not yet," he said. "But just wait until some asshole tries to rob me."

We rolled our way through the city. It was almost light out, and the idea of finding Burt Nelson started to seem a little insane. If he'd been willing to punch my mother, a slight woman with a soft voice, he'd have no trouble taking a two-by-four or baseball bat to my head.

"Do you want to go home?" I said.

"What?" Nick said.

"Do you want to go home? I'm tired."

"You asshole!" Nick said.

"What?"

"You asshole. Some fuckhead just punched your mother and you want to go home and get some beauty sleep?"

"I don't know," I said.

"Man, you're such a wuss. You're a fuckhead."

*I know it,* I almost said. *Take me home.*

Instead, I said, "Well, we won't find him now. Let's just go and get him later."

He pulled in front of the doughnut shop. I had registered for a few classes at the community college that winter, and had to be in class by eight.

"Let me pick up something at The Shop first," Nick said.

I wanted to wait outside, but that was no safer in the long run than going inside.

Plywood covered all the windows and the front door of The Shop. You entered through the back door, between two Dumpsters. The place was lit by a single bulb that hung from a busted light fixture above the counter. All around the store were dust-covered shelves and abandoned inventory. Dough was behind the register, all big and fat and white. He had a gun in a holster under his fat white arm. He didn't care what you took from the shelves if you were a paying customer. He liked to joke that he was carrying on the family business.

Sometimes Dough actually rang up your order, gave you the total, and exchanged small talk while he made change. It was like Mayberry gone haywire. You expected Floyd the Barber to be shooting up in the corner, or Barney Fife to come in tripping his balls off.

"Well, if it isn't Tweedledick and Tweedleprick," Dough said. He prided himself on making up nicknames. Last week, we'd been Licky and Dicky. His repertoire of insults lacked variety; they always were variations on a dick theme.

I let Nick go and buy his weed or whatever he was after, and wandered around the dark dusty aisles. I slipped some nail clippers into my pocket, and a pack of Q-tips. I liked the idea of all that free stuff, and couldn't help taking something every time I visited. I was amazed that there was anything left on the shelves at all, but I imagined most junkies didn't get excited about free zit cream or callus cushions.

WHEN WE PULLED INTO my driveway, I put my backpack together. Then I heard Nick say, "Well, look who it is. Right under our noses."

I looked up and saw Burt Nelson in the middle of the living room. He was in my dad's old chair, sipping from a mug and smoking a cigarette.

"Goddamn it," I said.

"You want my gun?" Nick said.

"Nope."

"You want me to go in there with you?" he said.

"No. I'll handle it."

"What are you gonna do, kick his ass by yourself?"

"Sure," I said.

"Fuck that. You won't be able to, Mikey."

"Sure I will."

"Let me come in there with you," he said.

"Nick, mind your own fucking business, okay? I can handle this."

"Fine," he said. "I gotta get to work anyway. I said I'd cover an extra shift today. It's Paczki Day. We'll be busy."

I was left in the driveway, scared about going into my own house.

"THERE HE IS," Burt said. "We were worried about you around here."

There was nobody else in the room.

"Your mother's still sleeping," he whispered. "She had a bit too much to drink last night."

I stared at him and then shrugged.

"I guess we all did, eh?" he said.

"Not me," I said. I had a watery feeling in my gut. My arm muscles were starting to twitch from lack of sleep.

"Well, that's good," he said, "since you're not even twenty-one yet."

He was wearing gray sweatpants and a sleeveless T-shirt. His forearms were thick and long, like a couple of logs.

"What do you think, Michael? Is it time to wake up your mother?"

"I don't care," I said.

"How about your brother? When does he need to leave for school?"

"He's got time to sleep," I said. "I gotta make his lunch."

Burt put out his cigarette in a Coke can that was on the edge of the TV table. I was still standing near the foyer in my coat, holding my backpack.

"You plan to stay here a while?" Burt said. He was standing up now, and he walked over to me. He was big. There was no way I could take him on, not by myself, not when I was this tired.

I went into the kitchen and took out the bread and peanut butter, and started working on Kolya's lunch. Usually it was my mother who did it, but I was trying to prove a point—with Burt Nelson around, she was slipping. When she woke up and saw that I had made my brother's lunch, she'd understand that.

"You know," Burt said, "I don't know what people told you, but I didn't hit your mother last night. We were having a fight, and I just grabbed her to calm her down."

"I don't care what you guys do," I said.

"Somebody told me that you were driving around looking for me," Burt said.

"You're lucky we didn't find you," I said.

He grabbed my arm as I was spreading jelly on bread. "Look, you and your little friends stay out of this," he said. "I'm not here for trouble, but I'll take it on if it comes."

I was trying to figure out if he was scared of my friends and me, or if he really was ready to fight us head-to-head. A glorious image came to my mind, of my fist in Burt Nelson's face.

I went to hit him with my free hand. He blocked me, and twisted my arm behind my back, then started wrenching on it.

"Say uncle," he said.

My arm burned. My face was hot. "Fuck, fuck you, okay, okay, uncle," I said. I was hoping Nick would burst in the door. Nick with his brass knuckles or a ball-peen hammer or a giant logger's chain swinging in a circle around his head.

"Say, 'I love you Uncle Burt,'" he said.

I said it and he let go and nudged me into the counter.

"You are a fucking pussy," he said and went back to the chair in the living room.

I went to my room and got into bed. An hour later, my alarm went off. I heard my mother and Burt talking in the kitchen. I heard my brother asking where his shoes were. I remembered what had happened, and put my pillow over my face. I tried to fall back asleep, but the adrenaline was pumping again. My veins felt heavy and my bladder was ready to pop. I sat up in bed.

"Fucking pussy," I said. I got up and took a shower.

BURT WAS NEW TO the area. He'd moved to Westland—a few suburbs west of us—after taking a job selling some sort of auto parts to the industry. He wore a suit to work. He had the too big, menacing quality of a Texas farm boy, and in fact had played linebacker at Oklahoma State. He was almost sixty now, the age where ex-jocks, about to be sent out to pasture by their employers, start getting nostalgic for their days of hard drinking and knocking heads.

Around my mom, he was sweet and smooth; he spoke in a forced drawl and had clean fingernails. He was nothing like the men of Maple Rock had been. On Friday nights, he'd come over and make a big pot of chili and a pan of corn bread. He painted the living room one weekend, and fixed my mother's car for her when the water pump exploded.

He went on business trips and brought her things like snow globes and silk scarves, airport gifts. Once when he'd been in Atlanta, he brought Kolya a Braves batting helmet and a tomahawk. The only thing he ever gave to me was a copy of the *Sports Illustrated* swimsuit issue that he said he had found on the plane.

Before long he began to sour, like old milk. His temper flared up more and more, over less and less. If he saw my mom talking to our new neighbor, a tall, dark Yemeni man who owned the Dairy Mart on the corner, he'd get jealous. "Why you talking to some Arab all the time?" he'd say. "You got a thing for men on camels? When I go on the road, does he sleep in your bed?"

When he got laid off, he started spending most of his time at our house, drinking beer and eating the food my mom was paying for and watching our only television sixteen hours a day. I found out then that he hadn't had a place of his own. His company had been putting him up at a Guest Quarters motel, and now that he was out of work, there he was, in the middle of our lives.

I know loneliness sends us into dark places. I know the day-to-day sadness most of us have to battle on a regular basis sometimes makes us be with people we normally wouldn't choose. I know all that now, but I didn't know it then. I just knew that my mother had disappointed me. In those years, she had a few boyfriends like Burt Nelson. I never stood up to any of them, and maybe that was not my role, maybe the son is not meant to defend the mother, maybe I am naïve to believe that my mother even needed my protection. She was older and wiser than me, she'd been through some things. But a flame of failure still burned in my guts anytime somebody like Burt Nelson would walk through our door.

WHEN I CAME OUT OF the shower, my mother had made eggs and bacon, which she never did before Burt came to live with us. Now it was eggs and bacon every goddamn morning. She looked tired. She would run around filling up coffee cups and orange juice glasses like she was waiting tables in Mel's Diner. She was working as a receptionist for a security company, dispatching mall cops and monitoring a panel of burglar alarms.

Kolya was at the kitchen table, buttering toast. Burt was mashing on a banana like a gorilla. I got myself some coffee, the last of it. It was burned and tasted like ashes. I added cream and sugar. Burt said, "Drink it black, it puts hair on your chest."

My mother flipped the eggs.

"You hungry, Michael?" she said.

"Nope."

"Thanks for making your brother's lunch," she said.

I looked at Kolya. He still had a pretty good shiner from a fight he had gotten in at school a few days ago. He was a smart kid, knew all the state capitals, could do long division in his sleep, won the sixth-grade spelling bee. But he was getting in trouble all day long, every day.

"Your eye's looking better," I said.

"I know," Kolya said. "Burt showed me how to punch yesterday."

"He's got to learn to defend himself," Burt said. "Every boy needs to know how to throw a decent punch by the time he is twelve."

"I don't want you fighting, Kolya," my mother said, setting eggs and bacon on the table. She was in one of the three business suits she had charged at Winkleman's when she started this new job. She had bought three colors—red, black, and charcoal gray— that she could interchange a bit, so it looked like she had more clothes than she did. Today, she was in the red blazer and the black skirt. She looked pretty. She looked too classy for a guy like Burt, who was sitting across from me in a flannel robe, his thinning hair smashed up on one side of his head.

"I could've taught you how to throw a punch," I said.

"He already knows how to punch like a girl," Burt said.

Kolya and Burt looked at each other and laughed.

"Burt," my mother said.

Burt shoveled eggs into his mouth, then folded a strip of bacon in on top of them. He really was a goddamn ape, in spite of those hairless, clean hands.

"Kolya," I said. "You want me to walk you to school?"

"Yeah," he said. "I'm almost done."

I went into my bedroom and got my backpack. I hadn't done all the reading I was supposed to do for class. I was a few weeks into my first semester. I was taking a few journalism courses, a literature class, and something called *Great Films of American Cinema*. It was supposed to be an easy class, but I was blowing it. The movies seemed destined to fuck me over. I was going to have to fight tooth and nail for a C minus. My first paper came back with a D on it, and the professor had written "Lacks sufficient understanding of film theory" on the back and nothing else.

I had signed up to work on the school newspaper too, and had written exactly one article for it about the problem of Canada geese shitting all over the school grounds, mucking up the park and the soccer fields. The headline read LOOK WHAT'S HITTING THE FAN ON CAMPUS. My mother was so proud to see my byline that she hung the article on the fridge, and there it was every morning when I got out the milk.

KOLYA HADN'T COMBED his hair, and it was sticking up everywhere. I was trying to smooth it down for him as we walked to school.

"You don't want the girls to think you're an asshole," I said.

"I hate girls."

"You won't forever, but if they think of you as the kind of kid who doesn't comb his hair now, you'll never live it down," I said. "Once an asshole, always an asshole. Look at Burt."

"Burt can punch holes in the wall. He did it in the garage."

I hadn't known that the new hole in the garage had appeared courtesy of Burt's temper.

"Ah, that's an optical illusion," I said.

He nodded and picked his nose.

"Don't pick your nose, either," I said. "You should have your hat and gloves on anyway."

"You should," he said.

We were walking down the sidewalk, between mounds of blackened snow. Everything felt dusted with icy grit. Kolya, skinny and small as he was, must have been freezing. All I had on was a denim jacket and a black hooded sweatshirt and I was cold. My Carhartt had been stolen at the Black Lantern last week. I suspected Tom Slowinski had taken it back. At least Kolya was wearing his boots and a real winter coat.

"So who is this kid who hit you?" I said.

"Larry DeSoto," he said. "He's in eighth grade."

"Why is an eighth grader hitting you?"

"I told him to go fuck himself."

"Why did you say that?" I said. "Even Nick wouldn't say that kind of thing to a bigger guy."

That was a lie. That's exactly the kind of thing Nick would have done. Maybe Nick could have used a little of Kolya's Ritalin.

"He beat up my friend Jason," Kolya said. "Someone had to do something."

"Why you?"

"I don't know. I was mad."

"Be more careful," I said.

I didn't have much to say to him. I was getting too old to worry about a twelve-year-old kid all the time. He'd learn the lessons the way I did, except he wouldn't have Nick to bail him out all the time, the way I did all through school.

"You need to make friends with somebody bigger and meaner than you."

He shrugged. We were at the front door of the school. I remembered walking through the same front door when I was a kid, and I remembered how low my stomach would sink and how some days I could barely get up the long, gritty staircase without crying.

"Hey," I said. "Be good today."

"Okay," Kolya said. He kicked the bike racks and then gave me a big smile. "Another day in the old salt mines," he said.

"Where did you learn that?"

"Burt," he said.

"Fuck him. Don't say anything he says. Ever. Now get to class," I said. The bell started ringing.

"Oh, fuck," Kolya said and ran down the hall.

THEY HAD PUT KOLYA on Ritalin a year ago, when he'd first started having trouble in school. In the middle of a spelling test, he went to the window and threw his workbook down to the playground below. Another time, he bit a girl's knee. He used foul language like a prepubescent Richard Pryor, with skill and flawless timing. He broke into the milk machine. And once, during an assembly, he tried to set his own hair on fire with a lighter he had found during recess.

On Ritalin, he had trouble eating. He was listless and lifeless, and he spent a lot of his time sleeping in front of a blaring television, his smooth white face lit green by the glow of frantic, flashing cartoons.

One night Nick and I stole a few of Kolya's pills, smashed them up with a spoon, and snorted them off the kitchen table. We went for a walk, barefoot, and had the idea of walking across the Ambassador Bridge to Canada, almost twenty miles away. We never made it. A cop found us on Michigan Avenue and brought us home.

AFTER I DROPPED OFF KOLYA, I had twenty minutes to get to my class, but I was willing to be late. Something about the great films of American cinema didn't have me all juiced up that morning. I wandered over to the doughnut shop where Nick was already working his first shift. Tom was there, drinking coffee. He did construction work on the new developments out on the edges of Maple Rock. Everyone was saying all the construction would make our houses more valuable and clean up our streets.

"I hear you wussed out of a fight last night," Tom said.

"I did not," I said. "I was tired and drunk."

"What's a matter?" Tom said. "You forget to take your Midol?"

"Why is that funny?" I said to Nick. "Why is this asshole here trying to be funny?"

Nick set coffee and a jelly doughnut on the counter in front of me. He shrugged. "It's not funny," Nick said. "But Tom's a Polack. He doesn't know better."

Tom was actually three-quarters Ukrainian, but his paternal grandfather was Polish and so Tom ended up with a Polish last name. Nick and I never let him forget it.

The to-go counter was swamped. All three of the brothers—Ray, Mario, and Joey—were running around filling up bags and boxes with doughnuts. Ray whistled over at Nick. "Nick! Counter! Now!"

We watched Nick step up to the counter. Tom and I looked at each other and smiled. We had never seen anybody give Nick an order before.

"Why do people always say Polacks are dumb? We invented Paczki Day, didn't we?"

Paczki Day is a Detroit holiday that falls on the Tuesday before Lent. It meant that all the Catholics in Detroit would gorge themselves on jelly doughnuts. Polish immigrants brought the tradition to Detroit years ago. But eventually all the Catholics—the Irish, the Italians, the Ukrainians— picked up on it. When we were kids, we'd even get doughnuts in school.

"What's so smart about a holiday when all you do is eat doughnuts until you're sick? No, Mardi Gras in New Orleans, that's the stuff. That's a holiday to have before Lent. I just read about it."

"You read too much," Tom said.

"People around Detroit are too busy working shit jobs to have real Mardi Gras," I said. "They came up with all of this shit about doughnuts so they could celebrate Fat Tuesday on their way to work in the morning."

"Shut up," Tom said.

"Plus, it's too damn cold for a parade or anything here. I'm starting to think New Orleans is the place to go when I get out of here," I said.

"What's so great about it?"

"It's not here," I said.

"What do they do at Mardi Gras?" Tom asked. He picked up another doughnut and shoved half of it in his mouth.

"It's all about getting drunk. Chicks run around showing their tits. Everybody fucks everybody."

"That's not true," he said.

"How many fucking doughnuts you going to eat?" I said.

"I like them. They have a calming effect, you know. In hospitals, they give them to people with ulcers, or ladies about to give birth, or even people who have had strokes."

"You're not only a dumb Polack, Tom," I said, "you're the dumbest Polack who ever lived."

"Hey, Mikey, I know what you can give up for Lent," Tom said. "You can give up being such a fucking pussy."

And with that, he grabbed a fourth doughnut and walked out of the door.

PROFESSOR HOWARD showed up for class with a box of jelly doughnuts and went off on how Paczki Day was such a hoot that he couldn't resist. He was originally from Manhattan, as he never failed to mention.

"Is anyone here from out of state?" he asked.

Where the fuck did he think he was? Yale? No hands went up. Then he asked how many of us knew about Paczki Day, and all of us raised our hands. He looked dismayed. He was set to teach us something about our history, and we already knew it. Most of us had doughnut grease sliding around in our guts.

So instead he gave a pop quiz that I failed because I had forgotten to attend the previous night's film screening.

I STOPPED BACK HOME for lunch. My mother was there, but before I said anything I looked around the place for the gorilla. He was gone.

"You're done with class?" my mother said.

I nodded.

"Here," she said. "I called in sick today. Let me make you some lunch. You want a BLT? There's some bacon left from this morning."

"No, I don't feel like eating," I said.

"You're sick too?"

"Just tired."

"I got you a present today," she said. "Maybe that will cheer you up."

"Why?"

She said she knew how hard it'd been for me lately. She promised Burt would be going back to Alabama soon. She said that with men like Burt, you can't really kick them out. You have to let them leave on their own terms or they'll never really go away.

She slid a package wrapped in gold foil paper across the table.

I opened the package. It was a book. *The Best American Short Stories 1993.*

"The guy at the bookstore suggested this. I told him you wanted to be a writer and he said this book had just been published."

She stood up and leaned over my shoulder and flipped to the back of the book. "See, here all the writers talk about how they wrote the stories and how they got their ideas and stuff."

"Cool," I said. And I really thought it was. She was doing the best she could. I resolved to cut her some slack about Burt.

"And in the very back," she said, turning the pages for me, "you get all the addresses of the magazines that publish short stories, so you can send in your own work."

I looked over the book. I didn't know the names of any of the authors, but what did I know? I couldn't remember ever reading anything by somebody who was still alive.

"It's not an easy thing to be lonely," she said. "That's all. I hope you understand."

She shrugged, turned her palms up to the sky, and tried to smile.

"Lunch?" she said.

"Sure," I said.


SINCE I WAS HOME that afternoon, doing nothing, I went to Kolya's school and waited for him at the edge of the playground. I figured I could walk him home, give him one day without getting his ass kicked. When you're a boy, you figure out pretty quick that there's always going to be some asshole hanging around the schoolyard, waiting to kick your ass. I always had enemies, but most of them were too afraid of Nick to fuck with me. They hated me from a distance.

Kolya looked happy to see me. His shiner had gone down some, and he was looking fresh-faced and innocent again. His backpack looked absolutely huge on him, and I pictured him as a soldier back from a mission. He had red jelly all over his lips.

"Hey kid," I said. "How's school?"

"Beats a sharp stick in the butt," he said. It was another phrase Burt had taught him.

"Wipe your mouth," I said.

He moved his sleeve across his face. "It's Paczki Day. I ate six of them."

"God bless you," I said. "You're a miracle man."

We walked a couple of blocks, both of us quiet. I was trying to say something that was comforting or wise, because it didn't look to me like he'd had a good day. Because he was on Ritalin, sometimes I felt like he was depressed; but then, how can you tell if a twelve-year-old is depressed? With kids, sometimes they're probably just thinking about Spider Man or whatever, and you think they're contemplating the Apocalypse.

"Stop," he said. "Let's turn around."

"Why?" I said, but I was already looking down the block, where a gnarly, pissed-off-looking trio of kids were taking turns jumping off a fire hydrant.

"That's Larry DeSoto. And all of his buddies. Let's take another street."

I wouldn't let him turn around. "Let's walk right by them," I suggested. "They'll see you with your big brother and they won't say a thing."

The kids jumping off the fire hydrant saw us coming. They stopped their silly game and stared at us, then stood three across the sidewalk. "Hey, it's the pussy patrol," they said.

"It's queer Kolya!"

"Hey, assface."

"Hey, man, your brother picks his nose and eats it."

"Yeah, his butt too."

We were only about ten feet away from them. Kolya was just looking down at the sidewalk.

I guessed that the biggest kid, a fat kid way too hairy for junior high, was Larry. He was standing in the middle of the three kids. He had a caterpillar of peach fuzz on his upper lip.

Kolya wouldn't look at them, like a dog trying not to make eye contact with the alpha. He started whimpering a little and backing away. I grabbed Kolya by the arm and made him stop. "Don't cry," I said.

Then I took a step forward. I looked at Kolya and showed him my clenched fist, but he just stood there, hands limp at his sides.

I hit Larry first, three times in the face. His nose was bleeding all over the front of his jacket. The two other runts tried helping him at first, and I got them each with a good gut punch and knocked the wind out of them. When they got their wind back, they hightailed it home.

Larry DeSoto was still on his back. He looked much younger that way.

"Fucking pussy," I said, but I could barely say anything. I wheezed, then coughed up some phlegm and spit on the ground. Kolya thought he knew what I was doing and spit a wad of saliva at Larry's face. Then he got something in his brain, and started kicking Larry everywhere he could, the nuts, the shins, the ribs, and even the face.

I finally had to pick him up and carry him away. He would have kicked Larry's fat face all day long.


I TOOK KOLYA OVER TO the doughnut shop so we could clean up in the bathroom and settle down a little before we saw Mom. It was almost four o'clock and the Paczki Day crowd had died way down. Nick was just getting off of work. He'd put in ten hours. He had six hours off and then he would come back for the night shift. He was hanging his apron up in the back hallway when we found him. I told him what had happened.

"Are you fucking nuts?" he said. "You beat up some kids? You'll go to jail for that. You're nineteen years old. You can't get away with that kind of shit."

"What was I supposed to do?"

"Not that," he said.

Just then two cops walked in the doughnut shop. I turned and hid my face.

"Relax," he said. "This is a doughnut shop. We get ten cops an hour."

One of the brothers came to the counter and waited on the cops.

Kolya laughed. "Can I get a doughnut?" he said.

"You already ate too many," I said.

"Let him have one," Nick said. "They have a calming effect, you know. You should have one too. They bring your blood pressure down."

"What the fuck is with you people?" I yelled. "Is everybody in this fucking neighborhood an idiot? They're just goddamn doughnuts."

One of the brothers called from the back room: "Nick, get your friends out of here if they can't talk like gentlemen."

BURT WAS ASLEEP on the couch and didn't move when we walked in the door. I tried to get a beer from the fridge, but old Burt had sucked the place dry.

I went down the hall and spent the evening in my room, looking out the front window every so often, half expecting the red-and-blue lights of a cop car to come shining and blinking into the driveway. But Larry DeSoto must not have thought to tell his parents that an adult had beat him up. He probably didn't know how old I was. Maybe he figured he had it coming. Anyway, the cops didn't show.

What I did that night, while waiting to be arrested, was read from my new book. In the table of contents, at the end of the list of stories, my mother had written in black ink: *"To Be Announced" by Michael Smolij (Coming Soon!).*

It was the kind of thing she liked to do, small gestures that made me see how much she believed in me, but that made it hard for me to be her son sometimes. She believed I was destined for great things, or at least destined for a better life, a different existence than the one she and my father had come up with in their time. That's just how mothers are with their sons, I guess, but I imagine some sons handle it better than others.

Eventually I drifted off to sleep in my clothes, on top of my covers, gut aching from doughnuts and coffee and worry. Later I woke to the sound of Burt Nelson yelling at my mother. I stayed in my room again. I didn't make him stop. Whether my mother needed me then or not, I don't know. I never gave myself a chance to find out.

In the end, my mother was right: about a week later, Burt Nelson would leave and he would not come back into our lives again, though I had nothing to do with that. I simply woke up one morning and found my mother cooking breakfast in her work clothes. She said, "Burt is gone and we won't have to deal with him anymore."

I nodded. Kolya shrugged.

The truth is, I had just sat back and waited Burt Nelson out. I still have a tendency to sit back and wait out the bad things that try and take over my life.

After a couple of weeks, I quit reading the new book my mother had bought for me, although I told her I had finished it. I said it was one of the finest books that I'd ever read. I said it had inspired me to write some of my own stories. In reality, I had just placed it on my shelf, where I forgot about it for a while. I was old enough to know a few things, and one of them was this: the best American short stories weren't written by people like me.

## a newcomer's guide
## to ann arbor

THIS IS WHAT you do:
Because you say you hate Maple Rock, on Friday nights in the fall, when things are still crisp and fresh, you and your pals drive out to Ann Arbor and pretend you are college students there and meet the girls and drink their beer and go to their parties. Nick tells you how it's done.

First of all, don't dress like an asshole. If you come to a party in a slick Banana Republic shirt tucked into some shiny Kenneth Cole pants, good as you might look, they're going to think you're trying too hard. It's better to dress in Levi's, with some low-maintenance brown leather boots. Wear a tight and clean white T-shirt when the weather's warm, since, after all, you do have muscles—you lug boxes all day or pound nails for a living or lift weights in your mother's basement out of endless boredom.

Don't slouch. Walk tall. Wear tennis shoes. If a girl asks your major, don't fucking tell her you're taking classes at the community college back home. Say, "I'm undecided." If you think the girl is smart, say you're leaning toward English, or history. But if the person you're talking to seems dim and shallow—as so many of them will, despite Michigan's stellar academic reputation—go ahead and say you're majoring in business. Say you want to get into the B-School at Michigan.

When you see an old high-school girlfriend—Sonya Stecko, for example—don't talk to her about old times. Don't say, "Remember all the good times we had? Remember prom night?" Because she won't remember, okay? She's over it. It's ancient times, man, ancient times.

Even though you could probably handle yourself, stay out of fights. The guys who go to college in Ann Arbor don't know the damage you can do to a human skull, and they won't think twice about using a beer bottle or a banister on the back of your head. And even with your friends, you'll *always* be outnumbered. Chances are, deep down these college guys will have as much meanness and anger in their hearts as you do.

More rules, Nick says:

Only go into parties with strobe lights, dark dance floors, loud music. Nobody will notice a stranger at these parties, and people are usually drunker and more open to widening their social circles.

Split up. Don't show up all together, like some dork field trip from Maple Rock. Two to a party, that's the ideal for scoring chicks, but if you can only find one good open-door party, stagger your arrivals. Every twenty minutes, send two more inside.

Get a beer. Have something in your hand when conversation lags. When a woman asks you something you don't know how to answer, you can take a long drag off the bottle while you figure out something to say.

Avoid the obvious. If you go for the girl in the tight black dress, the stylishly cropped blond hair, and the unabashedly hard nipples, the college boys will watch you like a hawk all night. Even if she comes on to you, blow her off. People get protective of these women.

Learn to dance. Guys who go to college in places like Ann Arbor hate to dance, they cannot do it. The trick is simple: have confidence. Find a few moves you can do. Be funny and loose. Act like you don't give a shit, which you don't. You get a girl on the dance floor, moving a few inches from you, getting a shiny gloss of sweat on her neck, you're doing well. Make the girl laugh, and you're home free.

Above all, remember this: these girls in Ann Arbor know what they want. The ones that want it, want it just as bad as you. They'll get you more than you'll get them. You want a piece of ass, and sometimes so do they. The girls at the Black Lantern in Maple Rock make you think that you're the only human being on earth who wants nothing more than cheap sex. But you're not.

The girls in Ann Arbor won't do this to you. They also smell better than the women in Maple Rock. They wear scents like Grass or Clouds or Tranquility. They won't choke you with flower smells. Girls in Ann Arbor smell like wind and fire. Their tongues taste like earth and salt.

Do not, do fucking not, Nick says, under any circumstances, fall in love with a woman in Ann Arbor. Do not wake up in their sunny apartments the next morning, in their messy rooms full of books and black-and-white photography, in their warm narrow beds that smell of beer and salt and sweat, and say that you're in love. You're not in love. You're an outsider. You don't belong in love with this woman. Leave before she wakes up, even if you feel like you're making the biggest mistake of your life. She won't miss you.

"I should have known you'd turn this into something poetic and meaningful," Nick says. "But it's not, Mikey. Trust me, it's not."

# the boy with
# the backward chakra

TWO WEEKS INTO MY JOB, a little kid named Manny Holloway died on my watch. He was an asthmatic. I was sitting on the lifeguard stand, scanning the pool. It was ninety-five degrees and the pool was packed. We had three lifeguards out there. I was a little hungover, I guess. I'd stayed out too late the night before. I was dreamy. It happens up there on the guard stand, in the heat, the sun, the water gleaming, the sound of kids and the nearly naked bodies of women all around you. You think about things. I can't remember what had my attention at that moment, but all of a sudden, some woman was screaming. I looked over, and there was this pale little kid with white-blond hair and a purple face slumped over the side of the pool. He was wearing one orange water wing. People crowded around yelling, even though a tall, bald man was shouting, "Stand back! Don't panic! Give him air, give him air!"

I had my mom's car that day, so I drove over to the hospital after I talked to the cops and everybody else. It had been a few hours by then, but the boy's mother was still there. She was a young woman, not much older than me, I thought. Later I found out she was thirty-three. She was wearing a black bathing suit and yellow flip-flops and had a hospital blanket wrapped around her. A couple of other women were with her, and some kids were off in the corner of the waiting room, playing. I was wearing my Burton Farms uniform, a too-tight royal blue polo shirt with white shorts. I still had my whistle around my neck. I looked like an idiot, like an extra from some bad 1970s summer-camp film. I sat alone along a wall. I could tell just by looking at the women that the kid was dead. They alternated between bouts of crying and long silences, where they just sat, holding their three heads together, like they were all joined by their skulls.

It didn't seem right that this grieving mother should be sitting there in a bathing suit and blanket. I got up and went to the nurse at the admitting desk. I said, "Can't you get me some scrubs?"

"For what?" she said.

"For that poor woman over there. Her kid is dead."

"I know," she said.

"Well, get her some fucking clothes, please. It's not right."

"Look," said the nurse. But then she didn't say anything else. She just picked up the phone, dialed three numbers, mumbled something, and looked at me. In about three minutes, an orderly brought me some green scrubs.

I walked over to the mother and stood in front of her. The other women were rounding up their kids.

"I'm very sorry," I said. I handed her the scrubs. She stood, dropped her blanket, and slid on the green pants, then pulled the shirt over her head. Then she sat back down and wrapped the blanket around herself again.

"Do you want me to call a priest or something?" I said. I don't know why I said that. I never had been in the immediate aftershock of death before. It seemed like the kind of thing to do. I figured Father Mack, my mother's friend, would come down and talk to her. He was probably at our house right now anyway, whipping up a pasta salad or cleaning out the garage.

"No," she said. "I'm not a Christian."

"A rabbi?"

"No, I'm not religious," she said.

I nodded. It was pretty fucking bold, I thought, not to be religious when your kid has just died. I wanted to say something else, who knows what, but a hospital staff member came through the double doors of the ER and ushered her away.

I sat down where she had been sitting. The two women who had been with her came back over with their kids. They were both blond, and they looked like sisters.

"Are you here for her now?" they asked. "If you are, we'll be going. We're so sorry about everything. We barely know her. We just felt somebody should be here."

"I am here now," I said. "I'll stick around."

They seem relieved to be rid of everything. Clutching their children, they raced out the automatic doors.

I waited for more than an hour at the hospital until the kid's mother came out to the waiting area again. She was still wearing the scrubs and holding the blanket around herself. She seemed surprised to see me.

"Your friends left," I said.

"I don't even know them," she said. "They're just mothers."

"Should we call someone?" I asked.

"Who?" she said.

I hadn't expected her to answer like that.

"I'm sorry," I said.

"It's not your fault. I had my eyes on him the whole time, and then I lost him. He was my responsibility."

She started to cry.

"I was the lifeguard," I said.

She looked down and shook her head vigorously, as if to disagree.

I WAS ALMOST twenty-three. I'd spent the year taking more classes at the community college, another journalism course and a literature class. I had written a few more dumb pieces for the student newspaper—TUITION RATES TO IN-CREASE, STRAY CAT BECOMES BIOLOGY DEPARTMENT MASCOT, BOB SEGER VISITS CAMPUS—and my mother had them up on the fridge along with Kolya's Three-Legged Race Champion certificate from Field Day.

I was still one semester shy of an associate's degree. My record was spotty and I had dropped a lot of classes. Still, although I hadn't told anybody this, a week before I started the lifeguard job, I'd driven to Ann Arbor to meet with somebody in the admissions office. Her name was Janice and she seemed to be about my age. She was dressed in a Michigan T-shirt and a khaki skirt, and had short blond hair cut into a bob. She kept tucking her hair behind her left ear as she talked. She spoke very fast and her legs were very tan. I wondered how she got so tan in that little cubicle. She had just graduated from Michigan herself, and recommended the school highly. I had expected somebody older, somebody in a smart business suit, behind a big desk in a plush office, but Janice was sitting in a small cubicle at a desk piled high with manila folders. For some reason, the casualness of the office made me more nervous than ever. I was wearing my only suit, despite the heat. Janice kept referring to me as a nontraditional student. She assured me that the university could accommodate my needs.

"What do you mean by nontraditional?" I asked.

"Well, you know," she said, "somebody who isn't coming to us straight from high school, somebody whose educational career may have a few gaps. A 'returning student,' we sometimes call them."

"Right," I said. "My grades are pretty strong. There's a C on there from my first semester, but that's because my film class was not exactly fairly graded."

"Will you plan to live on campus?" she asked.

I hadn't really thought of it. Maple Rock was less than an hour away, and I figured I couldn't afford to get my own place. I didn't know what to say. I didn't know what Janice wanted me to say.

"Sure," I said.

Janice put together a neat little packet for me and slid it into a shiny blue folder embossed with a golden block M.

"This packet has everything you need to get started," she said. "And my business card is in there. Feel free to e-mail me if you need anything."

"Right," I said. I didn't have an e-mail address, but I knew that was something I should keep to myself.

"I have a good friend who goes here," I said. "Sonya Stecko."

"I can't say that I know her," she said. "But there are more than forty-thousand students at Michigan."

"Right," I said.

"You do know that we also have a satellite campus in Dearborn?" Janice said. "It's closer to your house. And it also is a little less overwhelming than this place. It's huge here."

"Right," I said.

As I was packing up my backpack, Janice said, "What do you think your concentration will be, Michael?"

"Concentration?" I said. "I think it will be pretty good. I concentrate pretty well."

"No," she said. "That's what we call a major here—a concentration."

"Right," I said. "Philosophy."

"Oh," she said. "Wow. I sub-concentrated in philosophy. Who is your favorite?"

She was killing me.

"Um, I like most of them. It's hard to have a favorite," I said. My mind was blank. I couldn't think of one major philosopher. Finally, I managed to croak out the name Marx.

"Fabulous!" she said.

I pretty much ran out of there to avoid more conversation.

"Best of luck," Janice called after me. "I'll be rooting for you. And remember, we offer campus tours every Wednesday at noon."

I'd noticed, in recent months, a tendency for people to root for me. I wasn't exactly sure if this was because I was somehow charming and endearing or that I had a wimpy patheticness that encouraged people to cheer me on, like some wheezing last place finisher in a marathon.

The reason I had told Janice that I was interested in majoring in philosophy was because that summer I was taking something called Introduction to the Great Philosophers, which was taught by a friend of Father Mack's.

Father Mack was an old high-school friend of my mother's, and he'd been transferred back to a parish just outside Detroit. He came over a lot on Saturdays to do things around the house or take my mother out for pie and coffee. He was the kind of guy who had trouble hearing the word *no*. If he came over and offered to cook us hamburgers or replace the bathroom sink, there was no turning him down. When he encouraged me to take the Great Philosophers, I knew I had no choice.

It was Father Mack who'd found me the job as a lifeguard at a private swim and tennis club in Livonia, where his brother Stu was on the board of directors. Mack had five brothers, all of them rich, all of whom had followed their father into real estate development and construction, and all of whom, like Stu, served on many boards and committees and could get you just about anything you needed in the tri-county area.

Burton Farms Club was tucked away in a tree-lined neighborhood, far from any main roads. The members were rich, but not wealthy rich, just the kind of people I thought were rich back then—people with two cars, three full baths, four bedrooms. I didn't realize how rich people could really be until later in life.

Nobody paid much attention to me. Some of the young suburban mothers would drink too many wine coolers in the late afternoon and flirt with me, and I liked the attention. Every so often, on weekends, some pale, flabby businessman on the board would tell me that a toilet was busted or that the stripes on the tennis court needed repainting and I had to fix things like that. Still, I couldn't imagine easier work than hanging around with girls in bathing suits or flirting with bored and tipsy young mothers, while I sat in the sun, watching the pool. That is, it was easy work until the kid died.

THE MOTHER OF the dead child was named Holly. She asked me to drop her off at the place she worked, Burton Oaks Day Spa and Salon. She was a massage therapist there.

"My mother went there once," I said. "She won a gift certificate at a raffle at church."

Holly nodded. She had big eyes and her shoulder-length red hair, which had been wet from swimming, had dried into a mess of tangles and was sticking up in places, like the hair of a little kid who has been in the pool all day. This made her look younger than me, but when I took a moment to look at her watery eyes—a shiny medley of green and gray—I could see faint lines in her skin. She'd been crying so much that her eyes were puffy and her nose was raw and red. It didn't matter, I suppose, how old she was: she had a kid, a dead kid, and whether she was twenty-three or thirty-three, she knew and felt things I couldn't understand. It was something I should have seen then.

"One of the girls here will take me home," she said.

"Good. I don't think you should be alone."

"I won't be alone."

I almost asked her where the boy's father was, but I stopped myself. If he were around, he'd have been at the hospital. I was glad I stopped myself. It seemed one of the few mature moves I'd made in my life.

"Thanks for the scrubs," she said. She was still wearing them. They made her look a little like an inmate.

"I'm sorry," I said when she opened the door.

She was crying again. She just waved and closed the door.

I didn't go back to work that afternoon, or ever again. I was through with lifeguarding. I got home at six o'clock, a few hours earlier than anybody expected. Kolya was spending the weekend with a friend's family Up North. The living room was empty. I stood in the doorway for a while, trying to process the day. Just then, down the hall, Father Mack emerged from my mother's room in nothing but a white towel. His chest hair was matted and damp.

"Oh, good Lord, Michael," he said.

"What?" my mother said, coming out of the bedroom too. She was wearing a short black robe I'd never seen before. In the hallway's dim light, she looked closer to my age than her own, her face flushed red, her dark hair messed up and hanging straight down the sides of her face.

"Oh, hello," I said. I waved and went into the basement. Later my mother came downstairs dressed in shorts, a blue Michigan sweatshirt, and sandals. Her hair was pulled back in a ponytail. She still looked so young. Her face had changed some, but she looked basically like she did when I was very young.

"We were going to tell you," she said.

I exhaled and stared at the ceiling for a while.

"He's leaving the priesthood," she said.

"I'd hope so," I said.

"I didn't plan for this," she said. "But I'm not sorry it happened."

"That's nice for you," I said.

"In fact, Michael, I'm very happy about it."

"A kid died at work today," I said. "While I was on duty."

"Oh, Michael," she said.


OUTSIDE EVERYTHING was clouded by the haze and humidity. I stayed inside. We didn't have air-conditioning, but I had moved into the basement after high school and my bedroom was cool. I couldn't get very good reception on the television down there, so I was reading a lot. On the last Monday of every month, the Livonia public library had a book sale to clear out old and damaged books. For four dollars, you could fill a shopping bag. Sometimes I filled two. I didn't know what I was picking up, but I was willing to read anything. Some of it was hard to judge, I mean, if it was any good or not, because the books had those blank library bindings and there were no quotes on the back covers. I stuck to the literature and philosophy sections. At night, I listened to Ernie Harwell call the Tigers games on WJR. I was always awake for the last inning. I didn't sleep or eat too much. I knew exactly how Manny Holloway would have sounded when he was alive. I heard his voice anytime I tried to go to sleep. I dreamed about his mother a lot. I saw her in her bathing suit, wrapped in the blanket in the waiting room, with nobody she really knew around her.

FATHER MACK WAS at our house more and more. Or Mack. He asked us to stop calling him Father, but I still did. He'd quit wearing his black shirt and clerical collar. He looked flabby and older in a T-shirt and khaki shorts. He started to go to his family's office in Southfield a few days a week. He would tell us at dinner about some of the construction projects his company was working on, and then sometimes his voice would trail off, as if he had completely lost interest in his own story.

Mack was lucky: his father had made him a partner in the construction business years ago, though Mack had never really done anything, and had never collected any of his profits. His father hadn't been a religious man, and always believed that his son would eventually give up on the Church.

"He's eighty-three years old," Mack said one night when Kolya asked about his father. "And he's happy as hell that before he dies he gets to see my vocation fall apart. He said, 'I finally beat God. I got his Son, but he didn't get mine.' Then he laughed his ass off."

Mack had had a few beers, and he pointed at Kolya with a fork.

"He never believed I could hack the life of a priest," he said. "I guess he was right."

My mother put her hand on Mack's shoulder, as if she was reminding him not to talk too much about his situation. He looked at her, then looked at us, then attacked his pork chop with his knife.

Still, in general, Mack was a pretty happy influence around our house. He didn't have very many possessions and it only took him a couple of hours to move in.

"You're not wasting any time," I said to my mother. "He's just coming right in, huh?"

"Michael, what do you expect? Do you think he can drop out of the priesthood and hang around the rectory until he has a place to stay?"

Mack had started working out, and would always ask me if I wanted to go jogging with him. I never did go, but Kolya, who was fifteen now and taller and faster than me, had started to get interested in sports, and he would run with Father Mack. I was glad Kolya had some older guy as a role model. I wasn't up for it that summer.

One afternoon, after a run, Father Mack came downstairs and tried to talk to me about Manny.

"Michael, you didn't cause that boy's death. You witnessed it. It's not your fault."

"I was the lifeguard," I said.

"It was God's will," he said. "Who knows the mind of God?"

"Oh, knock it the fuck off!" I said. "Come on, Father Mack."

"Mack."

"Whatever."

"What?"

"You heard me," I said. "If God wanted that kid to die, he's nothing but a big fucking bastard!"

"Michael, that's not a very mature response," he said. "But it's an understandable one, I suppose. You know, that is why I suggested you take the philosophy course this summer—"

My mother called down the stairs. "What are you guys talking about down there?"

"We're fine," Father Mack said. He looked wounded.

I reached over to my nightstand and picked up a book. I handed it to Father Mack.

"Nietzsche?" he said.

"Yeah," I said. "Have you read it?"

He smiled and exhaled through his teeth: *sheesh*, said his breath, *sheesh*.

"Yeah, I've read it," he said.


"I WANT YOU," Professor Donovan said, "to spend the class period freewriting."

Most of the class moaned. It was obvious that a day of freewriting meant that Donovan had nothing to say, but felt too guilty about it to just let us go home.

"I want you," Donovan said, "to consider a moment when you have faced a philosophical crisis in your own life.

I want you to write about the philosophical questions that arose, and to discuss the philosophical conclusions that you arrived at, or the lack of a conclusion for that matter."

Most people groaned a little more and got out their "journals," hardbound black notebooks that Donovan had passed out at the beginning of the semester, and started to force themselves to write something. It was easy for me to write something: *While I was lifeguarding this summer some little kid died.*

I never minded freewriting, and I just did my best to tune out the other students, some of whom were still complaining. Inevitably someone asked, "How long does this have to be?"

"It's finished when it's finished," Donovan said.

"Are we supposed to write something like, 'To be or not to be?'" somebody else asked.

Randy Gardener, who always sat next to me in the class, not because we were friends but simply because he had been a few years behind me at Maple Rock High and knew my name, said, "Bud or Bud Light?" He slapped my arm. I glared at him and he said it louder. "Bud or Bud Light?"

The class started cracking up.

"Shut up and write!" Donovan yelled. Everybody laughed harder. I felt bad for Donovan. When he returned the journals during the next class period, he'd written, "Complex and thoughtful—A. Nice work." I showed the assignment to Father Mack. Not that I cared what he thought or anything, but I also wanted to show him I wasn't a complete fuckup.

"Good work," he said. "I'm impressed. Bob Donovan is a tough teacher."

I BORROWED Father Mack's old Buick Skylark one morning—
he let me use it whenever I wanted, since he was driving a
new company car, a red BMW, his mid-life crisis car, he
called it—and drove into Livonia to the strip mall that
housed the Burton Oaks Day Spa. I wanted to see Holly.
I wanted to see that she was okay, or at least almost okay. I
wanted her to see me and forgive everything or see me and
blame me for everything and beat me with her fists. I didn't
want her to be neutral. That would be too much.

I walked into the salon. A few women in sundresses sat in
the waiting room. The receptionist behind the front counter
was dressed in a black suit. The place smelled heavily of
woodsy soaps and flowery lotions. I thought I heard the sound
of water bubbling. A ponytailed woman in black baseball cap,
black spandex, and black sports bra walked into the place,
drinking from a giant bottle of water. She was so thin her ribs
were pretty much right out there. She looked unhappy to see
me standing in front of her. She huffed behind me, waiting to
talk to the receptionist. The receptionist was about nineteen.
Her skin was almost orange and her hair almost white.

"I'm here to see Holly," I said. "If she's available."

"Do you have an appointment?" the orange girl asked.

"No," I said.

"She's not here today," the orange girl said. "Monday
is her day off this week."

"Right," I said. "I forgot. It was just a whim."

"I can set you up with an appointment," she said.

The woman in the spandex and sports bra huffed again.

I rolled my eyes and the orange girl smiled.

"How's next Friday?" the orange girl said. "Are you free?"

I laughed at the thought of my not being free. "Yeah, sure," I said.

"One? Two o'clock?"

I nodded.

"Good," she said. She wrote down my appointment on the business card, and handed it to me. The woman behind me slid beside me and said, "I just need to buy some supplements."

I walked out looking at the card in my hand.

NICK AND TOM came around a few nights a week. One night, I was going through all of my old baseball cards, which I hadn't looked at in about eight years. I was trying to get them in some kind of order because I'd heard about an old guy at the American Legion hall who would pay cash for them.

"Hey, isn't it weird that the priest from Divine Child is cutting your lawn?" Nick said.

"Nope. That's just the lawn boy," I said.

"Mikey, I already know everything. Our mothers are sisters, you idiot. Father Mack is moving in with you guys."

"He's not a priest anymore," I said.

"Man, I don't know if I would stand for that," Tom said. "It's scandalous."

"Shut up," Nick said.

"What do you guys want?" I said.

"You should come out and get blasted," Tom said. "We were so shit-faced last night, we all had to go to work drunk this morning."

"Scandalous," I said.

"You really should come to Ann Arbor with us," Nick said. "Sunny's got a new house off campus now. She lives with six hot girls."

Sonya was heading into her fourth year of college. She'd taken a year off to travel around Europe and look at art. She had sent me a postcard from Milan, which I imagined was her way of saying, "Breaking up with you was the best thing I ever did."

"Dude," Tom said. "I can't believe how drunk everybody was."

"Are you sorting baseball cards, Mikey?" Nick said.

"I don't know about a party," I said.

I hadn't talked to Sonya much lately, and even though she sometimes invited Nick and Tom and me to her parties and things, I was starting to think that she only invited us because we were funny to her—the pathetic boys of her youth with shitty jobs, shitty clothes, awkward movements, and ungrammatical, profane speech. I pictured her writing poems and essays about us in her women's studies courses or something. I didn't need that.

I told this theory to Nick and Tom, but they ignored it.

"This one chick," Tom said, "she danced around in a bikini all night. She was hot. Dude, if her boyfriend hadn't been there . . ."

"You're not supposed to call them chicks," Nick said. "They don't like that. It's Ann Arbor."

"Well, they're not fucking here," Tom said. "So what does it matter?"

"Just watch it. You know you really fucking embarrass me whenever we go to Ann Arbor."

"You're just jealous that all those chicks want my twelve-inch hog," Tom said.

"Could you guys leave now?" I said. "This sounds like the kind of conversation that could happen elsewhere."

"Miserable Mikey," Nick said.

"Mikey's got dirt in his pussy," Tom said.

I didn't care about their teasing. I was just glad that they left.

HOLLY DIDN'T recognize me at first. She came in and filled out a little chart and asked me a few questions. Name? Date of birth? Did I have any chronic health problems? Allergies? Did I have any specific, recurring aches and pains? Any tenderness? Trouble sleeping? Loss of appetite?

She was scribbling away on the clipboard. Her hands moved quickly, and I couldn't read anything she was writing from where I sat. Then her shoulders gave way to a slight tremble, the hands shook, and she looked up at me.

"Hi," I said.

"I know who you are," she said.

"I'm sorry."

She wanted to know why I was in the office, and when I said, "A massage," she said, "No, really," and so I had to say, "I wanted to see if you were okay. I can't stop thinking about it."

I thought she might cry, but she didn't. She tilted her head back, took a deep breath, and smiled at me again.

"It was his asthma that killed him," she said. "If he hadn't had asthma, it wouldn't have been like that. He didn't drown, really. Don't blame yourself."

I just nodded. What did I have to say? I was twenty-two years old. Why did I always expect myself to act in ways that were tactful and brave? I just sat there.

"Okay," she said. "You can get undressed and get under this sheet here, face-down. It's up to you if you'd like your underwear on or not. However you feel more comfortable."

"Do you still want to do this?" I said.

"It's my job," she said. "You will pay me, right?"

She left the room and shut the door. I left my underwear on and got under the covers. It was not cold in the room, but I had goose bumps and my spine twitched under the sheet. My heart thumped around in my chest, offbeat and clumsy. It seemed like I was there forever under that sheet, waiting for her.

When Holly came back in, it was obvious that she had been crying. She explained a few things about massage, but I wasn't thinking about what she was saying. I was trying to keep from getting a hard-on under that sheet. I was glad to be facedown. I thought about baseball, but that wasn't easy to do once her hands and the apricot-scented oil were on my skin. This made me feel worse about myself. Really, what kind of person was I?

A few minutes into it, she started working on my back. She said, "This is interesting. This is really strange."

"What?" I said.

She didn't answer me for twenty seconds.

"Is there something that is burdening you?" she said.

"What?"

Again, a long pause.

"Are you angry with someone? Did someone you love disappoint you? Have you ever been abandoned?"

"What?" I said again.

"Are you afraid of something? Of success? Or change, maybe?"

"Why?"

"Well, your heart chakra is backward. It's the oddest thing."

She explained to me about chakras, about channels of energy that move in and out of your body, and how blocked chakras, or in my case backward chakras, could cause all sorts of physical and emotional problems.

"You're carrying around a lot of burdens," she said.

Then she didn't say anything for a while, just kept working on my muscles, and I almost fell asleep. When she was done, she said, "You know who else had a backward heart chakra? Manny, my son."

It was almost impossible to sit up. My limbs were heavy with water. I let the sheet drop from my body and I was in my underwear, dazed. I'd never been so relaxed in my life.

"Hold on," she said. "I'll leave so you can get dressed."

When I was ready, I opened the door and took out my wallet. I didn't know if I should tip, but I gave her three twenty-dollar bills, which was everything I had, and said, "I'm all set."

She thanked me. She said it was nice to see me.

Then I said one of the only appropriate, kind, and thoughtful things I had ever said in my life. I said, "I would like to hear more about Manny."

I meant it.

She smiled at me. I saw her eyes get watery again. "That'd be a nice thing," she said.

FOR SEVERAL DAYS after the massage, I did nothing but sleep and read. For the first time in my life I came down with a summer cold. I had a fever and woke up sweating, then woke up with chills, shivering and trembling. I stayed in my cool den of a basement, sweating it out. Going up the stairs for a glass of juice seemed to exhaust me. My mother and Mack would come downstairs and I would refuse to let them take my temperature. I refused Popsicles and chicken soup. Nick and Tom called but I didn't come to the phone. My limbs still felt so heavy. My head felt like it was full of water. I skipped my philosophy class on Tuesday morning.

Finally, on Wednesday morning I woke up and felt better. I took my first shower in days, ate a breakfast of three eggs and toast, then got dressed, borrowed Father Mack's new BMW, and drove down Highway 14. The sun was so bright it was hard to drive with both eyes wide open. I squinted into the light. I felt like I had sweat out all of the bad shit in me—the depression, the guilt, the boredom and hopelessness—over the last few days. The car still smelled new. I felt new.

Around noon, I found myself in the lobby of the admissions office at Michigan, waiting to take a campus tour. I had expected to be one of several dozen tourists and prospective students, but as I stood next to the giant maize M that said, GO BLUE! TOURS EVERY WEDNESDAY AT NOON, and the clock shifted both hands toward twelve, I realized that not many people would be joining me. A spry old couple in matching Michigan Windbreakers and baseball caps came walking through the lobby doors just as Janice came down the staircase from her office and said, "Michael!"

I was so shocked that she remembered me that I screamed her name back, doubling the pep and enthusiasm with which she had said mine. "Janice!"

We stood smiling at each other while the elderly couple came at us, the man thrusting his hand at us from several feet away. "Henry 'Hank' Wilson," he said, "Class of '49."

We shook hands, and his wife said, "Edna Fuller, 1951."

"Nice to meet you," Janice and I both said.

"I don't know if I really need a tour," I said. "I know the campus pretty well."

It was a lie, but I had pictured myself being able to blend in on a tour, not stuck in an intimate foursome with two geezers and a university tour guide.

Janice grabbed my arm. "You're not leaving me now," she said.

The tour was the usual rah-rah bullshit, peppered with comments about college life in the good old days from Hank and Edna. The dorms, the student union, the new building projects, the athletic hall of fame, and the state-of-the-art computing center. Toward the end of the tour, Janice led us into the Law Quad, an old Gothic quadrangle that looked as if it had been lifted right out of Oxford or Cambridge. She showed us into the law library's reading room and whispered to us that we should feel free to take a look around. It was like church, with the dark wood, the stained-glass windows, and the high ceiling. I walked up and down the main corridor. Each footstep echoed. A few students studying at the long oak tables stared at me. My mouth was probably hanging open. I peeked into the little alcoves, where small desks were hidden among shelves stacked with law books. Gold lamps were affixed to the top center of each desk.

"Can any student study in here?" I asked.

"Of course," she said. "The UGLI—the Undergraduate Library—is a little more fun. More socializing than studying, though."

When the tour was almost over, I thanked Janice quickly and bailed, sticking her with old Hank and Edna. I found a bookstore on campus and browsed around the textbooks for a while, until I found a summer course called American Dreams: Lost and Found. For three dollars, I bought a copy of *The Great Gatsby*—a novel I had heard of many times but had never read. I also bought a yellow legal pad and a GO BLUE pen. Then I wandered back to the Law Quad and the reading room of the law library, found a hidden alcove with a desk and chair, flipped on my own gold reading lamp, and read the book straight through, copying down the lines I liked best. I wondered if anybody knew I wasn't a student, and if anybody would ask to see my ID But nobody seemed to care that I was there. I read until the light faded from the stained-glass windows above me. I copied the words, "So we beat on, boats against the current, borne back ceaselessly into the past." It seemed like I had written them. My palms felt light. I was buzzing.

I CAME HOME EXHAUSTED, well after dark. Maple Rock seemed blander and more stagnant then ever to me that night. My mother was sitting at the kitchen table drinking a glass of wine, still in the skirt and blouse she had worn to work. She looked angry. I figured she was mad that I had taken Mack's good car without asking, but I had left him the keys to the Buick. I knew I was pushing Mack's limits, but I was curious. How far would he go to get me to like him?

"Look," I said, hanging his keys on the rack in the kitchen, "I'm sorry I was gone so long. Something came up."

I went to the fridge and got out a can of beer and sat across from my mother at the table.

"We've decided to move," my mother said. She never was good at having difficult conversations, and I knew she was nervous and serious when she came right out and said something.

"Mack's family has money," she said. "And now he does too."

I didn't say anything. I got up and looked in the fridge. I was ravenous; over the weekend, while I'd been sick, I had hardly eaten and I was suddenly so hungry I could barely get the food out of the fridge fast enough. I started planning a sandwich in my head.

"We've picked out a house in Northville. It's beautiful. Five bedrooms, Michael. Can you imagine that? Three baths!"

I took out a loaf of Italian bread Mom had bought at Beirut Bakery that morning. I cut the loaf of bread in half, right down the middle. Then I cut that half down the middle, lengthwise, so that the bread made one giant submarine bun. I got out the mustard and mayonnaise, spread them on the bun.

"It's on two acres of land, at the end of this beautiful gravel road that's completely covered in oak trees. In autumn, my God, it will be breathtaking."

I found some turkey and some bologna and lined each half of the bread with meat. I layered slices of American cheese on top of each half.

"I mean, I never, ever imagined that I would live someplace like that. Kolya will go to one of the best high schools in the state."

My head in the fridge, I found pickles and olives, half of a tomato, a cucumber, and some wilted lettuce that was still edible. I brought them to the counter.

"He's excited. I talked to him this morning. He might be on the swim team and maybe in the jazz band or ROTC or whatever. They don't have any of those things at Maple Rock."

I added some banana peppers, a little salt, and another layer of cheese. When I put the halves of the sandwich together, it stood almost eight inches tall. I garnished the side of my plate with one handful of potato chips, and then a second.

"And Mack and I plan to get married," she said.

I brought the enormous sandwich to my mouth and took the biggest bite I could. My mother stared at me. I flashed her the thumbs-up sign and chewed and chewed.

"Of course, you don't have to come," she said. "I suppose you could stay right here."

I gave her another thumbs-up, took another bite as soon as I had swallowed my first. My mother left the room.

That night the phone rang. I figured it was Nick or Tom, wanting to go out and get drunk.

"Hello," I said.

"You never called me," a woman's voice said.

"Holly?" I said.

"Hello," she said.

SUNDAY I WENT TO Holly's house, a small brick ranch in Redford. The yard was neat, with a few abstract, curvy sculptures and some flowers lining the front of the house. A statue of Buddha sat on the front porch, under the mailbox. The welcome mat didn't say WELCOME, it said PEACE. It was hot, and the air smelled like fresh-cut grass and heated asphalt. I remember that, because when Holly opened the door, everything smelled different. A lavender and peppermint scent washed over me, and I almost floated inside.

I might as well say it: I was taken with her beauty so suddenly, I was having a hard time keeping my basic bodily functions in order. She looked different than I remembered—taller. And her red hair seemed darker and deeper, almost auburn, and her gray-green eyes looked pale, almost silver. Even though it was summer, her skin was still very fair, and she had a tiny band of freckles dotting her nose and high cheekbones. When she smiled, her big eyes would get suddenly smaller and brighter, so it looked like two tiny gems of light were hidden under her eyelids. Her body was full of curves, with fuller breasts and hips than I remembered. Talking was hard enough, but walking was almost impossible. My limbs felt heavy one minute, and then I would take a step forward and my bones would turn to dust. My stomach was a swirling pit of water, and I worried that I might have to go straight to the bathroom.

Holly was dressed in a simple gauzy peasant shirt that was sheer enough for me to see the outline of the white camisole underneath. She wore a pair of denim shorts, cut high on her leg, and no shoes. Her toenails were painted purple.

The living room had wooden floors with small oriental rugs placed here and there. There was no television. There was a small stereo playing a tape of chants in a language I imagined was Indian or Chinese or something. A candle—the source of the lavender smell—flickered on a wooden table in the corner. There were some pillows on the floor, and a futon. "This is a nice place," I said.

"We're—I mean, I'm—just renting," she said. "Do you want a drink?"

"Sure, anything is fine," I said.

I sat on the futon while she went into the kitchen.

She came back a few minutes later with a small tea set on a wooden tray.

"I haven't had company in a while," she said. "This is nice."

She knelt on a small bench in front of me and poured the tea.

"It's peppermint," she said, handing me a small cup with no handles. "I think peppermint has a nice cooling effect in the summer."

I'd never been in a room like that in my life. I'd never seen someone kneeling on a bench like that. I'd never drunk peppermint tea.

"Mmm," I said, trying to hide the fact that I burned the shit out of my tongue. "Mmm."

We sipped our tea. I started to feel like it was a mistake to come and see her. What could she possibly have to say to me? And what did I have to say to her? Just as I was imagining a way to leave without hurting her feelings, Holly took the lead.

"How long have you been a lifeguard?" she said.

"Not long," I said. "A few weeks and then I quit."

"Because of Manny?" she said.

I nodded. I tried to look desolate. She leaped up from the bench like she had a great idea. She walked over to a small writing desk in the corner and started to shuffle papers.

"My parents came up here for the funeral," she said. "They're from Florida. My father retired early from Ford. They'd like me to move back down there."

"Would that be good?" I said.

"They drive me crazy," she said. "I grew up around here, you know. I came back here because my friend Annie opened a salon and said I could have a workspace there."

"Yeah, it's nice," I said.

"Michael," she said. "No, it's not nice. It's depressing. I can't think of anything more depressing than the Detroit area."

"I like it," I said.

"Where else have you been?"

"I went to Toronto once," I said. "And Ohio. Around there."

"You need to travel more," she said. "The world starts to feel small if you stay still for a long time."

"Tell me about it," I said.

She finished messing with the papers on the desk and started to stretch in the center of the room, like she was getting ready to run a race. She took deep breaths with each stretch. I could have watched her back arching, the rise and fall of her rib cage, all day long.

"How have you been doing?" I asked.

"Great," she said. "I mean, I think I am handling things remarkably well."

"You look good," I said.

"God, let me tell you the most scary thing, Michael," she said. I noticed she was saying my first name a lot, which gave everything she said an intense and urgent edge. "Some days I wake up and I think, well, I guess now I don't have to work so hard. I guess now I don't have to hold a steady job, have this house to live in, stay in one place, and think about school systems."

I just nodded.

"I hate this music," she said. "I mean, it's fine, but I've been sick of it lately. Chimes and sitars. I've been more into Dylan lately. And Fleetwood Mac. *Songs in the Key of Life* by Stevie Wonder. He's great. Do you know how great he is?"

I said I agreed, though I didn't know exactly which album she was talking about. She went over to the CD player. "Pink Floyd," she said. "I forgot all about Pink Floyd.

But it's good shit, really. In college, I listened to R.E.M. and the Smiths all the time. Pink Floyd was mostly for getting stoned."

"Sure," I said.

"God, listen to me," she said. "I've got diarrhea of the mouth or something. I'm thirty-three and I sound like I'm eighteen."

"I like it when people talk a lot," I said. "I never have anything interesting to say."

She smiled and tilted her head, like she was trying to look at me from a different angle.

"It's just, most days I think of Manny and can't move," she said. "Can't get out of bed, I'm so sad. And then some days—I mean, I'm still sad all the time—but I wake up and think, well, there's a lot less I *have* to do now. I can do whatever I want. I don't have to, for instance, try to get Manny's father to acknowledge his existence anymore, or to send child support. And I don't have to know where my next paycheck is coming from, and I don't even need a house, I can keep all my possessions in the trunk of my car and travel all over the country, or the world, because nobody cares what I do all of a sudden. And then I'm relieved. For just a second. Relieved! And then I hate myself and start crying again, not only for Manny, but for me, because I feel like a weak mother."

She stood and went to the window.

"How old are you?" she asked.

"Twenty-two," I said. "Twenty-three this fall."

"That's so young," she said.

She paced along the window.

"Why don't you come and sit down with me?" I said. "You're moving around too much. It makes me nervous."

She did. "You are a sullen creature for twenty-two," she .said.

I agreed with her.

"Are you sick of tea? I am. Do you want a drink?"

"Yes," I said.

"Tequila? It's summer. We should be drinking tequila with a little lime. I can make margaritas."

"Good," I said.

"Good," she said.

I followed her into the kitchen and watched her make the drinks. I had always thought margaritas were slushy drinks served in giant glasses, but she made them with a little ice, a lot of tequila, and a splash of some sort of flavored mix in a plastic bottle. She rimmed the glasses with salt and a wedge of lime. We went out to the back porch with our salty glasses.

I finally worked up the nerve to ask about Manny's father. She told me that Manny's father was never her husband and she had no idea where he was now.

"Somewhere in Spokane," she said. "A drunk to beat all drunks. That's all I know. I don't think he knows Manny is dead. I'll have to find him and send him a letter soon."

She told me that she didn't have many friends at work, other than Annie, the owner of the salon. And even Annie was just her best friend from high school; she had three kids and a husband who golfed, Holly said. All they really had in common was a nostalgic kind of loyalty.

"Most of the women there think I'm strange. They're nice enough, but they cut hair and put on makeup for a living," she said. "And I'm a practitioner of the healing arts and we just don't connect. I believe people come to me because they're spiritually needy and they believe people come to them because of split ends."

"Huh," I said.

"So no more lifeguarding? What now?"

"Finish school," I said.

"Then what?" she said.

I didn't answer right away.

I told her a little about my philosophy class, which made me feel very boring and immature. I told her that I still hadn't bothered to apply for a new job, even though my lifeguarding money was pretty much gone. Still, at least for a while yet, I almost always had access to Mack's old Buick, good free food at my mother's house, and a free place to sleep. I had always felt like I didn't have to know what I planned to do next, but now that my mother and Mack were moving, I knew I had to start thinking.

"God," she said, "I've always hated that question: 'What's next?' Why am I asking that? You don't have to know what's next."

"Well, that's good," I said to Holly, "because I don't have a clue."

We had finished our drinks. Holly went into the kitchen and I followed her. I watched her make another margarita for each of us. She handed me back a glass that smelled like it was pretty much straight tequila with a little salt and lime.

"I have to drive home." I said, taking another drink. "Go easy on me."

"You can spend the night," she said. "It's inevitable."

IN THE MORNING, when I came home, I found a FOR SALE BY OWNER sign in the front yard.

I stopped by Kolya's room. His door was shut and I knocked. He came to the door and opened it slowly.

"Oh, it's you," he said. There were three boxes on his bed and another one on the floor. I noticed he had a magazine called *Barely Legal* in one of the boxes. I remembered my first copy of *Barely Legal*. I'd stolen it from the Qwik and Cheap in eighth grade. My father had found it and confiscated it. Later I found it with his tools in the basement.

"Why are you packing already?" I asked him.

"We're moving in a few weeks," he said.

"So soon?"

"The house is ready. They're closing the deal in a few weeks. Mom was waiting to tell you last night, but you never came home."

"And you're going to the new house?"

"I can't wait," he said. "You know what my school is like. Full of assholes! A shithole."

"Still?"

"Don't you remember anything about high school?"

"So you want to move?" I asked him.

"Mikey, I hate Maple Rock," he said. "I hate this house and this street. I hate everything I know. I fucking hate Maple Rock."

"Wow."

"You should start packing soon too," he said.

But I had already decided I wasn't going, and I told him.

"Oh, well, that's rich," Kolya said. "That's too much."

I told him he sometimes talked like a fifty-year-old faggot and left the room.

THE NEXT NIGHT I drove by Holly's house before it got dark. Just seeing her front door in the twilight got me excited. I had to stop. As hard as I tried to remember it, the previous night was a blur. Skin and sweat, flailing limbs, thrusting in the dark. I wanted more of it. I stood on her porch for a long time, and rang the doorbell again and again. Finally she came to the door in a long blue T-shirt. Her hair was messy and her eyes were squinty. "You're persistent," she said. "I was sleeping. I thought you must be somebody from work coming to check on me. I canceled all my appointments today. That fucking tequila."

"Can I come in?" I said.

"Sure," she said and walked away. I followed her into the kitchen and sat at the table. She disappeared into the bathroom for a minute then came back and kissed me on the cheek with minty breath. She brought me some herbal iced tea, and leaned against me when she set it down. I felt her breasts against my shoulder blades and her breath on the back of my neck, which gave me goose bumps all over. My spine twitched and shivered.

Holly said, "How cliché is this? Thirty-something woman finds a young stud, gets drunk, seduces him, and fucks him over and over. How often has this happened to you?"

"Never," I said, which was the absolute truth. I had a

flash of Mrs. Gagliardi, the woman I had lost my virginity to the summer my father disappeared, but that seemed completely different.

"You didn't have to come back here," she said.

"Why? Didn't you want to see me again? Should I leave?"

"Well, I suppose it's what I needed. Look, it's just—no, I don't want you to leave. You're fine. I like you. But don't feel like you have this burden now. I don't want you to wake up in the morning and say, 'Holy shit, I got involved with an old woman who has a dead son.'"

"I won't," I said.

"Do you have a girlfriend?" she said.

"No!"

"Tell me the truth, because I don't want to end up with a screaming nineteen-year-old banging on my door and calling me a whore. I was nineteen once too. I know what can happen."

"I swear. I haven't had a date in months."

"Well, I suppose you better tell me about yourself then," she said.

Holly started to ask me all kinds of questions. I told her about my life in Maple Rock, about Father Mack and my mother, about the new house in Northville. I told her that my father had left for the moon.

She said, "I know. I can sense that in you, your disappeared father."

"I sometimes believe he really is on the moon," I said.

"Of course," she said.

"But, you know," I said, "of course, he's not."

She looked up at the sky, where the moon was now orange and low, the tentative brightness of a harvest moon underneath a flurry of stars.

"I don't doubt it at all," she said. "Of course he is there. Many people are there."

"You think so?"

"Sure. Why not?"

She went into the kitchen and I followed her and sat down at the table.

"But you can't come back from the moon," she said. "Not once you send your soul there."

She sat in the chair across from me and crossed her legs, pulled an orange from the bowl in the center of the table, and started peeling it. I watched her eat a few pieces of orange. Then she held one out to me, and I reached over and took it with my mouth.

"I need a shower," she said.

"Great," I said. "I'll take one too."

Afterward, skin still damp from the long shower, we went out on her back porch and turned all the lights off in the house and sat next to each other in our towels, glad for the faint breezes that stirred the air that night.

We drank herbal iced tea while we sat at an old wooden table next to the frantic flame of a citronella candle. Holly said she liked my company, and it wasn't just the fucking. I confess that I had never heard a woman talk about sex in the blunt and natural way that she talked about it. At twenty-two, it was thrilling as all hell.

———

WHILE MY FAMILY and Mack made plans to move, packed boxes, and picked out window coverings and carpet for the new house, I went to see Holly as often as possible. Some days, I would pick her up from work and we'd drive around in the last light of the evening, stopping to get dinner in one of the many strip-mall Middle Eastern restaurants near her house. Sometimes we'd go to the used bookstore in Farmington and browse through the fiction section while Skip, the owner, softly played banjo in the front of the store. Holly would point out novels she had liked, ones that I had never read—*The Stranger, The Immoralist, The Unbearable Lightness of Being.* I would buy them for myself and read them with a close eye, as if they were maps to her psyche. Sometimes we'd go bowling and Holly would let herself smoke a cigarette—a habit she'd quit some time ago. Sometimes we'd smoke a joint in her car and then head over to the bargain theater at Livonia Mall and see any movie that was playing. We saw some terrible movies. High and excited to be in the cool, dark theater, we'd giggle uncontrollably and stuff our faces with popcorn and Sno-Caps. There wasn't much to do where we lived, but we found ways to make the evenings interesting. At the end of the night we would go back to her house and get into bed. My heart still raced while we undressed, and my hands sometimes shook so badly it took me a while to undo my belt.

Some nights Holly and I would go straight back to her house and just sit on the chairs in the backyard. She would put her bare feet on my lap and I would rub them. I had never rubbed a woman's feet before, and the act struck me as so intimate that it occurred to me I would be more embarrassed if my mother saw me at it than if she walked in on me having sex.

I suppose what Holly really wanted me there for was to listen. Though she would often make jokes about how she was using me for my young body and tight ass, she seemed to want me there more than anything in the hours after we'd made love, when we would sit in the dark and she would tell me everything that was hanging around in the shadows of her heart. She would tell me about Manny and how she knew he wasn't long for this world.

"His soul, it was always just straining at the edges of this world," she said. "Maybe all mothers say this, but his spirit was too gentle for this world. His asthma reflected his waning light and energy."

I was not somebody who could come up with any sort of thoughtful responses to these proclamations, but I listened. Sometimes she would stop talking abruptly and leap up to go to the kitchen and make us some drinks. Other nights she brought out photo albums, and she'd show me pictures of Manny at the zoo, Manny with a balloon, Manny petting a kitten.

Once, after such a night, I went to see her at work the next day, hoping she'd have time for a quick lunch. The orange girl at the front desk of the salon told me that Holly had called in sick again and had canceled all of her appointments. She looked annoyed and said, "I hope you didn't have an appointment with her too."

"No," I said. "I'm her boyfriend."

"Oh, really?" the orange girl said, stretching out the word *really* with her high-pitched voice.

I went to my car and when I turned and looked back at the salon, four women were standing in the window watching me. I waved sheepishly. They burst into hysterics and began slapping each other on the arm.

There was no answer at Holly's house and so, for the first time, I let myself in with my key. I found her sleeping. She opened her eyes when I came into the bedroom and then she shut them again without saying a word.

The room was hot, so I turned on the ceiling fan. I undressed and got into bed next to her. When I woke up a few hours later, I heard the shower running and went into the bathroom.

"I think I need to paint the living room orange," Holly said. "I need a change in the energy here. Everything feels so stagnant."

"Let's do it," I said.

"You don't have to help," she said.

"No, I want to help. It'll be fun."

After our shower we drove to Home Depot and came home with a few gallons of a color called summer honeydew. I had on my good khakis and let them get covered in paint.

We painted together all night. She played some music—Chet Baker, which seemed to me to be the saddest music I'd ever heard. We stopped at midnight and made squash curry. It was too spicy for me, but I got used to it and we sat on the floor amid the drop cloths and paint cans and ate. Her face was sweaty and gleamed in the light of the kitchen. I had thoughts racing around in my head—could I live like this forever, with this woman, cooking curries and painting the walls honeydew? For a minute, I thought I could. I thought we would. The half-painted wall, one-third honeydew and two-thirds beige, seemed ridiculous and beautiful.

OUR HOUSE WASN'T the only house in Maple Rock that had gone up for sale that summer. Gradually the neighborhood was shifting. White families were moving out and new ones—blacks and Arabs and Mexicans—were moving in. Sometimes you'd hear racist remarks at the bar or in a grocery store, but to be honest, I don't think these new neighbors were the reason people were moving out of Maple Rock. They—the now-single or the remarried women of my mother's generation, mothers with children grown or almost grown—wanted to leave behind the lives that had fallen apart on them. Some of them were moving to smaller, cheaper houses; some, like my mother, were headed to bigger homes and better neighborhoods. But most of them wanted out. It was hard not to wonder what would happen if one of our fathers returned from the moon to find the locks changed, a new family sitting down to dinner while a stranger tried a key in their lock.

Still, despite the FOR SALE signs here and there, most of my own friends were still in Maple Rock. The Black Lantern was still open for business—Spiros's nephew George was the main bartender now—but I had lost interest in drinking at a bar once it became something I could do legally . Plus I liked being with Holly more than being with my friends. I liked having sex with her more than I liked drinking, loved the feel of waking up sweaty and spent better than the feeling of waking up dizzy and hungover.

One afternoon I saw Nick's rundown pickup truck in the parking lot of the Black Lantern.

"Mikey!" Tom Slowinski yelled. He and Nick were sitting at the bar. There was a half-eaten pizza between them, and an empty pitcher.

Nick put a few bucks on the counter and motioned to the waitress for another pitcher. "Let me get you a beer, pal," he said.

Nick and Tom were working construction. They started at five thirty in the morning at the site of the new mall on the other end of town. They knocked off at three o'clock most days and headed straight for the bar. The mud on their work boots, the sweat stains on their T-shirts, and the dirt under their fingernails made me realize how lazy I had been that summer.

Walker Van Dyke and Pete Stolowitz came over. They, too, looked as if they had just come out of some sort of mud pit. "Where've you been, Mikey?" Walker said.

Nick poured me a glass.

"His mother says he's been spending a lot of nights away," Nick said. "He's neck deep in pussy, I guess."

I shrugged off the comment with a smile. I didn't feel like telling them. I gave them a smile to let them know Nick was on the right track, downed my beer, and left.

"Ah, come on Mikey," Tom said. "Take a night off. Get shit-faced with us!"

I headed over to Holly's, and when I pulled into the

driveway in front of her house, I looked in my rearview and saw Nick's big red truck swoop in behind me. Nick and Tom were laughing, waving their middle fingers in the air.

I got out of my car and tried to get them to go away. But then Holly came out from around the side of the house. She was holding a watering can and dressed in her short denim shorts, flip-flops, and black halter top.

Nick and Tom tumbled out of the truck.

"Uh, these are some of my friends. They just happened to drive by when I pulled in," I said.

Nick and Tom made their introductions.

"They're about to leave," I said.

"Can I get you guys a beer?" Holly said. "You look like you just got out of some kind of hellish job."

"We'd love a beer," Nick said, while Tom winked at me.

We went around to the back porch and sat down. I sat in the chair facing the house, and Nick and Tom sat on the opposite side of the table. Holly went inside for the beer.

Nick whispered, "Older woman? Excellent."

"Did you see those tits?" Tom said. "Major league."

He grabbed at the imaginary female flesh and kissed it, making frantic gestures with his tongue.

"Oh, baby," Nick moaned.

Holly reappeared, holding four bottles of beer. "Is that for me gentlemen?" she said.

It was the first time I'd ever seen Nick's face go bright red out of embarrassment rather than anger.

He mumbled some kind of apology.

"They think you're a babe," I said.

"Excellent," Holly said, setting down the four sweating bottles. "Very sophisticated friends."

Nick and Tom could barely look at her until she said, "Aw, come on, boys. I'm just teasing you. I'm flattered."

They smiled sheepishly while they shook hands with Holly. I didn't like it, seeing Nick and Tom so close to Holly. I didn't like the fact that Nick and Tom knew what Holly looked like and where she lived, that they were on her back porch, that they were drinking her beer. It was like buying some beautiful cabin in the woods, on a secluded, pristine lake, and then having some developer building an amusement park right next door. All the stupidity and chaos of my life had followed me to Holly's house, and now she seemed less real than ever.

BY AUGUST, I had started to go over to see Holly every day. I had not found another job—not that I was really looking—and if I stayed home, I'd be stuck in the bustle of packing boxes and wrapping china.

Mack was waiting up for me one night.

"It seems like you have a new girlfriend," he said. "You're gone a lot."

"Hey, you've got no right to butt into my life," I said.

"I wasn't," he said. "I think it's great. Love—women, heck, let's be honest, women and their beautiful bodies—are the only thing that makes life worth living."

"What about God or whatever?" I said. "What happened to all that?"

"When you love a woman, when you know her intimately, that's when you know what God is capable of," he said. "That's all the proof you need."

I shook my head. I didn't want to hear that my mother's naked body was proof of a divine being.

What Mack wanted to tell me was this: he didn't need the money from the sale of the house. He was going to take down the FOR SALE sign.

"If you want to go Northville with us, great," he said. "But we shouldn't force you. If you want to stay here, well, welcome to your new home. It's all yours. We'll sign it over to you. We don't need the money, and well, given the fact that your parents bought it twenty years ago, it's got a very low monthly payment. It's almost paid off."

I asked Mack why he was doing this for me. I wasn't used to my mother dating men who had any concern for me at all.

"Because I'm bad with money, I guess," he said. "And because if I learned anything as a priest, it's to try and put myself in somebody else's shoes, and man, when I looked at your shoes, I could tell how hard it would be to move now."

"You don't have to do this," I said.

"Look, Michael, it's not like this place would sell very fast anyway," he said. "People aren't flocking to Maple Rock. Once you're on your feet, you can take over the payments and taxes. You'd be doing us a favor."

"Geez," I said.

"Anyway," he said. "This place is all yours now. And you can keep the Buick."

I managed to say thank you, but I couldn't think of anything else to say, even though the conversation seemed to beg for some closure.

In the morning, over cereal, my mother said, "I heard Mack talked to you last night."

"He did," I said. "Thanks."

She looked at me like I was this little kid who'd just come out of his room after a tantrum. "Don't thank me, thank him."

"I want Kolya to stay here with me," I said.

"Like there's a fucking chance of that!" Kolya hollered, then banged his spoon on the table laughing. "Mikey, you're so fucking miserable."

"Watch your language," I said.

"He learned it from you," my mother said.

The three of us laughed like maniacs. If you walked by our open kitchen windows that morning, we probably sounded insane. But laughing was all we could do right then, and sometimes it still is.


LATER THAT DAY, I asked Holly: "Do you believe in God?"

"God is within you," she said. "Within us. Don't you see God in me?"

I shrugged.

"I see God in you," she said.

"Me?"

"Look," she said. She opened her mouth wide and then came at my face. She put her wide-open mouth over each of my eyes. She was crawling up my shoulders, shoving her open mouth in my face. She was laughing so hard she bit my nose by mistake. I hollered.

We started kissing.

I felt out of control. She said she could sense it. She said, "Easy, steady your heart."

I said, "I see Him now."

"Him who?" she said.

"God."

"God is a her," she said.

I agreed. God, if anything, had to be a woman.


IN THE MEAN LIGHT of an August afternoon, I sat on the couch and watched my mother and Mack packing boxes. They never asked me to help, and I didn't offer. I wanted there to be some kindness between us, but I didn't know how to offer it. I knew already that their gesture—giving me a house—was vast and generous. Still, I was not ready to be happy for them. I watched them dismantle things I'd known all my life—a floor lamp, a kitchen table, a shelf full of my mother's old books.

It was a Friday, and the moving company was coming in a few days. Kolya came out of his room with a box of toys for the Salvation Army. I volunteered to take them to the drop box—I wanted a good excuse to leave—and I stopped by Holly's on my way.

She fell into me as soon I stepped in the house.

"I'm trying to clean out his room," she said. "And I can't."

She watched helplessly on the floor while I did the work. She said that she'd like to have a yard sale the next morning, and I took all the toys and children's books and old clothes into the garage. The rest of her house was airy and free of clutter that I was surprised by the amount of things Manny had.

"These are just things," she said. "These things aren't Manny. Something just spoke to my spirit and told me so."

Once Manny's room was empty, we started to move other things out of the house too—boxes of books, chairs, futons. Some of the furniture had come with the house when she rented it, but most of the landlord's stuff, she said, was hideous to look at that she'd stowed it in the basement and in the third bedroom.

"Don't you want any of this stuff?" I asked.

"My lease is month to month," she said. "I'm planning on leaving."

"Where are you going?" I said. "When?"

"I don't know. I keep thinking about the desert. I haven't been out that way for a long time."

"Will I see you again?" I said.

"I have a better question: If I send for you once I find a place, will you come?" she said.

"Yes," I said.

We kept packing up boxes and moving furniture. And I believed that she would send for me, that I would actually go and find her wherever she ended up after this. The desert was a distant and beautiful place that I had never seen, but I could picture the two of us there, in a small adobe house, with white linens on a clothesline in the yard, and a dog or two. I could see Holly dressed in a loose-fitting blouse and denim shorts and I could see myself wearing jeans and no shirt, snakeskin boots and a turquoise and silver belt buckle. My skin was a deep bronze color from the sun, and on my head was a dark cowboy hat that shaded my face and made me look older.

THE NEXT DAY, we sat in Holly's yard with a giant YARD SALE banner over our heads. The banner was decorated with rainbows and singing birds that Holly had drawn. We hadn't put prices on anything, and half the time when somebody asked Holly what something cost, she'd say, "That? That's free, take it."

"Why are you giving things away?" I asked.

"If I sense somebody has positive energy and really needs something, I don't drag money into it."

"You're a head case," I said.

She kissed me in the garage and we grabbed the cash box and snuck inside for a few minutes, leaving all of the sale stuff unattended. While we were in the bedroom, someone called out for us, and Holly yelled from the bed, "Oh, take anything you want. It's all free!"

By the end of the day, we took the few things that were left, along with the box of Kolya's old toys, to the Salvation Army drop box.

We got back to the house and Holly started to fix something to eat. The air filled with the smells of butter and garlic. I drank a beer and sat in the kitchen, watching her cook.

We ate noodles in tomato sauce, a boring, uninspired dinner for Holly. She looked drained and pale. She walked around the empty house and I suggested we go to sleep.

"It's been a hard day," I said.

"I'd like to be alone tonight," she said.

"Why?"

"I just want to be alone."

"Did I do something wrong?" I asked.

"Michael," she said, "you really have no idea what my world is like right now. I've lost a child. I've been through a dark, dark time."

"I know all that," I said.

"I've given you a lot of my energy and attention," she said. "And I feel drained."

The tone of her voice carried an accusatory undercurrent, and I realized it would be a long time before I saw the desert. That adobe house? Those blowing white linens? That tan image of myself in a cowboy hat and snakeskin boots on the porch of our adobe house? These things were no more real than any other future I had imagined for myself. I felt small and stupid, and I left Holly's house without saying goodbye.

I didn't want to go home that night and watch Mack and my mother continue to pack away my childhood. Part of me knew that I was being immature and melodramatic, but part of me believed that being any other way was too easy a surrender. I would let my mother move on and have her new life, I would let Kolya get a fresh start in a richer suburb. And yes, I would let Mack become part of our family, I would accept his generosity and his attempts at friendship, and my bitterness would turn to affection. But not yet; I wasn't ready.

I drove around Maple Rock until I found Nick and Tom sitting on Nick's front porch smoking cigarettes.

"Clyde Warren is over," Nick said. "We're out here so we don't drown in his sincerity. He bought me a TV-VCR combo for my bedroom. He felt bad because he and my mother are always watching old movies and hogging the TV."

Aunt Maria had started dating Clyde a few months ago. Clyde worked as a librarian at Schoolcraft College and was effeminate and thin. He was one of the nicest men any of us had ever met—considerate, generous, and soft-spoken—and he was intelligent. He loved art museums, classic films, and pottery. We all kind of hated guys like him in Maple Rock. Even my mother and Mack referred to Clyde Warren as Clyde Borin' when my aunt wasn't around.

"We're going to Ann Arbor tonight," Tom said. "Sunny's having another party. Mostly hippie chicks again, but lots of weed."

"Sure," I said. "Sounds good. Let's go."

"Seriously?" Nick said. "Where is your sophisticated lady tonight?"

"I think she's sick of me," I said.

"It was worth the ride, Mikey," Tom said. "Those tits were amazing!"

"He's grieving, asshole," Nick said. "Let the man grieve for lost pussy."

"I wish I had some other friends," I said.

But when we got into the car, and Nick and Tom started singing along to some hip-hop tape, I felt the old excitement of flying down the freeway, looking for trouble or fun or both. I felt glad to be with them. I hadn't outgrown them yet.

The party was visible from several blocks away. It was

a hot night and people spilled out onto the big front porch and down the wooden fire escape that ran up the side of the house. I hung around in a tiny third-floor bedroom, smoking weed with two dreadlocked girls, then wandered downstairs for a beer. Blues Traveler was the band of choice that summer, and an endless harmonica solo wailed from the speakers on the wall. In the dining room, which was empty of furniture, dancers swirled and spun on the hardwood floor. Sonya spotted me and came over to kiss my cheek and ask me how I'd been.

"I see a lot of your sidekicks around here," she said, "but you've been a total stranger."

I shrugged. "Been busy."

"Nick tells me you're dating an older woman," she said. She draped her hands on my shoulders and looked up at me, her beery breath in my face. "Does she do things to you that I couldn't do? Older and experienced is always a plus, isn't it?"

She was really drunk and I should have forgiven her for her comments. I think she was attempting to be affectionate toward me, and to make me feel welcome in her home.

"Sonya," I said, "to be honest, I barely remember anything we did."

"Fine, asshole," she said. She was still smiling, but I thought I'd wounded her a little, which felt almost good. She blew some cigarette smoke in my face and said, "Where's Nick? I want to make sure he stays away from my roommates."

I walked out to the front porch to look for some beer, but the giant cooler there was empty. I was about to head out for a walk, maybe go wander around the Law Quad, when I heard someone call my name.

It was Janice. She was dressed like she was dressed at work—khaki miniskirt, blue T-shirt, blue canvas sneakers. She tucked her hair behind her ears. Her tan was even deeper than it had been last month.

"This is so weird," she said. "What are you doing here?"

"I'm friends with Sonya," I said. "She lives here. Some people call her Sunny."

"Oh my god, my friend Monica lives here too!"

"Great," I said. She, like everybody else, was pretty drunk. She'd been drinking beer, she said, but her friend had gotten her started on Jell-O shots and now she was completely fucked up.

"I'm mad at you," she said and stuck her tongue out at me.

"Why?" I said.

"You left me with that old couple," she said, "and went away without giving me your phone number."

"Did you want it?" I said.

"I'm really drunk, so I'll be honest," she said. "I think you're really-really-really cute."

"Well, I'll see more of you then, I bet."

"Are you leaving?" she said.

"I was going to go for a walk," I said.

She grabbed onto my arm. It looked like she was coming along. I didn't mind. She had wonderful skin. She was closer to my age than Holly. She was drunk and obviously liked me. I figured she had an apartment somewhere and that we might end up in it.

We walked for a few blocks, passing house parties that looked exactly like the one we'd just left. We passed the sculpture of a spinning cube, which Janice had shown me on the tour. The sight of it launched her into a tirade against the campus. She said how sick she was of seeing it and talking about it, how much she hated trying to convince people to come to school there.

"This is not what I want my life to be like," she said.

"Let's not go there tonight," I said. "I'm not into self-pity."

Janice looked deflated. I could tell she wanted to have some deep, meaningful exchange.

It was the kind of invitation I'd accepted many times before, fueled by alcohol or drugs and a little sexual tension, and I knew how it would go. We'd talk about ourselves until we were so sick of talking about ourselves that sex seemed the only escape from the conversation. But I was thinking of Holly again, even though I had vowed not too. I didn't picture Holly as the jealous type. She certainly never called me her boyfriend or partner or anything like that. Still, I didn't want to talk to Janice about her post-college angst. I wished I had brought along a few beers.

"Well, nobody knows what they really want out of life," I said. It sounded terse and nihilistic—a term I only learned a few weeks ago, from Holly, but one that I thought I might struggle to embody from time to time. It seemed aloof and sexy. I was still waiting for the right moment to tell somebody I was a nihilist, but I didn't want to waste the line on Janice. She was sweet and bright-eyed and beautiful and drunk, and a little desperate for some sort of connection.

She was holding on to my arm , stopping to look at me when she spoke and to get me to look back. We walked through the Law Quad together. In the dark, with just the faint campus floodlights and sliver of a moon, the place looked even more imposing than it had before. I wanted to lie there on the grass and stare at the gargoyles and the Gothic towers. But it was Holly I wanted to be with, not Janice, tucking her hair behind her ears like crazy and showing me how her eyes even looked almost purple in the dark.

"See?" she said. She was about two inches from my face. "Purple!"

Halfway through one of the tunnels, she stopped walking. I leaned over and kissed her and I felt her tongue push into my mouth like a wave.

It took us less than ten minutes to get to Janice's apartment. I started to take her clothes off in the living room, even though she was laughing and telling me that she had roommates. I didn't care. I undid my pants and we rolled down onto the couch together. I tried to pull off her skirt, but she stopped me. She was too drunk, she said. The room was spinning. I complained that we should at least do something, so she used her hand on me. Nothing about it was at all gentle or tender. Afterward, while she was in the bathroom, maybe getting sick, I zipped up my pants quickly. I was headed for the front door just as a pretty dark-haired girl came into the apartment. She was wearing a strapless black dress and holding a pair of high heels in her hand. I winked at her.

"Who are you?" she said.

"Nobody," I said. "I think Janice is sick."

I went out into the fresh air. Back on the street, I had to stop into a pizza shop and ask directions back to the corner of Fifth and Jefferson, where Sonya lived.

As soon as I felt sober enough to drive, I got in my car and headed down M-14. I had a feeling that I would never get into school at Ann Arbor, that the whole world of that campus and those students were a world I would never get myself into, and that I was okay with that.

I didn't care how Nick and Tom got home. They were fools, I thought, going to Ann Arbor all the time, just to find a party. I wanted to convince myself that I was better than them, that I liked quiet evenings alone with Holly and that was all that I wanted. I tried not to think about Janice, but every time I thought about Holly, I'd see Janice's face, too. I pictured Holly in that rundown apartment, sitting in the corner watching me get a drunken hand job from a girl I didn't really know anything about. I made a vow that I would never go to a party in Ann Arbor again. I never wanted to run into Janice again. Besides, weren't there any parties in Maple Rock?

I SPENT MOST OF the weekend in my basement bedroom, trying not to listen to Mack and my mother packing up the house. They kept having this kind of exchange:

"Should we keep this?" Mack would ask.

"No reason," my mother would say. "Pitch it."

"Sentimental reasons?" Mack would say.

"It's junk!" my mother would say.

I stayed down in the basement and wondered what my

mother was calling junk. One of my first-grade art projects? Kolya's old soccer uniforms? My father's rusty pocketknife?

On Sunday night, Holly called and asked me to come over. She told me to pack an overnight bag. She wanted to take me somewhere before she left.

"I don't know," I said.

"Michael, " she said. "Don't play games."

When I got to her house, she was sitting on the floor in the living room, watching T.V.

"Where did you get that television?" I said.

"It's part of the landlord's stuff," she said.

Across the room, about ten small boxes and two large suitcases were packed neatly in the corner. There was also a guitar case, a small duffel bag, and two backpacks.

"I'm glad you answered the phone," said Holly.

"You never try to call me," I said.

"I want you to come somewhere with me," she said.

Friends of hers who owned a B&B near Lake Michigan had called to offer her a suite for a few days. They'd had a last-minute cancelation. Holly wanted me to go with her.

"It's about three hours away," she said. We can leave first thing tomorrow."

"Don't you have to work?"

"I quit," she said. "I'm leaving town, remember?"

"You never said it was official."

"I'm saying it now," she said. "Remember, I am going to send for you? From the desert?"

"Sure," I said.

In the bedroom, the closet, the dresser drawers, and the top of the nightstand were empty. The room was swept clean. I went to the bathroom. The clutter of lotions and candles and herbal oils was gone. I pissed and went back to the bed. I fell asleep in about thirty seconds, listening to Holly let out a series of long, slow sighs.

When she woke me up the next morning with a mug of hot coffee, her hair was wet and she was wearing a skimpy, clingy black sundress with thin straps, and black, high-heeled sandals that sculpted her calves. I'd never seen her in anything so shamelessly sexy, and it made the day feel full of promise. "Get up, brush your teeth, put some pants on, and let's get out of here."

She wanted to drop off my car in Maple Rock. She said the landlord was showing her place and didn't like prospective tenants to see old cars in the driveway.

"The sooner he rents it," she said, "the sooner I get out of my lease and get my security deposit back."

I parked the car in front of my house but didn't go inside. I figured it was pretty empty by then, and I didn't want to see.

Holly drove us west on I-94, and though she seemed a little happier, she didn't talk much. I would've talked, but I couldn't think of anything to say. I had never stood at the end of a relationship without hate and anger and hurt swimming around it. She rolled down all the windows and her little Toyota was like a wind tunnel. Holly didn't seem to mind. She listened to NPR and read the occasional billboard aloud. She woke me up when we left the freeway so I could help her read the map.

"You can quit pretending to be asleep now," she said. "We're almost there."

I had not even so much as checked into a motel with a woman before, and had never set foot inside a B&B. At first I felt like I was trying to pull off some sort of scam. But Holly's friends, Joe and Mary Carpenter, ran a nice place and mostly stayed out of our way. Joe, who wore his gray hair back in a ponytail, gave us a lot of guides to canoeing, biking, and fishing opportunities in the area. He kept talking to me about Hope College, which was nearby, I think because he wanted me to tell him whether or not I was still in college, but I didn't take the bait. Besides, I would be in college for at least a few more years, so my answer wouldn't help him figure out my age anyway.

Joe said to Holly, "I don't know if you still enjoy the occasional taste of the herb, but we have a little shed out back that is the appropriate place to partake of the peace pipe."

He looked at me and winked. "Purely for medicinal purposes."

"Hahahaha," I said. It sounded obnoxious and Holly looked at me with a twisted-up face that meant "Shut up."

Our room was called the Forest Room, and everything was made of wood. It had a bathroom the size of my bedroom at home, with a Jacuzzi. The first thing I did that afternoon was fire up the Jacuzzi. I kept waiting for Holly to take off her clothes and come in with me, but she got on the bed and fell asleep. When I finally got out of the water, my skin was wrinkled and steam was coming out of my pores. I toweled off slowly near the bed, half hoping that Holly would roll over and smile, grab my towel and pull me into bed, but she didn't. We went into town and had an overpriced dinner at an Italian restaurant packed with rich people from

Chicago in their weekend getups—designer Windbreakers, pleated Dockers, and long, loose dresses. Back in the room, I could tell Holly just wanted the night to be over. She undid my zipper, had me sit down on the bed, and took me in her mouth. She got up, brushed her teeth, and came back to bed in her pajamas. The whole affair took about three minutes, and she fell asleep right after we were done.

The next morning Mary, gray-haired and willowy, made us a wonderfully big breakfast while Joe highlighted some of the things we could do. Despite several cups of strong coffee, however, Holly and I went back to bed after breakfast. I woke up later, went for a walk along Lake Michigan, then came back to the room and hit the Jacuzzi again. After I was dressed, I woke up Holly and we went into town and ate fish sandwiches and fries by the water. We drank some beer and then watched the sunset on the beach. The wind pushed our hair back, and gulls circled and called above us. We were silent and tender with each other when we got back to the room. We moved in slow motion, and sometimes Holly stopped moving altogether and just stared at me, pushing my hair out of my face.

The next morning, we left the B&B after breakfast and spent the car ride home talking about Joe and Mary Carpenter. Holly told me their whole story—how they had been high-powered ad execs in Detroit for a decade before Joe had a breakdown, how Mary had miscarried twice and never conceived again, how Joe used to have long periods of time where he would go up north and live in the woods by himself, not contacting Mary for weeks at a time.

"And now I guess they've got things pretty well figured out," she said. "Don't they seem happy?"

"Totally," I said.

"It's a beautiful little place," she said. "It just proves to me that you can be happy no matter what, as long as you can carve out a quiet niche for yourself."

Near Detroit, we got silent again. As we drove through the streets of Maple Rock, every block seemed to give me some bittersweet memory, but to Holly they were just names—Mansfield, Whitlock, Sheehan, Elm. My stomach got that watery feeling again, the same feeling I had gotten the first time I had visited her.

My house was dark, and the FOR SALE SIGN was gone. Holly hopped out and opened the trunk. She handed me the duffel bag. She shut the trunk and threw her arms around me, then gave me a long, slow kiss on the mouth.

"Is this the last time I'll ever see you?" I said.

"Maybe," she said. "But I will send for you."

"This is my house now," I said. "We could live here."

"I suppose we could," she said.

We stopped and looked at the small, dark ranch as if we were really contemplating settling down there and living together forever.

"We could get married," I said, and suddenly it sounded like the perfect idea. "We could totally do that!"

"You're a sweet, sweet man," she said.

"I'm serious," I said.

"I'll miss you," she said. "A lot."

"Marry me," I said.

We kissed and she got into the car.

I was tapping on the window when she drove away.

———

I WENT INTO THE HOUSE alone and turned on all the lights. The moving company had done their work. The living room was pretty much how I remembered it. Mack and my mother had left me the couch, the two armchairs, the television and VCR. They were buying brand-new things for their house. Still, some things were missing: there were no pictures on the wall, and my mother's bookshelf was empty. In the kitchen, the cupboards were pretty much empty, though my mother had left behind some dishes and a few pots and pans. Her cheap silverware was in a drawer near the sink. There was a note on the table with their phone number. *Where are you? We'd love for you to see the new house. Please call us.*

I went down the hallway. Kolya's bedroom, the one I used to share with him before I'd moved down to the basement, was empty. There was no trace of him except for an old Tigers pennant sticking out of a garbage bag in the middle of the floor. My mother's bedroom was empty too, the hardwood floor freshly mopped and shining. When my father had lived with us, there was a deep blue carpet in that room, and the walls were a periwinkle color that my father used to complain about. It gave him headaches, he said, and made it hard to sleep at night. I could picture the two heavy oak dressers, wedding presents from my father's long-dead parents, and I could picture my mother and father and their matching white bathrobes hanging on hooks next to the door. I could smell not just my mother's fragrances—soft, lilac-scented perfumes and baby powder—but my father's Old Spice too, his stale coffee and cigarettes, his scotch.

I stretched out on the floor. My head was spinning amid a rush of dreamy memories. Did I hear my father's voice in the empty room, or did I feel my mother's cool hand touch my cheek? I did. Did I hear Kolya running down the hall, calling out for a Popsicle? I did.

Did I think of Holly? Did I miss her? Did I want her to appear, too, in that tormenting parade of ghosts? I did.

But it was just the floor and me. I thought about sitting up, but stayed there, flat on my back, until much later, until the light had come back to the windows, until the room was bright with morning, until I swore I could feel my heart chakra filling my rib cage with heat and flame. I felt it turning, burning, struggling to turn around and go forward.

## capable of love

MOST OF OUR MOTHERS, your wives, they've moved away. They now live in condos in Canton and Livonia and Westland, and some of them live with men, men who are cleaner, better dressed, and more polite than you ever were. They have steady jobs, retirement plans, crisp clean foreign cars, hairless knuckles.

These are the kind of men we, or anybody for that matter, should like. Still, we can't help it: we regard these men with suspicion, and when we are invited over for Sunday dinner, we feel as if we are dressed poorly or as if we look pathetic, waiting for roast beef or lemon chicken to be heaped on our plates.

When these men get up to clear the table, our mothers seize the moment we have alone and lean in, touch our arms, and ask, "So you're all right, honey? You're okay?"

Of course we are!

We still live in those houses, the ones you left. We've stayed behind, long past the time we should have moved out, and our mothers simply turned the houses over to us, moved in with their new husbands, worked their new jobs, lived their new lives.

On the walls of our houses, there are posters of retired Detroit athletes, such as my poster of Lou Whitaker and Alan Trammell, the Tigers' great second base–shortstop combo from the eighties. On the bookshelf, next to my high-school Spanish book, is a cigar box full of ribbons from a summer league swim team. On my dressers are buttons boasting photos of me and my old homecoming dates. Sweet girls. One of them now lives in Korea or Taiwan or somewhere with missionaries; one of them dates a golf pro with perfectly muscled, tanned forearms; one is earning a Ph.D. in women's studies.

It's hard to get rid of all this clutter when you've never left your mother's house.

Our houses—your houses—need new roofs and new paint and our driveways need resurfacing. These houses are rich with smells I can't explain, like clean, damp towels, like memories. On weekends, we mow the lawns and trim the hedges, we do all the maintenance we can that doesn't cost any money, and we look around at our yards, our trim lawns and sidewalks swept clean, and we say, here it is, here is the order in our lives, here we are in Maple Rock.

Sometimes we have girlfriends who move in with us, and they are impressed that we are homeowners. They look at our master bedrooms and white kitchens and think, this, *this* is a man I could marry. But sooner or later, something disintegrates: maybe it's our fault, maybe it's not. Sometimes, someone will break into the house, or there will be a rock thrown through the window, or there will even be gunshots in the night. Maple Rock is not quite what it used to be. Sometimes these incidents signal the end of our relationships. Other times, the women we are trying to love accuse us of moodiness, drunkenness, and indifference. They say we spend too much time and energy on our friends, on our *buddies*. They say the word *buddies* as if it's an embarrassment.

"When we look at you," they say, "it's as if your eyes and your minds are somewhere else, it's as if your thoughts are in outer space, as if you refuse to listen to us and connect to the things we say. You are incapable of love!"

We do not fight these accusations. We allow the women to leave without much pleading. We've long ago lost the idea of permanence as a possibility. We stagger around for a few days, drinking too much, finding their pink razors in our showers, their long brown, red, black, or blond hairs on our sheets, their washcloths drying by our sinks.

We do not discuss these women when we are sitting happily around a table at the Black Lantern, drinking pitcher after pitcher. The women seem to happen and then disappear. Eventually their scents, their strands of hair, go away.

When I think about you, the disappeared men of Maple Rock, I sometimes wonder if you all are capable or incapable of love these days. For the record, if you are now capable of love, we consider that unfair.

# knights of labor

W HEN GEORGE BUSH'S SON was running for president, he did not come to the Polish-American Hall in Maple Rock. We did not see George W. give any campaign speeches, though he did speak at a closed luncheon of the Detroit Businessmen's Club, which wasn't really in Detroit. It was in Livonia.

Still, we would boo W when he appeared on the television in the bar , throwing pretzels and popcorn at his smug, self-important little face. We did not want him in Maple Rock.

We despised him, the way he sauntered all over Washington, D.C., alongside his father. We hated watching him work the crowds at his campaign stops, his father—who had been president the year our own fathers disappeared— beaming with pride, shaking the hands of the Yale men who would get his son the job. We knew his father pulled all the strings, paved all the roads to get him where he was. When we got fired from a job or arrested for urinating behind the bar, or when the insurance rates went up on the rusted-out cars you used to drive, and when you, our fathers, were not there to help us, we hated George W. even more.

When George Bush Sr. would talk about his son, George W., he'd always say about how proud he was of his boy. Fuck him!

We didn't imagine you were proud of us. What did we care?

BY THEN WE WORKED, all of us, at the new Maple Rock Mall, on the west edge of town that used to be Rotary Park. The city had sold off the park to a developer because of the economic impact the mall would have on our region. Nobody seemed to care much. It was one less place for high-school kids to drink and screw.

So when the mall was finished, we got jobs there, as promised. Our grandfathers used to work the afternoon shift at Ford Rouge and Dodge Main, carrying busted-up metal lunch pails. At six o'clock they'd sit down to dinner far from their kitchens, eating cold cabbage rolls and city chicken, drinking lukewarm coffee from their thermoses. Our fathers walked into factories and warehouses and fluorescent-lit buildings every morning, brown bags stuffed with Fritos and bologna sandwiches and an apple or a banana. We ate our lunches and dinners every day at the Maple Rock Mall food court—chili dogs and cheddar beef sandwiches and Taco El Grandes—with the buzz of shoppers and elevator music around us.

We were walking into the food court. It was nine in the morning. We'd stayed at Happy Wednesday's well past midnight, drinking union-made Miller Lite, and my brain was a piece of steel wool scratching around in my skull.

"Be proud of what you do," Nick said. "That's what the man said."

"Who?" I said.

"Bill Clinton. Do you remember? When he was running for President and he came to Maple Rock? That's what he said: 'Be proud of what you do.'"

"We work at the fucking mall," I said.

"I know. But we work. We should be proud of that," he said. "At least."

"Okay," I said. "Fine. What brought this up?"

"It's an election year," Nick said. "I was just thinking about it. About pride."

"All right," I said. "I'm proud."

"But that's not enough. You need to take pride in your work, or at least in the fact that you get up for work every day."

"Okay, I'm proud."

"No. Not just proud, Mikey. You're a Knight of Labor."

"Okay," I said. "I'm a Knight of Labor. Will you shut up?"

"This will make us famous," he said.

The last time he had said that, we were twelve years old and he was trying to climb a TV antenna outside Channel Two. I was hoping his vision had evolved.

"What will?" I asked.

"You'll see," he said. "The wheels are spinning, Mikey."

OUR PAL TOM SLOWINSKI worked at Top Banana Smoothies and Shakes. He was the assistant manager. Most days, he worked alone, and he made up a special batch of Miami Mambo, a strawberry-banana-pineapple concoction that he spiked with vodka. If you wanted to partake of this special formula, you just asked for the Mall Employee Special. It cost five dollars. Tom wasn't greedy or stupid: he'd put three bucks in the register, to cover the cost of a regular Miami Mambo, and keep two for himself. Good weeks, he made an extra two hundred bucks in cash and nobody noticed. If you came to Maple Rock Mall in the late afternoon, there was a good chance that your sales associate was spinning pretty hard on a Miami Mambo buzz. It made the days go by with ease. It made $6.50 an hour seem almost worth it.

That was the year Spiros had a stroke and his nephew finally gave up on the Black Lantern. The bar became a falafel restaurant owned by some brothers from Yemen. We were well past twenty-one, however, and we did not need Spiros to serve us our liquor anymore. We drank in the new fern bars around the mall: George Monday's, Ruby Tuesday, Happy Wednesday's, TGI Friday's. I finally had an associate's degree in liberal studies from the community college and had moved on to taking night classes at UM-Dearborn. That was enough to land me a job as a shift supervisor at the Book Nook. Bookseller was a plum mall job and I knew it. Nick sold Philly steaks at Liberty Bell Subs in the food court and had to wear a patriot's hat. Still, he wore it with swagger and looked good in it.

Our other friends worked at places like the Sunglass

Hut, Ingenuity Unlimited, and American Pants. We flirted with the Maple Rock girls who worked at Victoria's Secret and Bath and Body Works, but nothing much came of it, because very few of the women who worked at the mall wanted to date guys who worked at a mall.

When the bars closed, we drove home at night, because we lived too far from the mall to walk there. That was something to miss about the Black Lantern, its proximity to our bedrooms, but we lived in the old part of Maple Rock, where there was nothing worth walking to anymore. Nick drove, and I rode and controlled the radio, our heads swirling, music blaring. I guess we knew we shouldn't have been driving, but we didn't care. We were careless. We were kings.


NICK AND I WERE sitting in Happy Wednesday's after work. It was Hump Day, so it was packed with mall workers like us drinking two-for-one margaritas and Mega-Mugs of Miller. The weekly Hump Day Honey Bikini Contest was about to start. The winners got $250 cash plus gift certificates. You could win every week if you were good enough—the favorite honeys kept customers coming back each week—and there were a lot of repeat performers. The year's all-stars, as determined by the managers of Happy Wednesday's and customers' votes, could compete in the national Hump Day Honey Spring Break Bikini Bash in February, with a grand prize of $100,000 cash plus a trip for two to Jamaica.

People were cheering. David Lee Roth's version of "California Girls" came on the stereo. The first contestant walked across the bar in a silver bikini. I had to stand to see, the place was that crowded.

Nick stood up and blocked my view.

He was looking at me, not at the stage.

"Have you ever heard of the Flint sit-down strike?" he said.

I moved him out of my way. The next contestant was walking up the stepladder. It was Ella Davis, a co-worker from the Book Nook. We had always been fairly friendly at work, and I knew a little bit about her. I knew, for instance, that she had a five-year-old son at home who had no father in the picture, and I knew that she wasn't on speaking terms with her parents. The only family she had was an equally beautiful sister, Margaret, a graduate student in Ann Arbor who would come over to help with child care on Wednesday nights and the occasional weekend.

Ella was wearing a white bikini that gleamed against her olive skin and long black hair. She was fairly short, about five foot three, with a slight but muscled figure and full, natural breasts. She'd have a tough time against the rail-thin tanning-booth fake-breasted blondes. Some of the women who entered the Hump Day contest were strippers who worked the airport bars in Romulus, and they were no strangers to the moves to make while walking across a bar top in heels and a bikini. Ella was a little less polished, and her eyes had a glimmer of anger when she smiled. But when she got on the bar, the crowd went wild. She twirled around so the men could see all of her and walked up and down the bar three times.

Nick said, "In 1937, a group of autoworkers at the GM factory in Flint ..."

Later, when Ella had been crowned the winner and was taking her victory lap along the bar, Nick was still talking. "I mean, in the thirties," he said, "this kind of shit happened all the time."

I looked at him, then looked at Ella. "Do you think she'd ever go out with me?" I said.

He stopped talking and turned to see Ella accepting her check.

"Fuck no, Mikey," he said. "Besides, if you had sex with a girl that hot, your dick would fall right off. It would go into shock. Now, listen, I want to tell you more about this sit-down strike at GM."

As I listened to him, I saw Ella Davis turn down the free drinks that about ten different men were offering. She took off her high heels and put on a pair of flip-flops. She slipped on a pair of gray sweats and a black sweatshirt, and threw a backpack over her shoulder. Some guy grabbed her arm and tried to give her a high five, which she met, slowly, as if it was causing her pain to raise her hand in the air. The man said, "You rule!" and finally let go of Ella's arm. When she was gone, the two hostesses at the Wednesday Welcome Wagon whispered to each other and laughed.

"Hey, Mikey," Nick said. "Are you listening?"

NICK HAD NEVER BEEN political. Really, nobody in Maple Rock had been political. We voted for Catholics when possible,

Eastern Europeans when possible, and usually settled on pro-labor Democrats. But we didn't always vote. I didn't even know if my father and his friends had been Republicans or Democrats.

Recently, however, Nick had brought politics into our lives. He was spending his days off in Ann Arbor, attending free lectures, book readings, poetry slams, whatever he could get into without buying a ticket. I had pretty much soured on Ann Arbor after my application was denied, and I also had outgrown the crowded house parties that used to seem so interesting and wild to me. But even after we stopped going out there for the keg parties, Nick continued to spend his days off wandering around the campus. Then, after Sonya Stecko had started her Ph.D. at Michigan, she introduced Nick to a bunch of graduate students there and he started to date the kind of women who would take him to gallery talks or art films or folk concerts. He invited me along, but I never went. I knew enough to know where I belonged and where I didn't, but Nick had a great gift. He never cared.

My mother once said, "If you could ever harness all of Nick's wild energy, you'd be unstoppable."

Lately Nick had begun to channel that wild energy by himself, and he was determined to bring me, and everybody else, along for the ride. He had met somebody in Ann Arbor—"just some woman," he said, which I knew wasn't true, because Nick had never called any of his girlfriends *women* before. He called them babes or chicks or girls, but not *women*. This one was always "this woman I've been seeing." When I asked who she was and when I would meet her, he said, "I will never bring her to Maple Rock. God willing, she will never have to see any of your sorry asses."

He had shaved his head and grown a goatee, and he worked out obsessively, lifting weights, running, and studying aikido at a gym in Royal Oak. He had acquired an earring and a jazz habit—he was always talking about some classic album he'd picked up for a quarter at Goodwill. And he started to read—history, philosophy, poetry, and anything by anyone he'd heard somebody talking about. He bought all of his books through me because I got a big discount, so I was able to keep track of his intellectual growth.

That night at Happy Wednesday's, he was telling me how he was sitting in on a class his girlfriend had turned him on to: History of the Labor Movement in America.

"It's a lecture of maybe two hundred people, and my girlfriend is the TA," Nick said. "I can just sit there and take classes at Michigan for free. Nobody knows who anybody is."

"You could get busted eventually," I said.

"No way," he said. "Besides, what would they bust me for? I ask more questions at the end of class than anybody. The professor loves me."

It was good to see Nick's interest expanding past driving around, drinking beer, getting high, and looking for fights. Still, the world of books and education had always been my turf. Nobody else in Maple Rock had really cared about it before, and I'd liked it that way.

"I'm thinking of going to college like you, Mikey," he said. "And then I'm thinking about law school."

I started laughing, and beer foam came out of my nose.

"No fucking way," I said.

"Fuck you," he said. "You'll see."

THE NEXT DAY AT the Book Nook, Ella was pricing a giant stack of remainders and I was trying to think of something to say to her. It was hard not to picture her in a white bikini and heels, walking across the Happy Wednesday's bar top. So I just said, "Congratulations."

She looked at me like I was a bug she'd forgotten to squash. "For what?"

"The Hump Day Honey contest," I said, and then immediately wished I hadn't. "God, you were there?" she said.

I nodded.

"Do you go to those every week?"

"Um, no. Not really."

"Not really?" she said. She shuffled around a stack of books. "It's easy money."

"I was just there for dinner. With my cousin Nick. Do you know him? He works at Liberty Bell Subs. Shaved head, goatee?"

"That's your cousin?" she said. "He's pretty brilliant."

I had never heard anybody call Nick brilliant before.

"He's cute too," she added.

"Brilliant? Cute?" I said.

"In Brooklyn, he's all the rage," she said. "Tough, hard-working, wears boots and Carhartt jackets. In Williamsburg, he'd be the hottest thing going."

"Are you kidding me?" I said.

"No. There was just an article in the *Times* about men

like him," she said. "My sister Margaret e-mailed it to me.
It was hysterical. Carhartt guys, they're called. I read all
about it in the *Sunday Styles* section."

"How ironic," I said.

"Exactly," she said.

"What?" I said.

"What?" she said.

"Am I a Carhartt guy?" I asked, then couldn't believe I'd
asked it.

"The tough guy thing," she said, "needs work."

"Thanks."

"If Nick's ideas come together, he might just be famous," she said.

"What ideas?" I said.

Our manager, Eddie Jones, came over and said it didn't
take a whole crew to price remainders, did it? He sent me
over to put out the new magazines. I tore the covers off the
old unsold issues and sent them back to the distributor for
credit. I could keep the rest of the magazine for myself. I had
a pretty good collection of coverless *Playboy*s going. Suddenly I was embarrassed by the thought of them. I decided
to throw them away when I got home.

Later, I found Ella having a cigarette out on the loading
dock.

"Do you know that in 1937, GM workers held a massive
sit-down strike in Flint?" I said.

"What?"

"I don't know. It seems workers had more rights then,
you know. They were better at fighting against shitty pay
and all of that."

"Yeah," she said. "I've heard all of this. I've already met Nick, remember?"

She was looking out into the distance, past a silvery stream of cigarette smoke, past an approaching UPS truck, past the vast parking lots and the smokestacks of an empty factory. I'd fucked up her cigarette break, I could tell. She didn't seem like she enjoyed talking to me. I was about to go back inside and get to work before Eddie came out and snapped at me again. Then she said, "You like me, don't you?"

She was smiling at me.

"Come again?"

"You're hot for me, is that it? You see me in a bikini on a bar one night, and now you can't think of anything but me? I don't know whether I should be flattered or insulted."

The list of appropriate comebacks was long and simple—*Don't flatter yourself* or *Hello, ego problem*—but instead I said, "I don't know."

"Say, Michael," she said. "Can you cover my shift for me this Saturday? Eddie didn't give me the day off because I need more hours to get my forty for the week. Trouble is, my sister is going out of town and I don't have anybody to stay with Rusty."

It was my only Saturday off that month. I had planned to go to Ann Arbor with Nick for a football game. There was supposed to be a party afterward, at the house of somebody he'd met at a socialist potluck. It didn't sound like much fun. Plus, an extra shift would earn me a day's worth of overtime.

"Sure," I said. "No sweat."

"Eddie's threatening to pull my benefits if I don't work a full forty every week until Christmas," she said.

"Can he do that?" I said.

"I think so," she said.

She flicked her cigarette off the loading dock and immediately lit another one.

"You know," I said, "I could watch Rusty for you. I used to watch my little brother all the time."

"I don't know," she said. "Do you really think you can entertain a little boy on a Saturday night?"

"I've got nothing else to do," I said.

"Okay," Ella said.

I pumped my fist in the air, like I'd just won a contest.

"Look," she said, "I'd feel better about it if you just stayed at the mall, you know, in case he needs me or something."

"Okay," I said.

"Maybe you can take him to the movies," she said. "And then I'll give you money for dinner and ice cream. You could take him to the toy store to kill time. He'd spend all day in there if you'd let him."

"I can buy him dinner," I said.

Ella put her cigarette out in the coffee can filled with sand that Eddie had labeled, BURY YOUR BUTTS HERE.

"You're sure?" she said. She looked upset.

"Are you sure?" I said.

"No," she said. "No sweat." She went back inside.

NICK AND I WERE smoking pot behind Victoria's Secret. Even as we embraced the intellectual world, we had some old habits that we didn't abandon. Going through the workday with a buzz was one of them. The loading dock for that store was on the far side of the mall, away from the roads and parking lot, and in the evenings, after all the deliveries were done, nobody was back there but a handful of mall workers getting stoned. We had five minutes left in our break, and we were trying to get high enough to survive until nine thirty. I was looking out at the wetlands and field that the mall developer had to leave to comply with state regulations, and all of a sudden this weird-looking dog walked out from some brush and stared at us, its tongue hanging out.

"Look at that dog," I said.

"That's a coyote," Nick said.

"There's no fucking coyotes around here," I said.

"Bullshit, coyotes are everywhere."

"No, they're desert animals. They're in places like Arizona and New Mexico."

"No, they can live anywhere. You just never see them around here. They're afraid of people."

The creature was thin and matted and looked a little squirrelly to be somebody's stray mutt. It froze when it saw us and then took off, with not even a little wag of its tail.

"Shit, that was a sign," Nick said. "An affirmation."

I started laughing and took one last hit off the joint. I was getting pretty bored with pot. It generally made me feel like shit the next morning and aggravated my allergies, but I was way more bored with working at the mall than I was with weed. Still, I had a story to write for my creative writing class, which I desperately wanted to do well in. I wanted the instructor to dub me an heir to the Hemingway magic. The previous week, he'd handed back my first attempt at a workshop story. On top of the first page, in bold red letters, he'd written, *There are no more interesting or intelligent stories left to write about drunks. Find a new subject and try again.*

"That was a sign," Nick said. "Talking coyotes, man, talking coyotes."

"Oh, yeah? Did he talk?" I said.

"Mikey, you don't listen to spirit animals with your ears. You listen with your heart."

I was getting a little sick of Nick the guru. I was ready for the old fuckface Nick who communicated by punching the hell out of my arm or throwing bottles caps at my head.

I walked Nick back to the food court. I hoped Tom was still on the clock. I was feeling depressed after the joint, and was thinking that maybe some Miami Mambo would do the trick. I would write my story the next night.

As we walked through the mall, a salesgirl from Banana Republic waved at us; a few guys at the Sharper Image and the counter woman at the Thomas Kinkaid Gallery waved too. At the Arby's, a few guys shouted out, "Comrade!" When we walked by the Successories store, a red-haired guy in a suit came to the entrance and glared at Nick. He was standing next to a Serenity Desktop Rock Garden display, but he looked anything but serene. When we were out of his sight, Nick said, "He's one of the only goddamn Republicans who works at a mall. You make eight bucks an hour and you're a Republican? Stupid shit."

"How do you know everybody who works here?" I said.

"Because I'm not an antisocial bookworm," he said. "I get out. I talk to the people. I sell submarines and frozen Cokes. And I find out what makes people tick. People know me."

"You're full of it," I said.

"For instance," Nick said, shrugging off my accusation, "for instance, the girl at the Banana Republic? She's trying to pay her way through college. And the guys at the Sharper Image? One has three kids, the other one has a wife on disability and a kid with diabetes. The art gallery woman? Newly divorced, mother of twins. Her ex-husband lost all of their savings in one weekend in Atlantic City."

"Man, you could write a book," I said.

"No way," he said. "I got bigger plans."

NICK DID HAVE A bigger idea than a book. For a change, I hadn't heard about it first. By the time he told me he already had about a hundred people who supported it. And, for another change, he seemed like he was actually hellbent on pursuing this idea, not just letting it die out in a series of barroom conversations.

"On the Friday after Thanksgiving," he said, "the biggest motherfucking shopping day of the American year, Maple Rock Mall will be the sight of the biggest sit-down strike since 1937. We'll be on CNN. We'll be on the cover of *Time*. They'll want to make movies about us."

"Why?"

"Man, if my fucking dad sees this, he'll shit himself. Yours, too. Can you imagine it?"

"What are you going to do?" I said. I was getting nervous.

My thoughts moved to worst-case scenarios: A bomb? A riot? A full-scale invasion?

"Sit my ass down. Me and more than five hundred of my fellow retail workers will sit our asses down."

"Really?" I said. "Why?"

"Have you not been listening to anything I've been telling you about 1937?"

"No," I said.

"You know," Nick said, "you tell me you go to college now, Mikey, but you're still one of the stupidest goddamn guys at the mall."

SATURDAY—FIFTEEN MINUTES before four o'clock, on a cold, drizzly October afternoon—I met Ella and her son, Rusty, at the fountain in front of JC Penney's. Ella was beautiful. She wore a gray skirt, black boots, and black V-neck sweater. Unlike the rest of the employees at the Book Nook, she was always well-dressed and professional. I knew she was hoping to become the manager if Eddie Jones ever left, and, since regional managers often dropped in unannounced, Ella made it a point to work hard and look good every day. Only out on the loading dock, during the occasional cynical rant on her cigarette breaks, could you ever guess how much she hated her job.

She looked so good that I didn't even see her kid until she said, "Michael, this is my wonderful son, Rusty."

I put my hand out and Rusty slapped it. I couldn't tell if he was offering a high five or rejecting my handshake. He was a cagey little kid, all knees and elbows, and he was dressed in blue sweatpants and a red Spider-Man sweatshirt and Spider-Man tennis shoes. He had white-blond hair, pale skin, and giant blue eyes. He didn't look a thing like Ella.

"Rusty, this is my friend Michael. He's going to take you to the movies and take you out for pizza, and then maybe a trip to the toy store. After that, the two of you will pick up Mommy at work, and we'll go home, okay?"

"Why?" Rusty said.

"Remember, we talked all about it this morning."

In that moment, seeing Ella squat down so she could look her son in the eye, I considered taking back my offer. Ella could stay with Rusty, and I would go to work for her, then give her all the money I made on the shift. But it didn't seem like she would accept charity, or would ever be interested in me if I blew off an outing with her son.

I squatted down next to them, so both of us were there at Rusty's eye level. I looked over at Ella and she smiled. The dimples in her cheeks made me want to jump on her right there in the mall. Instead, still looking at her, I said, "Rusty, if you want to see Mommy at any time, we'll just go over to the bookstore and watch her work."

This seemed to make Rusty relax a little.

"Should we go see that movie?" I said. Rusty nodded and grabbed onto my hand. His mother gave him a squeeze and a loud smack on the forehead, and then she patted my arm, thanked me, and trotted past the Foot Locker toward the Book Nook.

Rusty held my hand but did very little talking. I bought him a small soda and popcorn and we found seats near the back, which he said was where he liked to sit. *The Land Be-*

*fore Time* was pretty good, but midway through the movie, Rusty had to pee so I took him to the bathroom. He dropped his pants right in front of the lowest urinal and wizzed, getting some urine on the wall in the process. Then he pulled his pants back up, and I lifted him so he could wash his hands. We missed a good chunk of the movie, but he didn't seem to care.

After the movie, we checked in with Ella at the Book Nook. Rusty launched into a vivid description of the film's ending and Ella seemed relieved, but Eddie Jones was working the register by himself, so we didn't stay long. We went over to Pizza Pizzazz.

"What kind of slice do you want?" I asked. "Pepperoni?"

"No," he said. "Veggie Delight."

"Yuck," I said. "That's not what kids like."

"It has broccoli on it," he said. "I like broccoli."

"Rusty, your mom isn't here today," I said. "Get whatever you want. Wouldn't you like pepperoni, or ham? Sausage? Five-Cheese Fiesta?"

"No, the Veggie Delight is great," he said. "I have it all the time."

I ordered a Veggie Delight for him, and two pepperoni slices for myself. I'd spent less than three hours with the kid, and had already dropped almost thirty bucks on dinner and a movie. Not that I really minded. I thought he was polite and cute. I was starting to feel crazy in love with his mother.

Tom Slowinski came over to our table. I introduced him to Rusty. Tom nodded politely and then made a whipping sound effect behind my back.

"You are seriously p-whipped, my man," he said. "Maybe we'll see you at Wednesday's later. Or maybe not?"

"Later, Tom," I said.

After Tom had walked away, Rusty looked at me and said, "Why do you want to hang around with a little kid anyway?"

"Because it's fun," I said.

"Are you just trying to be nice to my mom?"

"Well, that's part of it," I said, "But I also like doing things with you."

"I don't believe you," Rusty said.

"Do you like toys?" I said. Rusty nodded. We kept walking through the mall. I saw a lot of mothers walking around with their kids, but not a lot of fathers. I could imagine a lot of the dads at home, in their recliners, watching college football. Or maybe they were away on fishing trips, or maybe they were out of the picture altogether. I tried to imagine what it would be like if Rusty was really my kid. Would I want to be here in the mall with him on a weekend, watching cartoons and eating pizza? Or would I see him as a burden, one of the many things in life I had to take care of, and would I just want his mother to take him to the mall and give me a little bit of peace and quiet?

Rusty and I made one last stop, at the toy store. It was the best part of the day for me. I ended up dropping sixty bucks on things I thought Rusty should have. I wasn't even sure he wanted them, but I hadn't been in a toy store since Kolya was little. I was amazed by all the cool things you could get for a kid now.

When we met Ella in front of the Book Nook, she

looked a little horrified by the huge plastic shopping bag that Rusty was holding with both hands. Still, she smiled and gave me a hug.

"You can't buy a kid's love," she whispered against my neck. "But, hey—go ahead and try."

"I will," I said.

She pulled away from me.

"Thanks so much," she said. "You're a lifesaver."

I asked her if I could take her and Rusty for ice cream somewhere. Rusty seemed excited to go, but it was past his bedtime, Ella insisted. And it was past hers too.

"A rain check?" I offered.

"Sure," she said. "We'll see."


I WALKED ELLA AND Rusty to their car, and then drove myself over to Happy Wednesday's. It was almost ten o'clock. After the dinner rush, the place was pretty much empty except for mall workers trying to drink their last shift away and not think about the next one. As usual, Nick had most people's attention, and I slipped quietly into the bar, ordered a Mega-Mug, sat in an empty chair next to Tom, and listened. More than two dozen mall workers were gathered around a block of tables near Nick. It was Nick's biggest crowd yet.

He was talking about 1937—the year of the sit-down strikes. In Flint, on December 30, 1936, hundreds of United Auto Workers members refused to work or leave the factories at GM's Fisher body plant. They gathered in the factory with banjos and mandolins and mouth harps and sang pro-labor songs while seated on pallets and crates.

Some men carried in jugs of wine, which helped the time go by more quickly. Women and children, forming the Women's Emergency Brigade, brought food, water, and blankets to the workers, hoisting the supplies up to the plant's windows. The strike went on into the desolate and gray chill of February, but the strikers stayed in the factory.

"Did they know what they were starting?" Nick said. "Did they feel themselves marching to the great drum of justice, changing the course of history?"

"Drum of justice?" I said.

"He's good," Tom whispered back to me.

In Detroit, there were more walkouts. Members of the UAW left their posts at GM's Clark Street Cadillac plant in the middle of a cold, flat January day, in support of the Flint sit-down. They carried signs that read MAKE DETROIT A UNION TOWN.

The next month, the National Guard attacked striking autoworkers at the Flint Chevrolet plant #4. They fired tear gas into the factory. Outside, sympathizing UAW members carrying two-by-fours and baseball bats swarmed the factory and shattered every reachable window, hoping to get fresh air to their brethren inside the building.

"Solidarity," Nick said, "is the most powerful weapon against power and wealth."

The National Guard poured into Flint. They surrounded the Fisher plant while the workers stayed inside, doing their best to continue the singing and chanting. GM had turned off the heat and water inside the plant. Around the nation, GM factories, unable to get the parts they needed from Flint, lay idle.

Finally, bowing to undeniable economic and social pressure, GM officials ratified a one-page contract recognizing the power and authority of the UAW. That spring in Detroit, sit-down strikes flourished. Workers from hotels and bakeries and cigar factories joined autoworkers in sitting down on the job. Workers at Dodge Main made Chrysler recognize their union; women who worked at Woolworth held an eight-day strike. The female workforce at Yale and Towne Manufacturing Company squared off against the Detroit police, who stormed the gates of the factory in the rain and pounded through doors with clubs in hand.

Even children joined the movement. One famous photo depicts schoolchildren picketing the home of a woman who took their baseball and refused to return it.

Those were the days that Nick wanted to resurrect. He imagined workers at malls across the country walking out during the busy holiday retail season, tanking the American economy until the minimum wage was raised to a living wage. He said he would risk having his face bashed in like Walter Reuther and Richard Frankensteen in the Battle of the Overpass outside Ford Rouge in May of 1937. Henry Ford's private security force had tried to stop the labor movement with brute force and wealth, but eventually even they had to cave.

"Do you think the mall's rent-a-cops will be as tough as the goons of Henry Ford?" Nick said. He had been telling stories of 1937 for more than an hour.

Everybody started laughing. I guess we were all pretty drunk.

A few of the guys Nick, Tom, and I went to high school with were there that night—Walker Van Dyke, Kyle Hartley, Mike Pappas. The others dressed like us, looked like us, laughed at the same jokes. It was as if even the strangers in that group had lived a life that paralleled mine. Nick had officially dubbed this crowd the Knights of Labor. Their mission was to spread the word of the sit-down strike to every mall employee who could be trusted. They were not to tell any owners or managers. To be honest, I had spent the previous weeks only half amused by Nick's quixotic campaign. I thought it was immature and ill advised. I thought it would fade away when he discovered a new obsession—the blues or Hitchcock films or German literature. But that night, I could see bright eyes shining in the smoky air, reflecting the lights of the beer signs over the bar as they looked up at Nick. And as Nick stood there in his leather jacket, his head shaved, his well-muscled shoulders and neck upright, his dark goatee framing his white smile, he looked a little like a revolutionary might look in the early days of a campaign—idealistic, fearless, strong. I realized then that these people were looking to Nick for leadership; he could take them on any path he chose. It was glorious and dangerous all at once. I realized then that I was willing to follow him anywhere, too. I, like everybody else in the bar that night, had nowhere else to go.

THE NEXT MORNING, I woke up and went to St. John's, the old Ukrainian church on Clippert Avenue in Detroit. I saw a few old ladies I recognized, and made polite small talk with them in my fading Ukrainian. My mother had stopped going to St. John's after she married Father Mack and moved to Northville, and very few of my friends went there anymore either. The neighborhood was getting worse. The drugstores and the credit unions and the burger joints were giving way to strip clubs and porn shops and check-cashing stands, and there were newer Ukrainian churches in the suburbs. St. John's had recently installed a wrought-iron fence around the perimeter of the church to cut down on graffiti and vandalism. I stood in the back of the church during Mass, the traditional place for single young men to stand in a Ukrainian church, and ducked out during Communion. The church seemed full of ghosts—some of them in the process of dying, some already dead. I could sense my father and his friends there, could almost hear them murmuring the responses and grunting as they kneeled for prayers.

Afterward, I drove to Northville and had dinner with Mom and Mack and Kolya. I told them a little about church, about my recent raise—twenty cents an hour—at the bookstore. Mack told me he had developed a genuine liking for real estate development, and Kolya gave me the rundown on how his math teacher was out to get him. My mother mostly folded her hands and stared at me and refilled my plate with chicken and potatoes the minute it was close to empty.

"Do you have anybody special in your life?" she finally asked. "Not to be nosy, but I am curious."

"Honey," Mack said, "go easy on him or he'll stop coming to visit."

"There's somebody," I said. "But it's not too serious yet."

"Oh? Somebody from school?" she said.

"Work," I said.

"Is she hot?" Kolya said. I wanted to say that she had just won the Hump Day Honey contest, but I knew that would give everybody the wrong idea. "She's very pretty and smart," I said. "She has a really neat kid."

"A kid?" Mom said.

"Kolya," Mack said, "help your mom with dessert. I want to show Michael something in the den."

Mack was the ultimate peacemaker. I hadn't really minded my mother's questions; in fact, I realized then that just talking about Ella made me incredibly happy.

"You know how moms can get," Mack said. "I avoided a lot of that by entering the priesthood at twenty."

"It's fine," I said.

Mack poured me a glass of cognac without asking. It wasn't really my thing, but I sipped it to be polite. I knew he was about to make me some sort of offer. He still had an almost unhealthy desire to help me.

"I have a friend who works in radio," Mack said. "And I asked him about the possibility of an internship."

"My job is okay for now," I said. "I don't mind it."

"Okay," Mack said. "I was just offering to make a connection."

"Thanks," I said. "I appreciate the thought. Let's get some of that dessert."

"Sure," he said. "Let's."

I spent the rest of the day watching football with Kolya, who kept trying to reenact exciting plays by tackling me and throwing me into the couch.

When I got home that night I had two messages from Ella. The first was an apology: she had forgotten to give me money for the movie and the pizza. The toys, she said, were my fault and she wasn't going to pay me back for those. Then she called an hour later to see if I wanted to come over and have tacos with her and Rusty.

"Give me a call if you get this message before eight," she said. "Okay?" She paused as if she was wondering if I was at home, screening my calls. I looked at the clock. It was almost nine.

"Okay. Otherwise, I'll see you at work tomorrow morning. Okay? And thanks again—so, so much—for your help yesterday."

I played the messages five or six times. That night, I could hardly sleep. I was so excited to get to work.

ELLA AND I WORKED together on Monday, but Eddie had us in different sections of the store, so we barely spoke. I went to find her when first shift was over and Eddie told me, a little perturbed, that she had asked to leave an hour early to pick up her son from day care. On Tuesday, I had the day off so I could go to class. I'd written another story that my teacher hated. Across the first page, he'd written, *Flat and clichéd female characters—even for a story about hunting!*

Wednesday our shifts overlapped for a few hours in the afternoon, but Ella was quiet and depressed. She had slipped a check for twenty-five dollars in my employee mailbox, with a thank-you card Rusty had made. He had signed it *Love, Rusty,* but Ella had not signed it. However, in the memo line on the check she'd given me, she'd written, *Thanks! XOXO.*

Ella won the Hump Day Honey contest again that night. It was her fourth straight win. She wore a black bikini this time, and black knee-high boots. She smiled a bit more from the stage, and carried a black belt that she playfully snapped at the men hooting and hollering along the bar. She was starting to pack in the crowds. But as usual, right after she won and collected her $250, she threw on her jeans and sweatshirt and headed for the door as fast as she could.

I followed her out into the parking lot. I caught up with her by her old white Dodge truck. She was fumbling with the lock. "You're becoming quite the champion," I said. It was a cold night and I was shivering.

She didn't answer.

"Over the hump," I said.

"I think it's pathetic that you go here every week."

"Sorry," I said. "At least I keep my clothes on."

"Hey, at least I get paid to be here," she said. "Do you know how much extra money I made last month? A thousand bucks, cash. Do you have any idea how much money that is for somebody like me? That covers rent and utilities. I've actually started a savings account. Do you have anything to say about that?" She put her hands on her hips and stared at me.

"I'm freezing," I said. My hands were in my pockets and my arms were literally trembling. It was hard to talk, my teeth were chattering so much. "Why don't you just swallow your pride and call your daddy and ask him for some fucking money?"

"Don't talk to me about things you know nothing about," she said. "You know, better yet, don't talk to me at all."

She got into her truck and started it, but not before I ran around the front end and hopped in the passenger seat.

"What?" she said.

"Sorry," I said.

"Once I have a little bit more money saved up, I'll quit," she said.

"Good," I said.

"But I'm not going to quit for you," she said. "This has nothing to do with you. The way I see it, if these assholes want me to strut up and down the bar in a bikini for five minutes and pay me two hundred and fifty bucks, they're the creeps, not me."

"They're the creeps," I said. "Totally. I just feel bad for you."

"Oh, and none of this Dostoyevsky-inspired stripper-with-a-heart-of-gold shit, okay? I know what I am doing and my heart isn't pure. I saw your staff picks. I saw *Crime and Punishment* up there. I'm not Sonya."

"I dated a girl named Sonya in high school," I said.

"Figures," she said.

"And I'm no Raskolnikov," I said. "I always imagined Raskolnikov with really greasy hair, a guy who smells like cold tomato soup."

She started laughing. "You've given this some thought, huh? Why would you think that one customer in Maple Rock Mall would ever be interested in reading Dostoyevsky?"

"I'm going to kiss you now," I said.

"No," she said, "you're not. That's all I need, for some dumb-ass jock to see the Hump Day Honey making out in the Happy Wednesday's parking lot. Look, I got to go home. Margaret's with Rusty and she probably wants to get home."

"I understand," she said.

"On Friday, Rusty is going to a children's play with Margaret and her boyfriend in Ann Arbor," she said, "and he's going to sleep over. Do you want to do something after work?"

"What?" I said.

"Figure something out," she said.

"What?" I said.

She looked at me and tilted her head. "Are you okay?" she said, slowly.

"Huh?" I said.

"I'll see you at eight?" she said. "Friday?"

"Yes," I said.

THAT FRIDAY, I WENT over to pick up Ella at eight o'clock. I was ten minutes early so I had to drive around for a while, and I started sweating as I drove, feeling sick. Ella lived in the Pink Flamingo trailer court in the old section of Maple Rock, not too far from my house. The Pink Flamingo was one of the few remaining trailer parks in Wayne County. Many of them had gone up along the edges of Detroit in the fifties, when the auto industry brought a huge influx of people to the area. They were mostly run-down now, though the Pink Flamingo was all right—it had a reputation of sorts among slumming suburban hipsters who liked the party lights, giant plastic flamingos, and fake palm trees that lined the perimeter of the grounds. The population of the place consisted of the drunk, the down-and-out, the recently divorced, and the young twenty-somethings who worked at the mall. The young people hung out on the porches of their trailers in the evenings, drinking cheap beer and wearing bowling shirts and polyester pants that they'd picked up at the Salvation Army. They wrote poetry or played in alternative bands or made short documentary films with camcorders.

I parked in the visitor's lot and walked up to Ella's unit, number eighty-six. I passed an old guy asleep on a folding chair on the sidewalk. There was a carton of empty Budweiser cans next to him. There were a lot of empty beer cans everywhere.

I knocked on Ella's door and a dog started barking. Rusty, dressed in jeans and cowboy boots, answered the door and a young yellow Lab wiggled onto the small wooden porch and started licking my pants. Rusty was holding a small rubber ball, which he hurled at me. The ball bounced off the porch railing and then shot back and hit me in the leg.

"Ha!" Rusty screamed.

I didn't blame him. If I'd been just a little bit younger when my mother started dating, I'd have done the same thing.

Ella came to the door. She was wearing a pair of plaid shorts that looked like men's boxers and a white V-neck T-shirt. She didn't look like she was going anywhere. She looked like she'd just woken up.

"Hey, I tried to call you," she said. "Margaret has the flu. Sleepover party was canceled."

"I didn't get the message. I didn't go home."

"The flu. That means Aunt Maggie is puking," Rusty said.

"And you already know this charming young man," Ella said.

"And that's Lucky the Dog," Rusty said. The dog came over to me and leaned hard into my leg, whacking me with his frantic tail. I gave him a good pet.

Then I put out my hand and offered it to Rusty and the kid shook it, dramatically pumping it up and down.

Ella laughed. "It's late, Rusty. Go brush your teeth."

He rolled his eyes and went down the hall.

"I'm sorry about this," Ella said. We were alone and the dog had gone and curled up under a coffee table with a large ball. "The place is a mess. And I'm sorry about that, too. Maybe I should write out all my apologies before you come inside."

"I don't care," I said. "It's nice to see you."

"Should we reschedule?" she said. "I'm not even dressed really. I should at least put on a bra."

I could feel myself blushing.

"It's okay," I said. "I've seen you almost naked on a bar top for several straight weeks now."

She smiled. "Finally you're developing a sense of humor."

I nodded, pleased.

"Do you want to watch a movie?" she said.

We got through half of something that night, a comedy about a therapist and an obsessive patient. We didn't watch much of it. She talked a little about her parents.

"The funny thing is," she said, "I mean, I've told you that they're loaded. But I think they're really loaded. My dad's in the oil business. He's played golf with Dick Cheney. He'd die if he saw where I live now."

"You don't see them much?" I asked.

"My sister talks to them a few times a year," she said. "Not me."

"Why not?"

"They're not worth talking to," she said. "They're corrupt souls and their money is corrupt and their souls are bankrupt."

"I see," I said.

"New subject," she said. "This is the longest story in the world and an old and boring one at that."

I asked her how she ended up in Maple Rock, and she shrugged. She said that she had met Rusty's father, Steve, on a backpacking trip through Europe.

"I'd been at Cornell for two years," she said.

"You went to Cornell?"

"Two years," she said. "I married Steve the summer after my sophomore year, after we'd spent one lousy week together in Greece—well, actually it was the only good week we ever had. Steve was from Livonia. He thought it'd be romantic to buy ourselves this trailer with the money I had in my savings account. He had plans to finish a novel, and make us rich."

"Oh, God," I said.

"Yeah. I was barely twenty-one. The sex was good. Pissing off my parents was even better. I got careless, then pregnant. I hated being on the pill—still do—so we used the trusty pull-out method. Steve was gone six months after Rusty was born."

"That's tough," I said.

"One bad decision after another," she said. "That pretty much describes my twenties. But I love Rusty. I love being a mom."

"Do you ever hear from Steve?" I asked.

"No. Not a word," she said. "His parents send a check at Christmas some years. They feel bad, but they live in Florida. His father is on oxygen and can't travel and his mother has MS and can barely walk."

"So here you are in Maple Rock," I said.

"What's your story?" she said. "It can't be more pathetic than that."

I told her my story, which I had told to so many women in my young life that I almost didn't believe it anymore. It sounded like some dumb pickup ploy, a pathetic tale meant to arouse sympathetic lust.

"When I was sixteen," I began, "my father went to the moon."

We stared at the movie in silence for a little while. It was supposed to be funny, but neither of us was laughing. Neither of us had followed the plot very well either, but the ending seemed to be happy. Around ten thirty, the credits were rolling and I had nothing to say. The tape reached the end and then started to rewind. The screen went snowy, sending flickering blue light onto the walls of the living room. Ella stood up from the couch and took my hand. I touched her bare smooth thigh with my other hand. She straddled me and we started kissing. After a few minutes, she said, "You should go."

"Okay," I said. "I understand."

I stood up and she pointed at the obvious bulge in my jeans and smiled. "Well, good night to you too, Mr. Happy," she said.

I blushed. Ella walked me to the door and we kissed again on the porch of the trailer.

"What the fuck," she said. "Rusty's a heavy sleeper. Come back in."

"I'd love to," I said.

"But you can't stay the night. No falling asleep," she said.

Afterward, as I was getting dressed in the dark, Ella, tucked under the quilt, flashed me a thumbs-up and whispered, "Excellent."

"When you're good, you're good," I said.

"I haven't had sex in more than two years," she said, "so don't get a big head."


THE NEXT NIGHT, Ella invited me over again. I didn't stay the night because she didn't think it was a good idea for Rusty to wake up and find me there.

"Once, I came home to find my mom in bed with a priest," I said.

"Oh my God," she said. "What did you do?"

"Well, I was older, it was just a few years ago."

"Yeah? What happened?"

"She eventually married him. He was an old high-school sweetheart. They live in Northville."

"That's almost romantic," she said.

"Almost," I said.

It became a habit of mine, waking up in the middle of the night and going home before dawn. After I left Ella's trailer, sometimes, if it wasn't last call yet, I'd meet up with Nick and the guys at Happy Wednesday's. I never got much of a chance to talk to him though. By now, he was swarmed by eager mall workers listening to the gospel of workers' rights. He'd started an e-mail list, and distributed information and rallying cries from a laptop he bought on credit at Best Buy. One night, we used the laptop to search our fathers' names on Google. We tried every variation of their names we could think of, but we found nothing.

UP TO THAT POINT, our days at the mall had flowed into each other, blurring. We were headed toward thirty, but we still didn't know what we wanted to do. We sometimes thought of moving or finding a new job, but it didn't seem to happen. We considered the bodies of our grandfathers, who died too young, just after retiring, wrecked and spent from day after day with the unstoppable gears of the assembly lines. Perhaps we were luckier than they were. Perhaps we weren't.

Perhaps we had dreams. To be honest, we couldn't remember them. We tried to imagine what we had wanted to be when we grew up. When we were ten, or eleven, or twelve, did we dream of becoming doctors or lawyers? Carpenters?

Teachers? Sportswriters? Auto mechanics? We didn't know. We honestly couldn't remember.

Perhaps you, our fathers, perhaps you know what we wanted from life. Perhaps you remember something we uttered as kids, some clues: *Daddy, I want to be a fireman. Daddy, I want to be a zookeeper. Daddy, I want to be a concert violinist.*

Once Nick said, "What would we be doing if they hadn't built this goddamn mall?"

And the silence was overwhelming. We didn't know.

But Nick had found a way, if only for a brief time, to make working at the mall seem interesting and full of meaning. The planned sit-down strike was all anybody would talk about at work. We wondered about media coverage. We wondered if mall workers around the country would follow in our footsteps. Would the Mall of America shut down? There was talk of launching a Web site on the day of the strike, so retail clerks around the country could log on and be inspired. We wondered which liberal celebrities would endorse our cause. Michael Moore? George Clooney? Drew Barrymore? Marlon Brando?

Managers overheard some of these conversations, and memos began appearing in our break rooms on a daily basis.

"The organization of a workforce must comply with all federal laws and regulations."

"Not showing up for work when scheduled is cause for immediate termination. Consider yourself warned."

"In recent weeks, certain planned pranks have been brought to my attention, and I am not happy. I hope that no employees of American Pants plan to be involved in these insurgent and unlawful activities."

"Show up to work on the day after Thanksgiving or you'll be shitcanned."

After work, we'd bring these memos to Happy Wednesday's and laugh wildly at them, letting their condescending tone fuel the fire in our guts.

ON ELECTION DAY, Nick convinced me to have a party at my house. Aunt Maria had just driven in from her new condo in Livonia and cleaned his place for him, and he didn't want to mess it up.

"Your mother still cleans your house?" I asked.

"Oh, come on, Mikey, yours does too. We're the first-born sons of Ukrainian mothers."

"Yeah, but it's not on schedule or anything," I said. "She just shows up."

"Same deal," he said. "Besides, your place is bigger and so is your television."

I had never been to, let alone hosted, an Election Day party. I bought a keg of Sam Adams because it seemed appropriate and patriotic, and the mascot on the bottle wore a hat that looked a little like Nick's Liberty Bell Subs uniform. I felt smart and sophisticated. I told Ella about the party and she said, "Maple Rock becomes an activist hotbed? This I gotta see." She asked her sister to come and baby-sit for her. When I told Nick I was dating her and that she would be at the party, he flipped. He sounded like the old Nick for a second, nineteen and brash and wholly inappropriate.

"The Hump Day girl?" he asked. "Did your dick fall off yet? I warned you."

"Don't bring up Hump Day while she's here," I said. She had lost the contest for the first time the previous week. She said the manager of the place gave her fifty bucks so she would keep coming back, but the tide had turned. Two new women, a blonde and a brunette, had shared first prize after they made out on top of the bar. I had missed all of the excitement. I'd been babysitting Rusty so his mother could walk across the bar in a bikini and earn a better life for him. It still was hard for me to think about—Ella half naked in front of all those stupid men. But anytime I brought it up, even jokingly, we'd get into a huge fight.

Most of Nick's hardcore followers showed up for our party, more than fifty people who worked at the mall. While we watched the election returns trickle in, people talked about the strike. They tried to predict how many people would join them.

"I mean," Nick said, "how many people will really do this?"

It was like he was testing the allegiance of his team.

Everybody started talking at once. They shouted out their predictions—one hundred, two hundred, five hundred—and Nick sat back and beamed. When they called out those numbers, this is what they were really saying: "We won't let you down, Nick. We're behind you 100 percent."

Suddenly, Tom Slowinski let out a loud, shrill whistle. He was crouched down by the television so he could hear it over the noise of the party. Everybody shut up and looked at him.

"Gore took Michigan!" he cried, and everyone went crazy. In the days leading up to the election, Nick had instructed us that a vote for the Democrats was a vote for the rich tradition of labor. He'd even handed out copies of the AFL-CIO's endorsement of Gore and plastered them in the break rooms and bathrooms of the mall.

We were in for a long night. Ella and I were in the kitchen opening some more bags of chips and jars of salsa. She pressed up behind me. "I like your house," she said. "It's very nice."

"Thanks," I said. "It's pretty much furnished and decorated with my mother's leftovers. I haven't done much to it."

"Well, it has character. It feels like a family lived here a long time."

"We did," I said.

From the other room, a chorus of cheers rose up when another state came in for Gore.

"Do you think anybody in there would have voted if it wasn't for Nick?" she asked.

I laughed. "Not a chance."

"Don't tell anyone," she said. "I voted for Nader."

"Wasted vote," I said.

She threw a tortilla chip at my head.

I asked her if she thought it would really happen, if she thought that Maple Rock Mall would make labor history.

"Tonight, for the first time," she said, "I do. I don't know why. I mean, maybe not labor history, but if nothing else, it will get some attention. Nick will have done something, and that's more than all of us can say."

Just then Nick stormed into the room with a red, shiny face and bellowed, "We're dry! We need more beer!"

It was strange to hear him shout this phrase, one I had heard him shout so many times in our lives, on this night infused with politics and history and vision. I almost wished the whole sit-down campaign would stop. It felt like we were being people we were not, people we had no right to be.

Gore had Wisconsin, Gore had Minnesota. We cheered wildly. Everybody was good and drunk by the time people started trying to call Florida, which was for the better. It was hard to watch. Tom made a run to the party store for more beer.

A few minutes later, my phone rang. Tom had been arrested on a DUI.

Ella and I drove Tom's fiancée, Tanya Jaworski, to the police station. In the car, Tanya leaned up from the backseat and said, "Mikey, I hope you're fucking happy. You and Nick are a train wreck. Nothing you do works out. It fucks everything up."

In the early hours of the morning, we watched Tanya post bail for her future husband with a credit card. The ride back to Tom's place was quiet.

"Fuck," I said, after we'd dropped them off at the door.

"She was just mad at Tom and took it out on you. You didn't make him drive."

I drove Ella back home to her trailer. There was a drunk teenager staggering across the road. I swerved onto the shoulder and just missed him.

"Do you want to come in?" Ella asked when we pulled in front of her door. "Margaret's probably asleep in the bed, but we can crash on the pull-out sofa."

"I better get back to my house," I said. "Make sure it's still standing."

She leaned over and gave me a slow kiss on the mouth.

"I love you," I said.

"Michael," she said. Then she touched my cheek with her hand and got out of the car.

THE MONDAY BEFORE Thanksgiving brought with it the first snow of the season. We still had no incoming President. Snow swirled over the roads as Nick and I drove out to Brighton and listened to public radio's coverage of the Florida recount. Nick was distracted and irritable and he kept telling me I was going the wrong way. We were headed to see Tom at the rehab clinic where he'd gone to dry out. Tanya had insisted he check himself in, a proactive step Tom's lawyer thought might get him a lighter sentence.

Tom ambled into the lobby of the clinic wearing jeans and a blue Michigan sweatshirt. He'd just been through his third day of detox. He was unshaven and thin and he said he hadn't been able to eat much. He was short, but normally a pretty stocky guy, and seeing him look pale and gaunt was a bit of shock. I tried not to stare at him.

"Don't I look great?" he said.

"Better than Mikey," Nick said.

Tom led us down the pristine white hallway to a room he called the lounge, which had a fridge full of Sprite and bottled water, and a hot-beverage machine that only served decaf coffee and herbal tea. We sat around a card table and drank thick, lukewarm coffee with powdered creamer. Across from us, a man in his late forties sat with two teenage girls. He was looking at a magazine, and he kept reading items out loud and trying to make the girls laugh. They looked like they'd been crying all day though, and they weren't in the mood.

"How bad is it?" Nick asked, lighting up a cigarette for Tom and then one for himself.

"It's not so bad," he said. "Man, I'd kill for a drink, you know? But it's not so bad. It might be the best thing that ever happened to me."

"Really?" I said.

"Sure," he said. Soft music played on a radio somewhere. "Margaritaville" came on, and someone turned the radio off. "I mean, how long can you be an asshole who drinks too much?"

"You don't drink too much," Nick said.

At lunch, the lady at the front desk told us that we were allowed to go out to McDonald's and bring some back for Tom. We got him a twenty-piece Chicken McNuggets, but Nick and I ate most of them. Tom just sipped on the milk shake we'd given him. He looked around and said, "I got two weeks in here, but I can stay up to six. Man, this is a helluva milk shake."

"Well, two weeks isn't so bad," I said.

"I think I might stay the full six," he said.

"Why?" Nick said. "You're not really an alcoholic. I don't think so. Do you, Mikey?"

"I think you should stay two weeks," I said. "You don't want to be in here at Christmas."

"No," Tom said. "But I don't want to be here ever again, either. I don't want to be that kind of guy."

"You won't be," Nick said.

"No way," I said.

"Gentleman, we need to step back for a moment and take a look at ourselves," Tom said. "Oh-fucking-kay?"

Normally this would have been just the kind of sudden and passionate Tom Slowinski speech that would have made us bust out laughing. Instead, Nick and I looked at each other and shrugged. Then we each dunked another nugget in barbecue sauce and finished our lunch in silence.

Finally, Tom spoke. "How are the strike plans going, Nick?"

Nick looked around the room, like he was afraid he was being tailed. "It's okay, Tom," he said. "It's going fine."

On the way home, Nick said very little. When we were back on the interstate I said, "I think old Tommy Too Slow is sad that he is going to miss the strike."

"Maybe," Nick said. "A few people are starting to bail on us, you know. About a dozen people have already told me they're having second thoughts. A lot of guys with kids. It'd be a shitty time to lose a job if you had kids."

"Who needs those guys?" I said. "Weak links."

I was thinking about Ella. What would she do if she lost her job over this strike? What would she get Rusty for Christmas? She'd have to win a whole lot more bikini contests to pay the bills without her job at the Book Nook.

The day was windy and some snow blew around, dotting the windshield with ice. The sky over the interstate was gray and the bare trees along the highway looked desperate for warmth, like they might snap in two if the wind picked up any more.

"It's not even Christmas," Nick said, "and I'm already fucking sick of winter."

---

THE NEXT AFTERNOON, Nick and I were on break smoking cigarettes behind Victoria's Secret. More snow was drifting down from the sky when he said, "I need to talk to you."

"We're talking," I said.

"I've called it off," he said. "Okay, Mikey? It's not going to happen."

"What?" I said.

"The strike. I've already got people spreading the word. It's off."

"Why?" I said. "Because of the election? All this recount bullshit? Is that it? Because if anything, now would be the perfect time to—"

"No," he said. "That has nothing to do with this. It's just not going to happen."

He threw a cigarette butt out ahead of him. It was still smoking when it landed. We were quiet for a minute watching it get covered in snow.

"I had a lot of trouble sleeping last night," Nick said. "And then I woke up and started making calls, telling people it was off, and that felt like the right thing to do. I don't know. Anyway, there's no use discussing it anymore. It's off."

"Whatever," I said.

"Look," Nick said, "people were getting cold feet. It would have been you and me out there all alone—a couple of stupid fucks against the world. Just like old times. We know better than that now."

"There would have been more people there. Ella would be there."

"Fine. You and me and Ella. Three stupid fucks against the world."

"Just like that? You can't do that. It's the only thing anybody has to look forward to right now. I hear people talking about it all the time. That's so goddamn like you, Nick. You don't stick with anything."

"My girlfriend is pregnant. We're going to get married."

"So? So what the fuck!"

"You think anybody is going to hire the leader of a sitdown strike? We're not in a real union, Mikey. There's nothing protecting us, no laws or anything."

"So? Who cares? It was a statement. You said it yourself, you said we'd be famous."

"I need the benefits for the baby. I've worked at Liberty Bell Subs for one year just to get medical insurance. I can't fuck this up."

I had never argued Nick into anything. I knew it wouldn't happen.

"So will I finally get to meet her? This girl? Is she the one from Ann Arbor? Will you have a wedding?"

"No. We're just going to the courthouse. She doesn't want a church wedding or a party or anything."

"Fine, fine. I'll be your witness!"

"Mikey. It's Sunny."

I just looked at him. He shrugged. Then I said, "You mean, Sonya? Sonya Stecko?"

"Right. She goes by Sunny now, you know that."

"I thought you were just friends," I said.

He shrugged.

"She's the one you've been talking about?" I asked.
"She's the beautiful, brilliant girl from Ann Arbor?"

"Mikey, are you pissed at me?"

"It was a long time ago," I said. "We were in high school.
Do you think I would care about that?"

"I know," he said. "But if you're mad, it's okay."

"I'm with Ella now. Who cares about Sonya Stecko?"

"I know. Ella's great. She's beautiful too."

"Yeah," I said. "She is."

"Mikey, Sunny is trying to finish a dissertation. I don't
want to be the guy who wrecks all that for her. So I've got to
make some money, pull down some benefits."

We watched each other as our hair and coats grew white
with snow. Then I quickly gave him a hug, thumping our
chests together and hitting him on the back three times.

"You're going to be a dad," I said. "Holy shit."

"Amazing," he said.

"Wow," I said. "Does that mean I finally have to start
calling her Sunny?"

Nick smiled and checked his watch.

"I have to get back to work," he said.

"Of course," I said. "Me too."

"I might end up getting a second job," he said. "Just to
save some money until the baby is born."

"Man," I said.

That night I called Ella and told her what Nick had said.

"I know," she said. "I heard. Some guy from American
Pants came in and told me. Maybe it's for the best."

"Maybe," I said.

WE HAD THANKSGIVING at Father Mack and my mother's house. Nick was with Sunny's family—Nick and Sunny had planned to break their news to Sunny's mother after she was calm and sleepy from turkey and wine. Aunt Maria was in San Diego with her new boyfriend, her first trip out of the state since she was twenty years old.

I picked up Ella and Rusty in the afternoon and, as we drove to my mother's house, I explained over and over again that Ella should not take anything anybody said seriously. That went for my mom and Mack and Kolya.

"Don't even listen to the cat," I said. "The cat is just as crazy as everybody else."

Rusty laughed from the backseat.

"Rusty, honey, pretend you didn't hear Michael say anything, okay?"

"Is your family crazy?" he said.

"No, Rusty. Michael was just being funny."

"No, Rusty, I mean it. They're wacko." I turned to my side and stuck my tongue out and made a funny face. Rusty found me pretty hilarious and it always made me excited to hear him laugh.

Ella lowered her voice. "You have to watch what you say around him, Mikey. He's like a tape recorder."

Rusty repeated her word for word.

The house in Northville felt like a strange place to have a holiday, even though my mother had been with Mack for a few years by then. Still, all of that dark wood and new china and silverware made me feel like we were staying in some country estate somewhere. We stood in the foyer shaking hands and hugging and everybody was exceedingly polite. After all, my mother and Mack had first coupled while he was under a vow of chastity, so they were kind of sitting in a glass house. They wouldn't say anything about something as common as a single mother. But Kolya was eighteen, in his fourth year of high school, and void of all tact. He said, "So, do you know who Rusty's father is then? Or do you not have a clue?"

"Kolya," my mother said, though I bet she wanted to know the answer too.

"Shut up," I said. "Everybody."

"It's okay," Ella said. "He's just not in our lives and we're okay with that."

"I've never even seen him," Rusty said. "Except when I was little."

Everyone nearly choked when he said that, his voice so young and sad and stretched out with longing.

"Sometimes that's for the better," Mack said. He still had some priestly instinct in him and was good at diffusing situations. "You've turned into a very smart and polite young man."

"I know," Rusty said.

It wasn't too bad of an afternoon. After dinner, Ella helped Mack with the dishes, Kolya and Rusty watched football in the family room, and my mother and I brought Christmas decorations up from the basement. Mom liked to decorate the house in a timely manner for each holiday, and the day after Thanksgiving seemed to be some urgent deadline in her world. I was glad that she wasn't working two jobs anymore. She seemed to have the energy she had when I was very young. As we untangled a mess of Christmas lights, my mother said, "Ella is beautiful and charming and smart. I'm glad you found her. And Rusty is too cute for words."

We had another round of pumpkin pie and coffee and then I drove Ella and Rusty home. I walked them to the door of the trailer, and Lucky the Dog started barking like crazy, so I came in to pet him. Ella asked me to stay while she got Rusty into bed, then she came back to the kitchen wearing an old plaid robe and gray flannel pajamas. This was the first time I'd seen her in this outfit, and in some ways, it was sexier than the short, shimmery nightgowns she wore in bed. Her hair was back in a ponytail and she came over and sat on my lap.

"Michael," she said. "I love you too."

"What?"

"A few weeks ago, after the party, you said you loved me and I didn't say it back."

"Oh, that," I said, trying to sound offhand.

"When you're a parent, I think you tend to give your love away a little less easily. It's hard to explain."

"That's okay," I said.

"But I do love you," she said.

I said it back.

"Will you stay the night?" she said.

"Sure," I said. I told her that I would take Lucky for a short walk and that I would meet her in the bedroom. She made a joke about the sexy flannel lingerie she was wearing for our first sleepover. I admitted that it would be nice not to have to drive home anymore, half asleep and lonely, at three in the morning.

Lucky and I walked slowly. He'd been inside almost all day and he wagged his tail and leaped around like a flea on a string, pissing on every tree and mailbox he passed. When we got back to Ella's place, I heard shouting. Lucky started to growl. The couple across the street was having a real knock-down-drag-out. It didn't feel right that Rusty would grow up in this kind of place, in a run-down trailer with people yelling "Fuck you" and "You fucking whore" every thirty seconds while he tried to sleep. Next door, some young hipsters were standing around a barbecue with cans of beer, still trying to get their turkey cooked. I went inside, latched the screen, and turned all three bolts.

When I got to the bedroom, Ella was still awake. She sat up in bed and helped me get undressed.

"I've been thinking," she said, "maybe we should do this anyway. We should make signs and try the sit-down strike without Nick."

"Are you serious?"

"What do I have to lose?" she said. "Right? One bad job? But what if it works? This could be something."

I loved her then, even though I knew she was only trying to keep me from crashing. She wanted me to be happy. I nodded. "What do we have to lose?"

I called Nick that night—Sunny answered the phone—and told him that we still planned to picket the mall at seven o'clock the next morning. We would urge all the other mall workers to join us. "We'll either see you there or not," I said.

"It's not going to work, Mikey," he said. "If I thought it might, I'd be right there beside you. But it won't. It just will not work."

"You don't know that!" I said.

"This time I do."

THE NEXT MORNING, Ella and I stood at the main entrance of the mall, near the food court. Rusty was with us, all bundled up and fairly interested in the signs we had made. This spot had been the designated rallying point. We put our picket signs behind some garbage cans and waited to see if anybody would join us. Walker Van Dyke and about eight other guys showed up and looked at the three of us.

"This is it?" Walker said.

"So far," Ella said.

"Nick bailed on us," somebody else said.

"Well, he's not the only guy that matters," Ella said.

I couldn't think of anything else to say. Rusty looked a little scared. He held my hand. A Channel Two news truck slowed down in the parking lot and watched us for a minute. Then Walker and the other guys talked among themselves and decided they had better show up for work.

For the past twelve hours, we had struggled to get the word to everybody that the strike was still on. We had woken people up in the middle of the night and tried to get them to listen to us. But it was hard to reach everybody, and without Nick and his dynamic, feverish leadership, nobody wanted to go out on a limb. Most of the workers looked at Ella and me and Rusty on their way into the mall and kept on going. A few of Nick's most ardent Knights of Labor showed up with signs made on poster board—MALL WORKERS UNITED and FAIR WAGES NOW—but dropped them in the garbage cans when they saw nobody else had joined us. Ella and I didn't inspire them and instill confidence in them the way Nick did. Nick was a man of many gifts. Nick had vision.

"You've got to have vision," he used to say, whether he was playing a prank on the principal or hitting on the hottest woman in the room or organizing a mass labor protest. "You've got to have vision, man."

A few minutes before eight o'clock, Nick appeared. He gave us nothing more than a glance and a nod, not even a discreet thumbs-up or an appreciative grin. His hands were plunged into the pockets of his denim jacket. He was wearing a navy blue watch cap. His shoulders were full and hunched, and his neck was slumping, pushing his head out in front of his body. He looked like his father. From his back pocket, his Liberty Bell Subs apron and hat waved like flags.

"Well, maybe you should go in to work too," Ella said. "We might as well not be the only two people who lose their jobs, eh?"

I was due in at nine o'clock, but Ella wasn't due until four. We decided that she would bring Rusty to work with her and I would take him home, feed him dinner, and put him to bed.

"Might as well," I said.

"Nick's just trying to be a good father," Ella said. "You know that, right?"

I nodded.

"Believe me, I wish Rusty had a father like him."

"I know all that."

"These things never go like you imagine they'll go," she said. "Dreams never do." She waited a moment, watching my face to see if I really was starting to cry. I cried all the time. I cried more than my mother and Kolya. I hated myself for always crying. What the fuck was wrong with me? I was going to have to go to a doctor and have my tear ducts removed.

"I know everything you're saying," I said.

"What's really bothering you then?" Ella said.

She was looking at me like she really wanted to know. People hardly ever look at you like that, like they really want to know the answer.

"I lost him. He's not the same guy," I said. "He'll never be the same guy again."

What she did then was take both of my hands and pull me against her.

"Well, you still got me," she said. "That's enough, isn't it?"

"It is," I said.

I held her. She held me.

I wanted it to be enough.

But it didn't feel like enough, not yet.

It wasn't even close.

# the warning signs and
# symptoms of depression, 2001

I WENT OVER TO MY mother and Mack's house for Sunday dinner. I'd just gotten off the early shift at the radio station, and I'd been up since 3 a.m. I should have gone home and slept.

Mack had made his famous pork roast. He and my mother had recently become Lutherans. They seemed happy to be back in God's grace in a church where the fall of a priest was more of a happy occurrence than an irredeemable sin. While he heaped meat and potatoes and carrots on my plate, he was telling Kolya and me about the brilliant, hopeful message they had heard in church that morning.

"This minister is really wonderful," my mother said.

I was staring at my plate, shoveling food in my mouth, and letting everybody else talk. I drained my second beer and got up for my third. My mother's eyes were on my back as I went to the fridge, and her eyes were still on me when I sat back down and flipped open the can.

"Kolya, maybe you want to tell Mikey your news," my mom said.

Kolya looked across the table at me. He took a huge drink of milk. He was a real lummox now, had failed his final year of high school because of his ADHD, and was now the biggest and oldest kid in school. He was six foot four and two hundred forty-five pounds. He played halfback on the football team, captained the swim team, and was a star pitcher for the baseball squad. I wondered if he dreamed about finding the bullies who used to pick on him before he had his growth spurt and inflicting a stern and swift justice.

"He won't care," he said. "He'll have some problem with my decision."

"Oh, now," my mom said.

"Boys," Mack said.

"Try me," I said.

"I've enlisted in the army," he said.

"Oh, you stupid shit," I said. "How could you?"

"See?" Kolya said.

"Boys," Mack said.

"Michael, we happen to be very proud of your brother. He feels very strongly about this."

"Not enough action in Northville, huh? You stupid shit."

"This is an important step for your brother," Mack said.

"Of course, we'll worry about him," my mother said.

"He's a stupid stupid stupid shit," I said. "After everything I've taught him."

"Fuck off," Kolya said. "You've never taught me shit. You're a pussy."

"Typical absent-father macho bullshit," I said.

"Did you learn that in college?" Kolya said. "You pussy."

"Everybody stop," my mother said.

It was October. It was 2001. The nation, including the crowd at my mother's dining room table, was stunned by tragedy and awash in patriotic fervor. I set down my fork and napkin and left.

"I told you," I heard Kolya saying. "He's got major fucking problems."

"Watch your language," Mack said. "Let's just finish this nice dinner."

"It is wonderful," my mother said. "I don't know how you do it, Mack."


I WAS WORKING AS the writer for the morning drive-time slot at a twenty-four-hour news radio station. The previous summer, after I'd finally finished my bachelor's degree at Dearborn, I had quit the bookstore, where I had clawed my way up to weekend supervisor. Mack had helped me land an internship at the station.

The internship was minimum wage, and it was weird to be a twenty-six-year-old working with a bunch of nineteen-year-old kids home for the summer from schools like Michigan and Northwestern and NYU. But when one of the station's writers quit in late July, Roger Rhodes, the general manager, called me into his office.

"You want a promotion?" he said.

"Yes, sir," I said.

"Herschel quit. Herschel made sixteen bucks an hour as a morning drive-time writer. But he had experience. How old are you?"

"Almost twenty-seven," I said.

"Herschel was thirty-seven, fifteen years of radio under his belt."

I nodded.

"Times are tough," the general manager said. "Really bad. Worst ever. I might have to let some people go. Can you do his job for nine bucks an hour?"

I'd recently heard that you should never accept the first salary you were offered. "How about ten dollars?" I said.

"Get out of my office," he said. "I got other interns to choose from. You're just the oldest and your copy is clean, but that doesn't mean everything."

"Nine dollars is fine," I said.

"Good. Be here tomorrow morning at four. Gunderson is your producer. Report to her."

The first few weeks, the job felt too good to be true. I had to crank out more than two dozen new stories in an hour, but radio stories were swift and compact. True, they weren't exactly hard-hitting, Pulitzer-contending pieces, but sometimes the pleasure of being able to compress the announcement of a tax cut or the initiation of a military campaign into eight sentences that could be read in thirty seconds was a thrill. I made sure all the nineteen-year-olds knew I was no longer a fucking intern. After working retail and other shit jobs for years, I was pleased to have a title: news writer. At nine fifty-two every morning, my name was announced on the air during the credits: "Our writer this morning is Michael Smolij." My mother tuned in to hear it. So did Ella, when she wasn't at work. And I was actually making money by writing. I started at four o'clock in the morning, but I usually showed up early just to read the wire stories from overnight, so I could crank out copy even faster than they could use it. It's embarrassing to admit it now, but for those first few weeks of work, it was hard for me to sleep. I was that excited.

IT WAS A MONDAY MORNING. I woke up at three, showered and dressed in about ten minutes, and drove down Warren Avenue to Telegraph Road. I stopped at Three Brothers for some coffee and then moved toward the freeway. All along the street, the Arab-owned party stores and gas stations flew giant flags and crudely drawn banners urging God to bless America.

Gina Gunderson was smoking outside the station's entrance when I pulled up. She was wearing a blue Michigan sweatshirt and gray sweatpants, and her gray hair was pulled back in a ponytail. She was too thin, and in the morning, despite a shiny set of blue eyes that hadn't aged, she sometimes looked a little skeletal. The good thing about radio was that you could wear jeans or sweats and nobody gave a shit, and you didn't have to comb your hair or work out or wear makeup like the TV idiots down the hall. This circumstance attracted the overweight, the bad-skinned, the prematurely bald, the chain-smokers, the yellowed drunks, and the chronically fatigued to the radio newsroom, and I liked being with them. It took the pressure off.

Gunderson was in her fifties and had produced the

morning newscast for almost thirty years. She'd raised three kids during those three decades, married and divorced three husbands, and spent three weeks the previous July drying out at the same clinic in Brighton where Tom had gone. She drove a 1976 Ford pickup with a ladder rack, and in the summers she rode a Yamaha motorcycle to work. She was a legend at the station. She'd been hired right out of college, and even as her life fell down a little every year—the bad marriages, the kids in trouble, the drinking—she stayed on, making her way in to work every morning. She had never had a promotion, but despite her alcoholism, it was said that she had never been late to work in her life and had never missed a deadline. She might drink off the clock and all weekend long, but never at work. She was on the wagon now.

"Not one goddamn second of dead air in my career," she would say to me. "Not one goddamn second."

Dead air was the mortal sin of radio broadcast. An error in the newscast, the wrong tape, or a miscued commercial could lead to the anchor's confusion, which could lead to fifteen or twenty seconds when nothing was happening, when the broadcast went silent. A good producer knew how to avoid dead air at all costs. Dead air made people change stations.

My job was to crank out twelve new scripts and tapes every thirty minutes, which Gunderson would then arrange into a twenty-two-minute newscast and run down to the anchors in the studio.

It was like a literary assembly line and I was well suited to it. I took pride in my work. It was the closest I was going to get to Hemingway.

That Monday morning, I passed Gunderson on my way in. It was still early, so I kept my eyes down. Gunderson didn't like people talking to her until she'd had her two cups of coffee.

"Look what the cat dragged in," she said.

"Good morning, Gunderson," I said.

"So did you know her name when you woke up this morning?"

"Whose?"

"Whoever's naked ass was in your face when you got up today," she said. She laughed until she had a minor coughing fit.

Monday mornings were usually slow, but in recent weeks, there were always stories to write. Terrorism was good for the round-the-clock news business. I wrote a few pieces about a party store on Evergreen that had been raided by the FBI. The Palestinian man who had owned the Beer Wine Bungalow for ten years was denying any links to terrorism. I wrote some more pieces, recycling wire copy on cleanup efforts in New York City and Colin Powell's statements on yesterday's telecast of *Meet the Press*. I found some tape from an interfaith rally at a Dearborn mosque and started to work a script around the sound bites.

And then something happened. I passed out on my desk. Gunderson was kicking at my shin when I woke up.

"It's five minutes until five," she said. "Where the hell is my lead story?"

"Oh, fuck," I said. I shook my head. I'd fallen right to sleep, my face on a legal pad, a pen jammed into my forehead.

"I won't tolerate drunks on my shift," she said. "When I drank, I kept it out of the office, you understand? Are you hungover, Michael, or are you still drunk?"

"No. No, not at all," I said. I handed her a hastily arranged set of scripts and tapes. She started eyeing them, checking them over for fuckups. "I guess I'm just tired."

"Tired?" she said. "Thirty years. I'll show you tired."

Then she winked at me and smiled, smacked me lightly on the back of the head with the stack of scripts. "Get some coffee, hon," she said. "You've got another seven hours."

WHEN I CAME HOME from work, my mother was in my kitchen. She still had a key, and though I had repeatedly told her that she shouldn't bother, she would sometimes come over while I was at work and drop off food for me. Sometimes she cleaned the kitchen or the bathroom.

"It was so filthy, I couldn't stand it," she would say.

Once my mother found Ella sitting at the kitchen table in nothing but her underwear, eating a pint of ice cream. I had already left for work, and Rusty was at school. Ella stood up, placed one arm over her breasts, and, as if nothing out of the ordinary had occurred, offered my mother a spoon.

Ella had none of my concern for rules and I loved her for it, but I had not been spending very much time with her since I'd been promoted at the station. During the week, I went to bed around eight thirty in order to get up by three. Rusty was usually awake until nine o'clock, so Ella and I didn't have much time alone together. Sometimes it didn't seem worth the trip over there just to sit around and eat dinner while listening to Rusty recap the adventures of a first grader. I know that sounds bad, but there it is. This is how I sometimes think.

Today my mother had found an empty kitchen. No Ella. Something was cooking on the stove when I walked in.

"How's my little newsman?" she said.

"Fine," I said. I knew she would never break her habit of referring to me as her little this or that. She would never stop calling me Mikey. She would never stop bringing me food. I accepted these things. After all, she had been through a lot in her life. And she had never gone anywhere without me knowing where she was. She had never been unavailable to me, not even for one minute.

"I was sorry how it went yesterday," she said. "I brought you some leftovers. Are you hungry?"

I wasn't, but I said I was. She started to fix me a plate.

"You need a real set of dishes," she said. "It's time you ate off real dishes. I saw some on sale at Target."

"How's Kolya?" I said.

"I think he was pretty upset by your reaction to his big news."

"How could you let him, Mom? Why would you let Kolya do that?"

"What choice did I have?"

"I don't know. Couldn't you have stopped him or something?"

"We tried. In our own way, we gave it our best shot. Now we can't do anything but be proud of him."

"Please," I said. "Ma, don't you realize he could go into the army and never come back?"

"No, Michael," she said. "That thought has never crossed my mind."

She stopped spooning out mashed potatoes from the Tupperware bowl and slammed the spoon on the counter. Then she quickly wiped a spattering of potatoes from the wall with a paper towel.

"Please, Michael. Give me some credit," she said.

She set the warm plate on the kitchen table and I sat down in front of it.

She sat across from me. "Here's two other things I brought you," she said.

She slid a book over to me. It was a copy of *The Best American Short Stories 1984*.

"Are you still collecting those?" she said. "Mack found it at a garage sale."

"Thanks," I said. "That's great. Thank him for me. That's an old one."

"Do you still write?" she said.

"Just at work," I said. "News stories."

She nodded. "There's something in the book, too."

I opened the book and found a pamphlet inside. On the front cover, a frowning handsome young man, hands in his pockets, was staring down at his shoes. A pretty black-haired woman was resting her head in her hands and staring off into space. In red block letters at the bottom of the pamphlet were the words, "Are You Depressed? A self-quiz about your emotional state."

"Mack was worried about you," she said. "You're acting different lately. He was at the doctor for a check-up and happened to pick this up for you."

"Fuckin-A, Mom," I said.

"Don't you want to eat?" she said.

"I do," I said. I looked down at the pamphlet in my hands. I was exhausted again. I was having trouble even staying on my feet. "But I'm just not hungry."

I flipped through the pamphlet and looked at the checklist: "Loss of appetite. Difficulty doing things done in the past. Feeling of hopelessness, pessimism."

"Mom," I said, "I'm fine."

NICK CALLED. He woke me up from an afternoon nap.

"What are you doing?" he said.

"Sleeping. Taking a nap."

"Why?" he said.

"I had to be at work at four this morning," I said.

"That's sad," he said. "I'm unemployed."

"I know."

"Your mother told my mom that you're depressed," Nick said. "Are you?"

"No," I said. "I'm just tired. Busy and tired."

"Sunny doesn't have class tonight," he said.

"When *does* she have class?" I said.

"Very funny," he said. "She'll be home with the kid. Let's get some beers tonight. I'll call Tom."

"Fine. Good. Fine."

Nick and Sunny's baby, Natalie, was four months old. Sunny was still trying to finish her Ph.D. in women's studies and Nick had been working sixty hours a week at Liberty Bell Subs. Aunt Maria had moved back into the house in

Maple Rock for a few months to help with the baby, but she kept the condo in Livonia she owned with Clyde Borin'.

Around the time Natalie was born, the man who owned Liberty Bell Subs suffered a stroke. Within a few weeks, a Subway had replaced Liberty Bell Subs. The new owners offered Nick a job at four bucks less an hour and no benefits. He passed on it. Tom Slowinski (who was still working at the juice stand but—now on the wagon—no longer offered his Miami Mambo specials) told me later that you could hear Nick yelling all through the food court "Go fuck yourself and your Subway! I'll give you six dollars an hour right up your franchised ass."

I met Nick and Tom at Happy Wednesday's, where we hadn't gone for a few months. Tom had gotten married to Tanya Jaworksi after rehab, and she was six months pregnant with their first child. He was sober now, and working a double shift at the juice stand and the Hot Dog Hut. He and Tanya lived in the Slowinskis' old house around the corner from me. Mrs. Slowinski lived with them.

The three of us had a few drinks and ordered nachos and some Wednesday Wings. Tom ordered a Coke. I know I should've been proud of him, but something in the way that once-heroic drinker said "Just a Coca-Cola, please" broke my heart. I thought Nick might even tease him about it, but I guess we'd gotten too old for that kind of thing.

We bitched about our jobs, or in Nick's case, lack of a job. It felt good to be there, even though the restaurant had some bad memories for me—my mall job, Nick's failed labor movement, my current girlfriend, broke and without options, walking half naked across the bar to the cheers of countless men. I tried not to think of these things. I thought of how different we were all starting to look, older, a little thicker, our stubble darker. I had the warm glow of a full pitcher inside of me, and I had not felt this good in weeks. My face went numb, and I thought how fine it would be if my brain could go numb like that too for a few weeks or months.

"I have a little business proposition for both of you," Nick said. "Rather, a business opportunity."

Nick had just bought a used Dodge Ram with a snowplow and a trailer. He was planning to open a lawn care and snow removal business, like the one his father used to run. If Tom and I wanted to invest some money in a second truck and trailer and a little equipment, we could get in on the ground floor.

"When it's warm, we cut lawns, do landscaping, clean pools, whatever," he said. "In the winter, we sit in our trucks, listen to the radio, sip hot coffee, and push snow around. We dump some salt on the walkways. There's real money in all of this, and you'll never work for anybody but yourself again."

"No way," Tom said. "Not with a kid coming. I need something more reliable."

"I figured you'd be too dumb," Nick said. "What about you, Mikey?"

"I don't know," I said. "I mean, I just got a promotion this summer."

"Look," Nick said. "In a way, it's the perfect job. You're helping people, really. By making their yards look nicer, by making it easier for them to get to work in the morning, you're doing a great service. It's a true vocation, boys."

We just looked at him and laughed.

"I know, I know," he said. "Nobody wants to get involved with me and my plans anymore. You all too mature for that?"

Tom said, "God, I hope so."

"I'm just really happy working as a writer," I said. "I guess that's it."

"That's not writing," Nick said.

"It makes me happy," I said.

"You're happy?" Tom said. "My mom ran into your mom at Kmart last week. She said you were depressed."

"Oh, for fuck's sake," I said.

"He's Miserable Mikey," Nick said. "Just like always."

We drank, we insulted each other, we laughed at each other, and then we drank some more.

In the parking lot at the end of the night, Tom offered to drive all of us home, since he was the only sober one. Nick and I decided to take him up on his offer, figuring we'd worry about our own cars in the morning. As we drove home through those familiar streets, we could've been sixteen again. It seemed we were just as confused and aimless as ever.

"You know, Nick," Tom said, "sometimes I want to do just what you're doing. Chuck away these goddamn mall jobs and start all over, work for myself."

"You call me if you change your mind," Nick said.

We pulled up in front of my house. It was completely dark.

"Looks like you're the only guy not living with his mother," Tom said.

"Well, that was a lot of fun," I said. "It was good to blow off some steam."

"That was fun?" Nick said. "Man, I thought it was just depressing."

"Who's miserable now?" I said.

Later, when Nick plowed through his first blizzard, I rode in the truck with him. It was just work, the moving of snow and the melting of ice, but it was real work and it was our work and later, in my memories, God, that night we were so happy.

THE NEXT MORNING at work, Gunderson was on my case.

"I don't know what her name is," she said, "but she's keeping you up too late. There's not enough stories here to fill an hour. Start cranking."

She waved a stack of scripts at me.

"So who is she?" she said.

"I wasn't out with anybody last night. I mean, just the guys, some pals."

"Don't hold out on me, Michael. I live vicariously through you young ones."

"Really," I said. "I was just out with a few guys drinking some beer."

"That's even worse," she said. "Drinking is harder on you than sex. When I was your age, Michael, I was a bottle. A real fucking bottle."

She brought me coffee and a doughnut a few minutes later.

"I've worked with a lot of writers," she said. "Thirty goddamn years' worth of them."

I nodded.

"And you're the best one I've seen."

I didn't know how she could tell that from my thirty-second radio pieces, but I was glad she'd said it.

"You say that to all the boys," I said.

"Fuck no," she said. "Most of the boys I tell to get the fuck out of the news business. You? You'll go places," she said. "That's for sure. You won't spend thirty years in this windowless newsroom. Cleanest copy I've ever seen."

It was the reputation I was developing. Cleanest copy. By the end of the day, Gunderson had the morning anchors calling me Mr. Clean. It wasn't the kind of thing you could go out into the world and brag about, but it was nice to know.

Ella and Rusty came over for dinner that night. They hadn't called first and I was pretty plowed when they showed up. I had stopped off after work—at one o'clock—and bought a six-pack of beer. Then I came home, got out a yellow legal pad and some newly sharpened pencils, and tried to write a story. Gunderson's compliment had me thinking that I had this terrible talent and I was wasting it. But when I sat down to write, I knew that I hadn't been wasting shit. I had nothing to say. When Ella showed up at my door with Rusty, some root beer, and a large pizza, the six beer cans and the legal pad were both empty.

"Are you busy?" she called, knocking on the door, then pushed it open before I could get there. She had her own key.

"We got pizza!" Rusty yelled. He made a beeline for the kitchen table.

Ella handed me the hot pizza box and the two-liter bottle of soda and started clearing the kitchen table.

"Were you writing?" she said. "Oh, I'm sorry. We should go."

"No. No. I was just figuring something," I said.

"Figuring?"

"Yeah, yeah. Sit down. How was your day?"

"Full of annoying customers," she said. "Buying shitty books at big discounts."

"Sounds like a perfect day at the Book Nook," I said.

"Are you okay?" she said.

I shrugged.

Ella looked a little disappointed, so I struggled to smile.

"It's just I haven't seen you for almost a week, and once I mentioned to Rusty that we should surprise you with pizza, there was no stopping him."

"Oh, I know, this is fine. It's great. Has it been a week?"

"Are you drunk?"

"No, sit down, sit down," I said. "It's only been a few days."

"You are drunk," she said.

I held up my thumb and index finger to indicate the tiniest amount of something and mouthed the words, "A little."

Rusty was already pouring himself a root beer, sloshing a big wave of it onto the kitchen table. Ella came over and soaked it up with a towel, and then she got Rusty a couple of slices and put them on a paper plate.

"We got pepperoni *and* ham *and* bacon," Rusty yelled. "Because you like meat!"

"Indoor voice, Rusty," Ella said. She motioned with her head toward the living room, then left the kitchen.

"Meat-a-licious," I said. I followed Ella into the living room. The truth was, I didn't want them there. I didn't know why. I didn't know what was wrong with me, which is why, when Ella asked me that very question, I just shrugged.

"Why would you be drunk? Especially this early in the day and all alone?"

"I get up for work at three," I said. "I have to start early."

"I mean, what's wrong with you? Why are you drunk at all?"

I shrugged again.

"Just relaxing," I said. "Just chillin'."

Rusty hollered from the kitchen. "Hey, don't you guys want pizza?"

"Chillin'?" Ella said. "Just chilling?"

"What is wrong with *you*?" I said.

"Your mother called," she said. "She thinks you're in trouble. She says that you're depressed."

"Please," I said. "Please, please, please."

"Are you?"

"At work, they call me Mr. Clean. I've got the cleanest prose they've ever seen."

"That's great," she said. "How nice for you."

"Yeah," I said. I leaned in close. "You want to sneak off and see if you can get Mr. Clean to be Mr. Dirty?"

I buried my face in her neck and sucked the salt off her skin.

"I'd like that more than anything," she said, "if you were sober. But there's a six-year-old boy in the next room who desperately wants you to sit down and get really, really excited about the pizza he's brought over."

"It's a deal," I said, and slunk back into the kitchen.

"Fucking pepperoni *and* fucking ham!" I shouted.

Rusty looked at me with tomato sauce and grease running down his chin. Ella said my name, softly, behind me. "What's wrong, everybody?" I said. "Come on! Three cheers for three meats! Hip-hip!"

"Hooray!" Rusty cried, thrusting his fist out and knocking his root beer over.

"Oh, that's fucking great," I said. "Hip-hip, hooray!"

Ella went over to the table and wiped the pop off of Rusty first, then went to work on the table. I was drunk enough to find all of this very amusing. I believed we were a beautiful sight. The fucking Waltons, the Bradys, the Cleavers, they had nothing on us. I said something to that effect. Ella packed Rusty up and got ready to leave without saying good-bye. She took the leftover pizza with her.

"See you later," I said. When Rusty was out the door she turned around and flipped me the bird. I didn't know what she was so mad about. It's not like I asked for this. It wasn't like I'd invited anybody over.

I STARTED TO SOBER UP and felt down again. The house was too quiet. I paced around and looked over the depression pamphlet my mother had given me. *Loss of interest or pleasure in regular activities. Decreased energy. Feelings of fatigue.* I made little marks in the boxes on the checklist. I tried calling Ella before I went to bed. I would say to her, "Look, let's talk."

She didn't answer the phone and I didn't leave a message. After "Let's talk," I had nothing else planned to say.

I slept poorly. I was about fifteen minutes late to work. The novelty of writing for a big radio station seemed to have shut off with my alarm that morning. The prestige of being Mr. Clean had washed off in the shower. By the time I got into my car and headed onto Warren Avenue, it was just work, a shitty-paying job that required me to wake up at four in the morning.

"Late!" Gunderson snarled as I walked into the newsroom. "There was a chemical spill in Wyandotte last night. You've got to get me some tape from the police department PIO for the lead story."

"Why?" I said. "Why do we need a public information officer's sound bite? Will people not believe us if we just say there was a chemical spill? I am so goddamn sick of sound bites."

"Get on the phone now—555-3355," she said. "That's Wyandotte police and fire.

"At two thirty this morning," said the night-shift police sergeant into my rolling tape recorder, "a chemical tanker overturned on the railroad tracks in downtown Wyandotte. Police and fire crews were able to evacuate all residents in the area, and a Hazmat team is on location now. Jefferson Avenue will be closed until at least nine a.m."

"Thank you, Sergeant," I said. I hung up the phone and hammered out a script.

"For your lead story," I said, handing the tape and the script to Gunderson.

At nine o'clock that morning, I got a phone call. I wondered if it was Ella, still mad about how poorly things had gone the night before. But it wasn't Ella, it was the assistant principal at Rusty's school. It seemed that Rusty was sick, and I had been listed as the emergency contact.

The principal must have heard the surprise in my voice. She said, "You are Rusty's stepfather, right?"

I almost told her that I was too busy. I almost explained to her that, in fact, I certainly was not Rusty's stepfather. I almost said, I'm sorry, but I am a news writer and I am in the middle of the morning drive-time broadcast, the station's most important time slot. But then I pictured Rusty on a cot in the antiseptic, yellow-walled nurse's office, and I remembered those poor kids in grade school who would get sick and spend all day on a cot, puking into a garbage can, because there was nobody around to get them.

I nodded, realized the woman on the phone couldn't see me, and whispered, "Right. I'll be there as soon as I can."

I logged off and explained things as best I could to Gunderson. She was still mad at me, but she said, "If your kid is sick, your kid is sick."

"Well, he's not my kid," I said. "Really."

"If the school calls you when he gets sick," she said, "he's your kid."


RUSTY LOOKED MISERABLE. He was sitting in a green chair and his face matched the plastic of the chair. The school nurse said he was running a fever of 102 and he had been throwing up all over the place. Now, she said, he had nothing left to throw up, so he was probably done with that.

"What do I do now?" I asked.

She looked at me for a second, and it dawned on her that I really didn't know what to do.

"Get him into bed," she said. "He just needs to sleep it off. You can give him some children's Tylenol for his fever. You can use a cold compress on his forehead too. And start with clear fluids. If he can tolerate those, maybe tonight give him some crackers and chicken noodle soup. But if his fever doesn't go down soon, you should call his doctor."

"Who would that be?" I asked.

"I don't know, sir. You would have to know that."

"Right," I said.

I put Rusty in the backseat of my Buick and got behind the wheel. In the rear view mirror, he looked slumped and hot and miserable. I wished Ella had a cell phone. I didn't know what to do with him.

"I'm so cold," said Rusty. He was shivering.

I drove over to Nick's house. It was close by and I knew he'd be home. He was a dad now, and maybe Sunny or Aunt Maria would be there, and between them, they could help me out.

Nick was in the driveway, working on the engine of his red Dodge pickup, which was equipped with a giant yellow plow and a dump bed.

"Welcome to my office," he said. "Did you come over to beg me to let you get in on the ground floor? I'm still seeking an investor, so you're in luck."

"No, not that," I said.

"Is that Ella's kid in the car?" he asked.

"Yeah. He's sick. He has a fever, chills, the whole works. I don't know what to do with him."

Sunny and the baby were out at Sunny's mother's house for the day, and Aunt Maria was back at her place in Livonia, but Nick was pretty competent on his own. He made up the guest bed for Rusty, gave him some children's Tylenol, and brought him a grape Popsicle. He carried the TV in from the kitchen and set it on the dresser across from Rusty's bed. He turned on some educational show with puppets. Rusty was out cold pretty fast. I checked on him every five minutes to make sure he was still breathing. His fever was going down, his face no longer so hot to the touch.

When I finally got hold of Ella, she said she had just come in with groceries.

"I have to go get Rusty from school in a minute," she said.

"Rusty's here," I said. "They called me from school to pick him up."

"Oh, God," she said.

"He's fine," I said. "We're at Nick and Sunny's place. He's in the guest room sleeping. His fever broke."

"I was going to tell you," she said. "About being listed on his emergency form. Margaret is the first contact, but she must have been out too. I didn't know anybody else I could trust, so I listed you second. I never thought they'd actually have to call you."

"It's fine," I said.

"I plan to get a cell phone," she said. "It's just fifty dollars a month I don't have.

"I said it was fine, Ella. I'll bring Rusty home."

AFTER RUSTY HAD had a bath and been put to sleep in his own bed, Ella and I ordered Chinese food. Neither of us had enough cash to pay for it, so we put it on Ella's Visa card. Once we realized that were going to have to charge the meal anyway, we ordered a ridiculously large amount of food, five entrées and three appetizers, laughing about it while we ordered. But Ella looked tired and worn. Her hair was dull and so was her skin.

I told her how surprised I'd been by Nick's calmness and competence.

"Well," Ella said, "he's a father. It's not rocket science. I'm glad he was home."

"Me too," I said.

"I was driving around looking for another job today," she said. "Filling out applications everywhere. You know, a degree in art history doesn't go very far. Especially when it took you three colleges and seven years to finish it."

I helped myself to some sweet and sour chicken, but now the sight of all that unpaid-for food was overwhelming and a little depressing.

"You're going to work two jobs?" I said.

"I'm getting a little too old to win bikini contests," she said.

"No way," I said. "You could win any Wednesday of the year."

"Not that," she said. "I mean, for a while it was kind of poetic—young educated feminist using institutional sexism as a weapon against itself."

"I just thought you were showing off a wonderful rack."

She tossed a fortune cookie across the table.

"Anyway, I can't do that kind of thing anymore. Although I did consider Hooters. I thought I could write a book about working there after a year or so and get rich. I could call it *More Than a Mouthful: A Mammary Memoir.*

"Great. It would sell," I said.

"Anyway, I need to do something. The trailer park is not a good place for Rusty. I mean, I grew up with rich parents and a nice place to live."

"You should call them," I said. "Ask for help."

"No way," she said. I could tell there was no room to push the issue.

"Move in with me," I said.

"Wow," she said. "The thought of Hooters must have horrified you, if you're willing to offer that."

"No. No, I think I'm serious," I said.

"You think?" she said.

"This place is a shithole. It's not even safe. And Rusty loves me, you know? I mean, I pick the kid up from school when he's sick. That's a real dedicated stepfather."

"No way," Ella said. "Not under these circumstances. We shouldn't move in together out of desperation."

"Why else do people do anything?"

"That's poetic," she said.

"I've got that big house," I said.

"You've got a big, bleeding heart," she said. "Too big."

"It's a serious offer," I said.

"Michael, you couldn't even handle it when we dropped in unannounced last night," she said. "Do you know what it's like to have a kid twenty-four hours a day? It's a lot of work. Not a lot of down time."

"I know all that," I said.

"Let's go to bed," she said.

Ella was asleep in a few minutes. I stared at the ceiling for a long time. At three o'clock in the morning, I was still wide awake. I turned off the alarm before it could ring and wake Ella. I got out of bed. It was time to go to work.

A FEW DAYS LATER, I went in to work with the flu. I'd caught it from Rusty, I figured. I had the chills and every muscle in my body was heavy and aching. I was thinking about how to get some sympathy from Gunderson, and maybe permission to go home early, but Gunderson wasn't in the parking lot smoking cigarettes and drinking coffee. I went into the newsroom and the news desk was empty. Gunderson's desk was clean. Even the pictures of her kids were gone. Nobody had made coffee. Larry Miller, who usually did the afternoon production slot, was sitting at his desk, typing at his computer. He wasn't much older than me.

"Hey, Michael," he said. "Man, I don't know how you work this shift. It's not human to be up this early."

"Where's Gunderson?" I said.

"I don't know," Larry said. "I got a call last night after dinner. They said they needed me to cover the a.m. for a few days. I'm working double shifts for the next week. My wife is *not* happy."

"Did you make coffee?" I asked.

"I don't drink it," he said.

Larry's wife had just had twins, and she called the station for him every thirty minutes. Larry was a good guy.

My first day as an intern, he had taken me aside and said, "Look, I know all the old-timers around here will complain to you—about the pay, the hours, the bad coffee—but believe me, this is a dream job. This is what I always wanted to do, I always wanted to be a reporter, and here I am, working my dream job."

I had just nodded. "Thanks, Larry. That means a lot," I said. I felt bad for him.

"You want to crank out some stories so we don't start the morning drive-time with dead air?"

"Sure," I said. "I'll crank something out."

We fucked up a few times. One time, the anchors got the wrong tapes and played the sound bite of the mayor talking about jazz instead of the story about Dick Cheney's heart condition. Later in the morning show, I'd written "President Clinton" instead of "President Bush," and neither Larry nor the anchor caught the mistake. These things seemed like big deals to me, but they really freaked Larry out.

Around ten o'clock, Roger Rhodes came into the newsroom, tapped me on the shoulder as I was typing and said, "My office. Pronto."

I thought he was about to give me the boot or chew me out for the mistakes on the newscast that morning. I followed him down the hall to his office. He had a little putting green all set up and he was using his putter to hit an imaginary golf ball.

"Sit down," he said, swinging at the invisible ball.

I sat.

"You're about to get two promotions in one month," he said.

"I am?"

"Let me finish. We had to let some people go, and we have some openings, including one for a new reporter. And your name has come up. You know, get out of the newsroom a little, stretch your legs . . ."

"Did you let Gunderson go?"

"She took early retirement," he said. "A few of the old-timers did."

"Did they have a choice?" I said.

"Look, I'm offering you a raise to twelve bucks an hour. I'm going to make you a reporter. You're young, you're single, you're good-looking and outgoing, and you're the kind of man who can work long hours out in the field and make a good name for this station."

"What about Larry?"

"Larry's a pussy. Larry needs to sit at the news desk. He'll be fine."

"Where's Gunderson?" I said.

"You know how many kids would kill for this job?"

"I know," I said.

"We take care of our employees here. We're CBS News. That's big time. A few people need a little nudging out of the nest. You, Michael, you have the chance to step into the spotlight. We'll have you out and about, getting tape, doing interviews. Heck, you can even file a few stories and get some real on-air experience."

"That all sounds good," I said.

"Don't thank me," he said. "You'll be in the prime-time world now. You'll need to put on a tie."

"Oh, I'm sorry. Thanks so much. This is a good thing."

"It is," he said. "You'll do great. You don't golf, do you?"

I didn't. I had never held a club, except for one time in a fight, when I'd swung a putter at somebody's head and missed. It seemed like a hundred years ago.

"Sure," I said. "A little."

"We should get on the course someday, then," Roger Rhodes said. "I'll bore you with some stories about when I was a green reporter."

Later, Larry came out of Roger's office and told me that he was stuck with mornings. He had been moved to Gunderson's old post.

"My wife will hate this new schedule," Larry said. "She needs me around in the morning to help with the twins."

"It's too bad," I said. "About Gunderson."

"I know," he said. "Good for you, though. I heard you got a fucking promotion."

I tried to find Gunderson's home phone number, but there were hundreds of Gundersons in the phone book, none of them named Gina.

I stopped of at my mother's house after work. I told her about the promotion. I wanted somebody, at least, to be happy about it.

"Well, that's amazing, Mikey," she said. "My little reporter."

"You know," Mack said, "most people are getting laid off right now, and you're getting a promotion. That's impressive."

"You have no reason to be depressed," my mother said. "See?"

————————

ON CHRISTMAS DAY, 2001, Gina Gunderson killed herself. I didn't find out about it until five days after it happened. The funeral was evidently a brief, private affair, and nobody from the radio station was wanted in attendance.

We found out about her death in a short memo from Roger Rhodes that didn't mention the suicide, just informed us of a random death, as if she'd gone in her sleep. It was Larry Miller who tracked down one of Gunderson's daughters and got the real story: she'd been running the car with the garage door closed. The car radio was tuned to our ridiculous all-news station when they found her. I wondered if the daughter had added that detail out of bitterness and anger, or if it really was the case, if Gunderson, in her last moments, was remembering her work and the way she'd lost it. It probably was true, I decided, and so did Larry Miller. We had trouble getting any work done that day, or that week. The newscasts were bland and perfunctory. Another memo listed an address where we could send donations to a scholarship fund the station was establishing to aid journalism students at Wayne State University, Gunderson's alma mater. Who had extra money to send to a scholarship fund? The memo ended with this line: "We are deeply sorry that Ms. Gunderson did not live to enjoy the full blessings of her much-deserved and long-awaited retirement."

ON NEW YEAR'S DAY, Ella and Rusty and Lucky the Dog moved into my house. It had been my idea, and it took some real convincing. I pointed out what an unsafe and inappropriate environment the trailer park was for a young boy. I noted that Ella struggled to make her monthly payments, and would never save up enough money to move to a better place, no matter how many Hump Day Honey contests she won. I reminded her that the three-bedroom ranch had been given to me and that I lived there all alone. I said my brother's old room would be perfect for Rusty. I said that my room seemed to want two people in there at night. In my dreams, I said, I was always alone in vast open spaces.

When I told this to Ella, she said, "What do you think that means?"

And I said, "It means I need you there at night."

Ella didn't have that much stuff she wanted to keep, so Nick and Tom and I spent one Saturday morning carrying most of her old, beat-up furniture to the curb. Within minutes, somebody from another trailer made off with the couch or recliner or wobbly kitchen table we'd just dumped. Ella had been able to get $20,000 for the trailer and the lot, a little less than she and her husband had paid for it eight years ago, but she didn't care. It was as if she'd hit the lottery. She planned to pay off her credit cards and her student loan, and she'd dragged me to the mall to buy all sorts of new shit—toilet brushes and wastebaskets and curtains—for the house in Maple Rock.

We loaded the boxes of Ella's remaining belongings into the back of Nick's new truck and moved them to my house. It took three trips to get everything over there, but it was only a two-mile run. One of the trips was nothing but boxes and boxes of books. Another trip was for Rusty's bedroom furniture and toys, and one trip for Ella's clothes, kitchen stuff, and photo albums. By the end of the day, Ella's trailer was empty. To thank Nick and Tom for their help, Ella and I cooked up a big pot of chili and my two best friends and my girlfriend and her son sat around my table sharing a meal. My mom and Mack dropped by a little later.

My mother said, "It's nice to know that this house has a family living in it again."

After everybody had left and Rusty had gone to sleep in his new bedroom, Ella and I did our best to wash dishes, but we were so exhausted that we undressed and tumbled into bed without brushing our teeth or washing our faces. We did not make love, but in the morning, when I woke her up, she rolled over and said, "This is good."

# please don't come back from the moon
# (reprise)

IT WAS LESS THAN two years later when the moon finally
called our names, and we found ourselves gathered in a
familiar parking lot, staring at a familiar sky. The moon was
flat and full above us, a silver nickel tossed into the night.
We stood in silence for a long time underneath it, as if we
were waiting for it to fall. We had not planned to gather
here in this way, and it was apparent that we had nothing
to say to each other, and no explanation for how we'd arrived there together. We looked down at each other only
briefly, and made minimal eye contact, slump-shouldered,
heads down, submissive as dogs. For the most part, we were
sober and in sound mind. Some of us had not spoken to
each other in weeks or months; in some cases, we had not
seen each other for years. The air was hot, with the occasional gritty breeze that passes for pleasant in Maple Rock.
Worried men, I think, have trouble sleeping on such brief,
sad August nights. There we were, in the parking lot of
what used to be the Black Lantern, some two dozen of us

answering a mystical ringing that had sounded unexpectedly in the middle of the night.

A FEW HOURS EARLIER, I had been driving around in the news truck, on the overnight beat. It was two in the morning. Three kids had been shot in a drive-by on the southwest side of Detroit, and I was standing on the patchy lawn across the street with all the other journalists, holding my notebook. Even though the sun was long gone from the sky, it was hot and I was sweating. I had a tape recorder slung over my shoulder, and the attached microphone shoved into the back pocket of my jeans. I was waiting for somebody to come around and give me the details and a sound bite, so that I could get out of there and go home to Ella. I could already picture her, asleep on the couch in one of my old tank tops and her underwear, three fans pointed on her, trying to stay cool. Rusty would be asleep upstairs in his bedroom, with the racing-car wallpaper I'd put up for him last weekend. Our newborn daughter, Nina, would be asleep in her crib, in an infant's deep-breathing slumber.

I often thought such long thoughts while driving around in the news truck that summer; I often imagined what my house was like with Ella and Rusty and the baby in it, what they were doing and thinking while I was working late, what Ella was wearing, if she would be awake when I came home.

I imagined that there might be some leftovers from dinner, and I would heat them in the microwave. Ella might get up and sit across the table, with lovely sleepy eyes and matted hair, and I would tell her about my night, about three wounded kids and all the reporters lined up at one end of the street, wanting and not wanting the story at the same time. That all might make it worth it, I thought, somebody—somebody beautiful—waiting for me at the end of the long night shift.

One of the sergeants came over. The reporters gathered in a semicircle around him. The cameras rolled, and we all held our microphones out as far as we could, as if the sergeant was some kind of god and we were his worshipers.

"One of the children has died," the sergeant said. "The other two have been airlifted to the University of Michigan Hospital and are in surgery."

We reporters called out our speculative, pleading questions.

"We have a suspect in custody," he said. "We believe the shooter knew the victims. He was the father of two of the children. The third was his stepchild."

And then, as if the sergeant needed to say something editorial about the whole, pitiful night, he added, "This is a great tragedy."

We begged for the names. Give us the names and ages of these victims! Let us tell the story to our readers and listeners and viewers in all its graphic, lurid horror, we said.

"Out of respect for the families involved, we can give out no further information at this time," the sergeant said.

He walked away, stopping and bending like a jackknife to get under the line of yellow police tape that surrounded the house.

I waited around a little while longer, until I saw some kids trying to break into the news truck. I chased them away and left the scene.

I went back to the station, put up my tapes and my scripts for the morning drive-time newscasts, for poor Larry to arrange and make sense of, and all the while I was picturing the startled listeners—those much-coveted a.m. drive-time commuters waking up to hear the brutal, sad news of children gunned down, right here, right in their own world.

ELLA WASN'T ON THE couch when I got home. She was already upstairs asleep. Lucky the Dog was curled up on his bed, keeping warm. He looked at me, let out a moaning yawn, and tucked his nose down again between his paws.

Hanging my windbreaker in the front closet, I could hear the wave machine that we'd just bought for Rusty's room. Rusty was maybe the only eight-year-old insomniac on record. It wasn't just monsters under his bed and all the standard stuff that keeps kids awake at night—bogeymen, fear of sudden death, a noise in the wall, a light in the window. He would sit in bed awake, looking out the window, eyes frozen and wide with worry. So we bought the lull and crash of an electronic sea to accompany him to sleep, and it seemed to be working fairly well. He'd slept through a couple of nights in a row.

I dropped a metal hanger on the tile floor, then scrambled to pick up the jacket and put it away. Afraid of waking Rusty from his fragile dreams, I left the closet door open. I didn't want the squeaking tracks of the door to rouse him.

And then, suddenly—yes, that's the only way I can describe it: suddenly—my careful quietness irritated me.

Maybe I was still reeling from my shift, crazed from breathing the stale and sticky air of urban crime scenes, but I found myself filled with anger. In the kitchen, when I opened the oven door to find some leftover pizza warmed to a hard half circle, I shut the door with a satisfying, metallic thud. A few minutes later, I was eating the old pizza in front of a not-so-softly-tuned television and drinking my second beer when I heard Rusty call for Ella across the hall. Then Nina began squalling from her crib. I pressed the mute button on the remote control.

I heard Ella groan and get out of bed, the squeaking of the tired mattress, the slap of her slippers. "Michael," she called from the bedroom. "Is that you? Are you home?"

I went to the edge of the staircase and peered up into the dark hallway. Then I went back to the foyer, opened the front door, and left the house.

WHERE DO YOU GO at three in the morning, when you are a grown man and you can't sleep and the walls of your house seem so close and confining that, as hard as you try to want to, you cannot go up the stairs and get into bed with your wife—cannot, irrationally and without explanation, go up the steps and hold your own crying baby?

I didn't know, so I just started walking.

Even at that late hour, the air was still and thick. Mosquitoes landed on my exposed neck as I walked. My shirt was already damp from working all night, and it stuck to my back. It had been a few years since I walked around this neighborhood in the middle of the night. And I had not snuck out of the house to do it since I was much younger, living in the basement of the house where now I lived with my family.

Maybe it was the windless, humid air, but the neighborhood felt heavier and more tired than I remembered it. I was still holding a bottle of beer, and I pressed it against my forehead. I looked around. The houses that had once seemed so sturdy and solid looked weak and worn out. The lawns were patchy with crabgrass and weeds, driveways sagging and broken. Grit and trash lined the sides of the streets, and in the heat, the night smelled vaguely of garbage and burning tires.

I lived in a dump.

I walked up Warren Avenue, following the nearly empty street and its flashing yellow lights past the darkened neon signs and marquees for pizza shops, party stores, and check-cashing places. Some of the signs were in Arabic as well as English now, and here and there, gang tags and anti-Bush slogans marked the brick walls alongside the stores.

I came to the parking lot that used to belong to the Black Lantern and now belonged to Uncle Al's, the falafel joint that had replaced our neighborhood bar. A few old-timers, Ukrainians and Poles and Greeks, still met there every afternoon for coffee as if nothing had changed.

For the first time that night I looked at the moon as I walked, and this is when I felt my feet leave the earth: I started walking a few inches off of the ground, as if I were following some invisible staircase.

Within a few seconds, I was six or seven inches off the ground, and then, as quickly as it happened, I stumbled on nothing, some invisible obstacle in the air, and landed hard on the ground, rolling my left ankle.

I sat on the asphalt for a minute, my ankle starting to pulse and the palms of my hands raw and smarting from my landing.

As I tried to get to my feet in the darkness, still dazed, I saw a shadow of a man approaching. He was large, with wild curly hair. It was dark, but he appeared to be shirtless.

Ever since I have become a father, I have been somewhat afraid of the night. In the darkness, whether I am walking through my own neighborhood or driving down a stretch of rural highway, or even peering out my own front window into the darkened yard, I have had the sense that something, someone, is out there in the shadows, prowling and stalking, waiting. In the night, when I can't sleep, my heart tends to race and I imagine the worst scenarios, people coming to harm my family, breaking down the doors and overpowering me, hurting my wife and children. This is one reason I agreed to the night shift at the radio station. I was having trouble sleeping anyway, and thought some months spent awake and working in the darkest hours of the twenty-four might help me overcome my fear.

The man stopped in front of me and looked down. It was Nick.

He was wearing a pair of running shoes and blue jeans and nothing else. He said, "Mikey, what the fuck are you doing on the ground?"

THAT NIGHT, NICK HAD been up late in his garage, as had become his habit that summer. He was drinking beer and listening to Springsteen's *Nebraska* album—best fucking album of all time, he said—when he went to change the spark plugs in his truck. It occurred to him as he worked his wrench that he hated the old pickup truck in front of him. It looked ridiculous, he said. He couldn't stand to look at it anymore, with its rusty extended cab, jacked-up all-terrain tires, and ladder rack, the sign that said KOZAK'S SUN & SNOW. All that he had intended to do was change the spark plugs, he said, but the idea of doing any more maintenance on the old engine suddenly infuriated him. He wanted a new truck, but of course, he and Sunny had just had their second child and money was tight. Plus, he said, the economy was shitty and people had started mowing their own lawns and he figured that they'd be clearing their own driveways that winter. Money, he said, was just not available to him.

All he wanted was to do a little preventive maintenance to keep his equipment running through one more winter. And then, he said, he fell apart.

"I was just trying to get through the motions," he said. "And I was kind of praying, you know, not to God or anything, just kind of hoping that we'd get a winter with some heavy goddamn snow, for a change.

"And then I thought of my father, and how he did the same goddamn thing for so long, how he spent every winter for almost two decades hoping there would be enough snow, and there never was, never close to enough snow to pay all the bills."

"And then what?" I asked him.

"I decided I wanted a goddamn Volvo or Saab or something," he said. "I decided I didn't want to be a guy who drives a pickup with a ladder rack anymore."

I laughed. I couldn't tell if he was serious or not.

"And then I started walking," he said. "And I walked here."

IF THE BARS OR party stores had still been open, Tom Slowinski would have been drunk already. He'd been sober for more than two years by that point; that night, he said, he woke up at midnight, after his wife and kids were fast asleep, and the only thing he wanted was a drink. It had been so long, really, since he wanted anything that it felt almost good to battle an urge like that. He was out of work again, this time because Gorski's Family Hardware on Warren Avenue, where he'd worked as the assistant manager, had shut down a few weeks earlier. He'd just put in his application at a new Home Depot out by the mall, but for the first time since it had opened, the store was not hiring. It was now one of the best jobs in Maple Rock, working at Home Depot, and the slots filled up quickly.

Tom had developed the habit of watching his children as they slept.

"It isn't like I just look in on them," Tom said. "Not normal father-looking-in-on-his-kid stuff. I mean, I poke my head into their room"—he had twin boys, one-year-olds—"to check that they were sleeping, but then I get the idea in my head—it's fucked up, I know it—that if I leave them alone they'll stop breathing in their sleep.

"When I was drinking," he said, "I never got thoughts

like that. But now—man, it's the only kind of thought I get. So, anyway, I end up, half the night, sitting on a tiny chair that's between their two beds, looking at Joseph for a minute, and then over at James, and I can't believe they are alive and so dependent on me. Usually, I finally fall asleep sitting in that chair, and when I wake up again, it's close to dawn, and I feel like I can finally leave them sleeping alone."

That night, Tom said, after he left them, instead of schlepping down the hall to get into bed with Tanya, he went into the living room.

"I used to keep a bottle of scotch right next to my chair," he said. "So I wouldn't have to get up from there while watching TV. It was easier to stay drunk if I didn't move."

AND THEN THE others arrived:

Peter Stolowitz had driven in from West Bloomfield, where he worked as a dentist. He said that something in the way the light of the moon came through his window woke him up. He said his wife looked blue in the light. He said he had three kids, and a fourth on the way, and sometimes, when he tried to sleep, all he could imagine was the ocean, and the noise of the waves—imaginary goddamn waves of all things—kept him awake. He had his head down when he arrived; he's the richest and most successful among us, and it made him sheepish and humble in our presence. We only saw him at weddings and funerals, and even on those occasions he'd duck out early.

Walker Van Dyke was working as a third-shift janitor at the mall. He was trying to wash some graffiti off a bathroom mirror when he felt a little odd, like he might faint. He put down his bucket and brush, blaming the fumes of the industrial cleaner he was using, and went outside to the loading docks for some fresh air. After about fifteen minutes, he said, the last thing in the world he could bring himself to do was to go back into the mall and clean that bathroom stall. For a while, he just stood staring at the service entrance, and then looking at the key ring in his hand. And even though he had a whole four hours of work to go, he went to his truck and drove to the parking lot of the old Black Lantern.

Michael Pappas was working at the tire factory. His vision started to cloud up, and then his head spun, and the foreman came over and relieved him. He got sent to the urgent care clinic and the doctors said that maybe he'd developed a migraine.

"But I never had a goddamn migraine in my life," Michael said.

Then he drove straight to the parking lot.

Jimmy Nelson was working on a painting, a still life of a gas can, some red roses, and a bottle of beer. He had been taking an art class at the community college, and painted still lifes in the evenings to help himself relax. He was a manager at UPS, and the stress got to him.

"At night, I don't sleep," he said. "I paint pictures of things."

J. J. Dempsey, who sold life insurance, had been watching the Discovery Channel. It was Shark Week and J. J. said he had been staying up all night for a week, watching the same shark documentaries over and over and over.

"I should have been a marine biologist," he said. "I could've lived in the sea."

Pete Ziggouris was still at the warehouse he owned. He was known around Detroit as the Restaurant King, and he sold food service supplies all over the state. He said that he'd been putting off going home that night, and eventually it was midnight and then it was three and then he finally got into his car, but instead of heading to Novi, where he lived now, he turned the opposite direction and came back to his old neighborhood.

"I just felt like I couldn't do it," he said. "I felt like going home would ruin something for me and my family. Like if I went home without really wanting to go home, something terrible would happen to us."

Kyle Hartley was still driving the same old work van, a 1984 Dodge Ram. We heard him coming from a quarter of a mile away, that troubled engine of his grinding its way down Warren Avenue.

They came from all the corners of our neighborhood, and from the city and its widespread suburbs, they came with hair messy from sleep and faces shadowed by stubble, they came worn out, they came overweight and under-weight, they came with their stories, their marriages and divorces, their births and their deaths, their baptisms and their sins, they arrived one and another and another, and the moon, whistling above them, sang the melody we had forgotten to fear, sang the soft and hushed sound of our names.

---

THE QUESTION I HAVE to ask myself is probably the one you are asking: After all those years—twelve of them—did I really still believe that my father was on the moon? The truth is, of all the men from Maple Rock who disappeared so many years ago, not one of them has ever reappeared. We have done Internet searches and scanned phone books and hired private investigators. The truth is, they're gone. There's no trace.

It's possible that our fathers were geniuses, that they conducted an elaborate, organized, and flawlessly executed disappearance scheme that persisted for more than a decade. Or it's possible that their abandonment was more spontaneous, a simple case of one following another following another, and that they still roam, individually and aimlessly, around the earth. Or it is possible—as all things are possible—that they discovered a way to get to the moon, and that indeed they live a new and secret life there that we will never understand.

When I was a younger man, such thoughts obsessed me. I can admit that, because I believe that such a story would obsess any young man for years and years. But now as I get older, now that I am a father, to be honest, I no longer think about my father and all of the other disappeared men every day. There simply isn't the energy in my guts to worry about it anymore. There isn't the desire and pain that is necessary to fuel endless speculation and wonder. They were men who failed at something in my eyes, and failure is not something we dwell on in the Midwest, in Maple Rock.

In either case, I don't see much difference between the things that never happened and the things that are believed to have happened and the things that are inevitably going to happen. I don't see a whole world of difference between our deepest wishes and our deepest fears.

They all merge together eventually.

We do what we can.

FOR A LONG TIME that night, nobody knew what to do. We stood there in the parking lot, talking in low voices, looking around at the streets and the sky, waiting for an explanation or a sign. There were about two dozen of us by the time the stream of nighttime pedestrians and roaming headlights stopped coming into the parking lot. We talked in quiet groups, catching up with one another or talking about the day at work we just had. We told each other how we had arrived at this place, how our lives had gone or had been going or how they were striving to go. Our conversations were serious, perhaps even a bit melancholy, but really, there was nobody voicing any sort of disbelief or nervousness or shock at the spontaneous and mystical nature of our gathering. We had a common thread of memories. We had spent years believing in a story that nobody else really believed. We had been through things, and maybe we were like soldiers at the end of a long war, who watch with calm resignation as the air raids come into their cities. It was no surprise to us that our worlds would eventually lead us to this point.

Maybe we were waiting for something. Maybe we were waiting to be reunited with our fathers, maybe we believed they were about to be returned to the earth, or maybe we believed that we were about to be taken to the moon. Either way, nothing else happened. Around six in the morning, the sky quickly filled with light.

Like we were sixteen again, we all looked at Nick, and Nick said, "I'm going home."

So we did too.

I went home and slipped into bed next to Ella. I wasn't quite asleep when her alarm clock began to chime.

THAT MORNING, like any morning, I got out of bed and came downstairs for coffee. It was after ten o'clock, but because of my work schedule I often slept late. Nobody seemed to be suspicious of me. Rusty was in the living room watching *Sesame Street* and Nina was down for the first nap of the day. Ella was at the kitchen table, with a textbook open in front of her. She was in her white bathrobe, with wet hair, and she crossed her legs, which were tan and lean. I remember thinking that she looked like a good omen for the day—tangible and clean and real. She wrote tiny, barely legible notes in green ink on a yellow legal pad. The lines of her book were highlighted in blue and orange and yellow and pink, and next to the book were the four highlighters. It was a scene of order and ambition. In hopes of someday getting us into the realm of financial prosperity, Ella had started law school at Wayne State, at the urging of Sunny, who had become her best friend. Sunny hadn't finished her dissertation yet, not with two kids, but she was pushing Ella to finish school. Once, at a party, I overheard Sunny saying, "Look, it's not like every one of us has to give up on our dreams. You weren't born here. You have no reason to behave like the rest of us."

Ella looked up from her book for a second and muttered, "Fresh coffee."

Ella is not a morning person, but since I was working nights, she had to be the parent who got up early with the kids, made breakfast, and started the day. Understandably, she was not always in a good mood when I got up, but this morning she seemed particularly terse.

"A lot of work to do?" I said, sitting down across from her with my coffee. It did not taste fresh; it tasted bitter and burned, and so I got up and added milk and sugar to it.

"Yes," she said. She waited until I had my coffee and had taken a sip and then she asked, "Did you come home last night and then leave again? Did you leave after I called you to come upstairs and help with the baby?"

I sipped my coffee and leaned against the counter. With my white cotton pajamas, my messy hair, and my steaming Detroit Lions mug, I must have looked like the very symbol of domesticity—the sleepy and happy husband, the hapless sitcom dad in a minor bit of marital trouble—not someone who wanders off at night while his wife deals with an insomniac child and a squalling infant.

"What's that?" I said, though it must have been obvious that I'd heard her and was only stalling for more time. She did not repeat herself, and I was left to take a second to ponder the wisdom of lying about the night before.

"Yes," I said. "I did."

"Well, that's great, Michael. Why did you do that?"

"It was a rough night at work," I said. "Three kids were shot and I covered it."

"I saw it on the news this morning," she said. "I figured you were there."

"It was awful," I said, though, I have to be honest, I had not given it much thought since I'd been home. It sounded like a good excuse, but I'd become used to such tragedies while working the night shift in Detroit. They rarely kept me up at night anymore.

"You need a new line of work," she said.

"I know."

"Where did you go?" she said.

I shrugged.

"Wandering," I said. "I just kind of wandered."

WHEN ELLA LEFT for class, Nina woke up and I got a bottle of breast milk Ella had pumped and brought Nina into the family room where Rusty was still watching cartoons.

Nina looked just like Ella, in my opinion, already with a head of dark hair and big, watery eyes. But my mother said she looked like me.

A few nights after Nina was born, I woke from bad dreams and went into the front yard and sat down on the curb. We had the heat on fairly high for the baby, and I had woken up in a sweat, my face burning and my throat dry. I was happy, not even officially married for a year, yet already father of a newborn. My life had shifted so much in the last three years that some mornings I woke up and could hardly remember its details: I had a wife. I had a newborn daughter. My mother had remarried. My brother was in the army, overseas. I had a full-time job that paid better than minimum wage. I was in the process of officially adopting Rusty.

Thinking on these details out in the night air, my chest tightened. It was late March and still cold. I went back in the house, dressed quietly, took the car keys, and went back outside.

I went driving that night. I got into my car and headed down Mansfield Street, then north on Warren Avenue, which seemed to me to be the direction of the moon. Fat flakes of snow made their way down from the sky, crumbling onto my windshield and melting. I liked to leave the wipers off for ten seconds or so, just to cloud my vision a little. My heart pumped away, skipping beats, on the verge of implosion. I drove out of the city, out of Detroit and up toward Flint, then farther still, toward Alpena. By sunrise, I was very far away from the life I was living.

I don't know what made me turn around and head back home. I'd like to tell you that it was something altruistic, or some epiphany that appeared suddenly in front of me, but there was none of that. I just felt bad for leaving. I made up an excuse about being called in to work, and that was that. The next night, I stayed in bed where I was supposed to be.

I thought of that night while I sat in my home, the morning after we men gathered in the parking lot of the old Black Lantern. I was holding my baby, watching Rusty play with his toys in the family room. I was overwhelmed with love for them, for their tiny and innocent hearts.

I called Rusty up to the couch and let him hold the bottle and feed Nina with me.

But I worried—worried about the man who went driving north in the night, worried about the man who stared at the moon, worried about the man who felt his feet leave the ground when he went walking on a sleepless night. I worried because I knew that the man who did those things would do them again.

THAT AFTERNOON, on my way to work, I dropped the kids off at my mother's house in Northville. She was cleaning the screens of the house, and was dressed in shorts and a Maple Rock High T-shirt, and wore a blue kerchief around her head. She was tan and had lost weight. She had recently begun to take a yoga class at the Y.

She wiped her hands and came down the front yard to meet us.

She took Nina from me and Rusty skipped up to her side, singing, "Grandma!" He had never had grandparents he knew until my mother and Mack entered his six-year-old life like some great and sudden dream. I was happy for him, happy for my mother and Mack, who seemed just as delighted by his existence as he seemed by theirs.

"Well, Ma," I said, "I have to get to work."

"So soon?" she said. "I didn't think you started until seven."

She was right, I didn't, but I lied and said someone had called in sick and I was covering a shift so they could leave. The explanation was clumsy and I mumbled most of it, and my mother said, "What's wrong with you, Michael?"

"What?" I said.

"Something's not right with you today," she said.

Her face had shifted from annoyance to concern to fear.

"Michael, what aren't you telling me?"

"Nothing, Ma," I said.

She looked like she might cry. It had been a rough summer for her. Kolya had been stationed in the Persian Gulf for most of it, and she watched the news too much and spent her days angry and nervous. But I wondered, what did she sense in me that afternoon? The last thing I could tell her about was the night before, my old friends and me staring at the moon. What could I tell her about the way the world felt? How could I explain that I thought, maybe, that it was getting too small for me? What could I say about the way my feet felt ready to drift off the earth, carry me away?

"Love you, Ma," I said, and got in my car and drove away.

NICK WAS IN THE front yard with Natalie, his oldest daughter. She was running around the grass patting a beach ball, and she started laughing when I pulled into the driveway. She recognized my car. "Moo," she said, when I got out of the car. "Moo."

This was what she called me.

"Why does she call me that?" I asked Nick.

"She thinks you're full of bullshit," Nick said.

Sunny came out to the front porch. "Hi, Mikey," she said. "Come on inside and get washed up for dinner, Natalie."

Once they got Natalie to agree to go inside, Sunny said,

"Maybe you can get Nick to tell you where he goes at night, Mikey."

I looked at Nick, and he motioned for me to follow him to the garage. He got two beers out of the fridge he kept there.

"I guess you know why I'm here," I said.

"Free beer?"

"What happened last night?" I said. "What was that?"

"You know what it was," he said.

"But you don't believe that," I said. "Do you?"

"What else do you believe?" he said.

I shrugged. I had to get to work.

"It didn't get us yet," Nick said.

Natalie had come back outside to where we were sitting and she wriggled her way onto Nick's lap.

"Eventually, it might," Nick said. "Eventually, it might win."

THAT FALL, I WAS switched to the day shift. Driving the news truck in the glare and shadow of the bright autumn afternoons hurt my eyes, and I could never take off my sunglasses, a cheap pair of aviator shades I'd picked up at the Rite Aid. I'd not gotten into the habit of shaving in the mornings, and I wore a few days' worth of stubble most of the time. With the heavy equipment on my shoulder, the glasses, and the beard, I looked like an extra from a bad war film.

I felt disoriented in the truck, with all the sounds and lights of daytime traffic around me, and I missed those long, quiet nights, when at two in the morning I could be the only car in my lane for miles. Merging in and out of traffic on Telegraph Road and the Lodge Freeway exhausted me, and I'd come home in the evenings with a quiet, racing heart and shaky hands. It was good for me to be home with the family at dinnertime, and my mother and Mack loved being with Rusty and Nina when I was working and Ella was at class. Mack would pick up Rusty from third grade every afternoon and bring him to our house where my mother was looking after Nina. More often than not, my mother would cook a big dinner and when Ella came home from class and I came home from work, we'd sit down together as a family and eat.

We were blessed, and I knew that. It wasn't this tranquil, if dull, domesticity that rattled me that fall. I didn't feel smothered by any of it. Instead, I felt a profound and relentless doubt; I didn't believe I belonged there. I believed, sooner or later, that I would destroy all of it.

Most nights, I couldn't sleep: I couldn't stop thinking of the night we'd all wandered into the parking lot of the old Black Lantern, staring at the sky. The end of each day brought voices, starlight, the fading sound of machines, the constant grinding of wheels on pavement, the smell of smoke, a thick layer of burning ash, and then when I did finally drift into dreams, they were dreams that left me still half awake, not dreaming really, just drifting, floating off to somewhere else. I'd stay in bed and wait for the dreams to pass, for the feeling of floating to pass; I tried to ignore the recollections that came at me in fragments and jagged shards. I would just tough it out some nights, stay stone-faced and sober until morning, and then I would get up, not rested but restless, and the world was awake and bursting with dawn all around me.

Ella's worry and confusion turned to annoyance. We were short with each other. She urged me to find a therapist or consider medication; we made love less and less often as the days got colder. Sometimes I didn't come to bed at all, but stayed in my chair in the living room, in my state of half sleep.

At work my job performance suffered. I made careless mistakes. I mislabeled tapes. I didn't verify my facts. I misquoted my sources.

My mother would come to visit the children, and I would barely talk to her. She would forward me e-mails from Kolya when he was able to get a few minutes on the computer at his base, but I never wrote to him. I had his mailing address, but didn't even send him a postcard.

Nick and Tom said I was acting strange. "Man," they said, "you just have to forget some things, Mikey. Not everything is important. Pretend it never happened."

"What if it happens again?" I said.

"You can never be sure, Mikey," Nick said. "Don't ask 'What if?' so much. You'll drive yourself crazy."

BY THE MIDDLE OF November, the gold-and-red leaves had been erased from the trees, and the air turned relentless once again, windy and damp. The skies held the color and smell of wet concrete. In the mornings, the bare black branches of trees were slick with frost and mist, skeletons of obsolete machines.

I went to see Nick one day on my way home from work.

He was in the garage in his jeans and quilted flannel shirt. He'd grown his beard again, and when I pulled up, I noticed his face had gotten thinner. His sad blue eyes stood out from his shadowed face like pale, smooth stones.

He offered me some coffee from his thermos, and handed me a chipped Lions mug. We sat on two milk crates. I took a sip of my coffee and held the cup to my face long enough for the heat to warm the skin of my cheeks and lips.

There was something unbearable, that year, about the thought of another winter. I found the fact that each day grew a little more cold and damp almost terrifying. I was having that feeling just then, when Nick said, "I make most of my money in the winter. But this year, I'm starting to wish the winter would never come. I don't trust this winter. I feel like bad things are going to happen to us this winter."

A FEW WEEKS LATER, I woke up around midnight. I'd had only two hours of sleep. I heard, from Rusty's room, the dinging of Lucky the Dog's collar and tags. He was scratching himself, or maybe moving into Rusty's bed for a better, warmer sleeping spot, but whatever he was doing, he kept on doing it. The room felt cramped and hot, and then I heard Lucky's collar again. I was facing the wall, tucked into that side of the bed because Ella could not sleep next to a wall. I got out of bed, climbing over Ella's naked body. She didn't stir.

In the hallway, I flipped on the light and squinted into the yellow glare. At the thermostat, I rubbed my eyes and turned the furnace down a few degrees. Just before I made my way back to the bedroom, Lucky the Dog appeared in the doorway, his leash in his mouth. We had forgotten, I supposed, to take him for a walk before bed.

Outside, the night was cold but lush. The first snow of the season was coming down in thick flakes. A small covering of white powder was dusting the sidewalks and streets. It had turned windy, and the trees and shrubs on my street, some leafless, made a snapping, rustling sound as they moved in the wind among the snowflakes. My hair blew back, and I had goose bumps. Lucky the Dog sniffed at the air and sucked the wind in through his cheeks. It was late, nobody was out. I let Lucky off the leash and he sprinted up and down the sidewalk, ecstatic to be free, sniffing and marking every tree and fire hydrant he could find.

I looked at the moon and walked ahead, following the dog. More clouds seemed to be merging with their purple shadows and the stars were disappearing. I felt tiny droplets of snow hit my forehead. The rate of snowfall grew more intense. I kept my eyes on the ripe, heavy moon, until it was lost in the clouds. It was hard to keep my eyes open with the swirling snow. My body left the sidewalk, and I stepped in midair for one, two, three, four strides, getting higher and higher, as if I was walking up an invisible set of steps. I was walking straight up to the moon, off of the earth, free of gravity, released.

Just then, Lucky the Dog started barking. I fell out of the sky and onto the grass. Lucky ran at me full tilt, halted at my fallen figure, and licked my face, whining. It was just a dream, he seemed to be saying, just a dream. I shook my head, pushed the dog away, and slowly stood up again. We stayed where we had stopped for twenty minutes or more, just kind of looking around, me searching the sky and Lucky sniffing the wind.

By the time we turned and headed back, it was a little after one in the morning. There were very few cars on Warren Avenue, and the snow was falling harder so that the few cars on the road seemed to be moving in slow motion. I put Lucky back on the leash and we went home.

Back in my own house, I went into the living room and turned off all the lights in the house as well as the light on the front porch. I opened the curtains and moved an armchair into the middle of the room, so I could look out of the picture window and out onto the street. The snow was coming down harder now, and it was difficult to see even the large shrubs at the end of our yard. Above, the streetlamps illuminated halos of falling flakes, turning the sky blurry and pink in the air above the roofs of our houses.

I got up and made some coffee, then returned to the window and waited to hear the sound of Nick's truck coming down the street. Because of budget cuts, the city always ran behind on plowing snow from the residential areas. Last winter, Nick had started to plow a few of the neighborhood streets himself. He did our driveways for us, too, if the snow was particularly heavy, and my driveway was usually first.

By dawn, Nick still hadn't plowed my driveway. I had the day off and I didn't have to be anywhere, so I didn't care. But I also knew that Nick had always gotten started before first light in the past. I hoped that he simply had too many paying customers this season and was too busy to do anybody any favors. The day grew lighter and lighter and the snow continued to pile up in our yards, on our cars, on the sills of our windows. Rusty had a snow day and got to stay home from school, and I stayed inside with the baby while Ella and Rusty built a snowman in the yard. Around eleven o'clock, Sunny was calling. I picked up the phone and she said, "Michael, where is he?"

His truck was missing. His clients had been calling all morning, wanting to know why he hadn't arrived yet to clear their parking lots and roadways.

By noon, Maple Rock had eight inches of snow, and nobody had plowed our streets. I knew what was happening. I could almost picture Nick driving north, or worse, parking his truck somewhere and walking off into the air. Ella asked me if I was going to shovel the driveway. Like all the garages in Maple Rock, ours was a detached structure in the backyard, at the end of a long, narrow driveway. Ella had class that evening and needed to get the car out, but so much snow had blown in through the open garage door that the car itself needed some digging out.

"I could do it," she said. "Would you like me to do it?"

"No," I said. "I'll go and do the walk. Nick will be by soon. He'll plow the driveway."

After I cleared off the front porch and walkways, I bundled up in my hunting boots and down jacket and walked the few blocks to Nick and Sunny's house. I stood on the front porch for a little while before I rang the doorbell.

I waved my gloved hand at Sunny when she opened the door.

"Don't you tell me what you're going to tell me, Michael," she said. "I don't believe in the bullshit you guys believe in. I'm not that naïve."

"I just wanted you to know something," I said.

"What?"

"Nick loves you," I said. "He'll be back soon."

From the way Sunny looked—the way her arms were folded, the way her body weight rested on her left leg, the way her eyes seemed too tired to look up at me and focus on my face—I knew that she wasn't sure if she should believe anything I was saying.

I wasn't sure if I believed all of it, but I knew that the first part was true.

One day passed, and then a second.

A full week went by, and the next one started.

Nick stayed away. All that week, the snow piled up on our streets.

VALENTINE "BUNNY" Slowinski was found dead on December 5, 2003, in a Super 8 Motel, just off the interstate in Effingham, Illinois. He had been living there for three weeks, the manager said, paying $120 in cash every Monday morning. He had just taken a job at a Home Depot nearby. The night he died, he had come back to his room after his first day, an eleven-hour stint in the lawn and garden section. He heated a can of spaghetti on a hot plate, turned on CNN, and died of a massive heart attack. He was fifty-four years old. The smoke alarm went off in the room a few hours later—because of the burning can of spaghetti—and the night clerk found Bunny dead.

"Bunny was a nice man," the motel manager said on the phone. "He was working here part-time to pay his bill."

"That's nice to know," Mrs. Slowinski said, before she started crying again. "I hate him, you understand."

"I'm sure you have your reasons," the manager said. "We watched *Monday Night Football* at Applebee's last week. Bunny was a Bears fan too, unless they were playing the Lions."

Mrs. Slowinski said, "No, I don't hate him."

"I'm sorry," the manager said. "This must be hard."

"Oh God, Bunny," Mrs. Slowinski said. "What were you thinking?"

And the manager said, "We're very sorry, ma'am."

Tom came over and told me the news, and we called down to the motel a few minutes later. Tom did the talking while I listened in on the extension.

"Well, it was very odd how he showed up here," the manager said. "It was early in the morning and I had been taking the trash out to the Dumpsters, when I saw this man in a dirty white shirt, walking out of the acres of empty fields behind the hotel. He had no luggage except for a brown grocery bag, and his face was covered in dust. He had a rather large cut on his arm, and I asked him if he needed help. And he said, 'No, just a room.' When I took him around the building to the front desk, he pulled out an old wallet. He said his credit cards had expired years ago, and his driver's license—which I require from all of our guests—had expired in 1992. But I could see he needed some help, so I offered him a room for free, just so he could clean up, drink some water, and sleep. I sent my son into town to the Wal-Mart, and I got him a change of clothes. I could see he was in trouble. All alone in the world."

"Thank you," Tom said.

"It was the Christian thing to do," he said. "What would Jesus do? My wife is into all of that."

The news of Bunny Slowinski's mysterious reappearance and death spread across our neighborhood and into the suburbs and cities far away, and by evening, a stream of friends and family came to Tom and Tanya's home. Tanya worked in the kitchen with other women from the neighborhood, fixing sandwiches and borscht and potato salad, while Tom held his sons and showed them off to the visitors. My mother and my aunt Maria greeted friends and family as they arrived. People stood in circles and spoke softly. To be honest, if it hadn't been for Mrs. Slowinski sitting and crying, exhausted and pale, in a small rocking chair in the corner, the evening might have felt like any of the gatherings we used to have in our neighborhood, a first communion or christening or graduation party.

The new priest from the Ukrainian church, Father Marion, a tall, bearded man who had just arrived from Ukraine, came to the home and said prayers. He didn't seem to know how many of us had stopped going to church in recent years, or maybe he didn't care. He walked around and gave a lot of warm hugs, but he couldn't really know what the discovery of Bunny Slowinski meant to the rest of us. The house was full of our old friends, the mothers of our old friends, and small packs of old men we hadn't seen in years. Tom's grandparents drove down from Toronto to mourn their son. The house smelled of the wool of heavy winter coats and rye bread and beets.

We all gathered there because we were good friends,

because the Slowinskis were part of the extended family of Maple Rock. But mostly, I think, the mourning over Bunny—a good, well-loved, and funny man when we knew him—was so vast and intense because the discovery of the dead body of Valentine "Bunny" Slowinski meant one thing: he was not on the moon, and maybe nobody was.

THE NEXT MORNING, well before it was light out, Ella and I woke up and drank coffee together. I could tell she was worried about me, and usually, when she is worried, I try to reassure her. I try to convince her that my sadness is temporary, that my dark moods and depressive spells will be gone soon enough. Sometimes I feel like marriage is one long lifetime of reassuring each other of our sanity. But that morning, I felt sadness that didn't seem capable of ending, and when Ella came and put her hands on my shoulders, I just hung my head and cried. Then we showered together, and I packed a bag and dressed. I kissed Rusty and Nina while they slept in their beds. Just as I finished lacing up my boots, Tom pulled into the driveway with his van and I kissed Ella goodbye. She handed me a thermos of coffee and walked me down the driveway, where she hugged me again and then pressed her fingertips to the windshield and smiled at Tom.

Tom and I pulled out of the driveway with a few flakes of snow falling onto the windshield. Tom was playing a tape of Ukrainian music that his father liked. I thought it bordered on the maudlin, but I didn't say anything. Who knows how I might have acted if my father had been the one they'd found dead in a Super 8 Motel?

Our journey was a maudlin one, to be sure. The hotel manager in Effingham had arranged for a mortician to embalm the body and prepare a casket. Tom and I were on our way down to pick up the casket and drive it back to Detroit for the funeral. There were services you could hire for this kind of thing, but Tom insisted he didn't have the money. That was probably true, but part of me believed and still believes that he craved this road trip as a ritual, that he longed to drive and get his father's body back because it would make the surreal situation seem more real, make it mean something. I knew he was mad at Nick for not being there, and I was too.

It was three in the morning, and I-94 was empty and dark, the only traffic an occasional semi passing us on the left, blowing a smoky dust of snow over the windshield. The forecast included the possibility of an early-winter blizzard. By the time we made it to the long, flat stretch of I-57 that runs down through Illinois, blowing snow would occasionally swell up from the endless prairies and obscure our vision. The going was slow. We took turns driving, but neither of us slept. The roads seemed treacherously empty, and the areas around us flat and gray in all directions, and for a minute, I thought perhaps we'd driven off the earth.

When we reached Effingham, it was daylight and the snow had stopped and we were most definitely still on the earth.

THERE WAS A SMALL BOX of Bunny Slowinski's belongings at the Super 8, in which these things were found: a collection of rough, gray pebbles in a Milwaukee Pickles jar; a handful of dirt in a sealed plastic bag; and an assortment of autumn-painted leaves, pressed dry and flat into the pages of a hardcover copy of *Awaken the Giant Within*. These things were returned to the Slowinskis, along with the remains of Bunny Slowinski.

Also this: an unsealed Super 8 envelope, with Tom's name on it. The envelope sat on top of a blank sheet of Super 8 stationary and a Super 8 pen. The only words on the stationery were *Dear Tom, There's no.*

We must have looked exhausted, because the clerk at the Super 8 offered us a free room to sleep in for a few hours, but instead we asked for directions to the funeral home, which was just up the street, sandwiched between a Kinko's and a Dairy Queen. We paid the funeral home director, and he let Tom have a few moments alone with the body before we loaded the casket into the van.

I started out driving on the way home. We stopped at a Wendy's and got some burgers and Cokes, and the mood shifted. As we pulled back on the interstate, even with the body of Bunny Slowinski in a casket behind us, we started to make jokes.

Tom said, "You know, I fucking *tried* to get a job at Home Depot and couldn't. And my fucking dad is down here working for them and nobody knows about it."

We laughed the best we could. We passed a gorgeous red-haired woman in a red pickup truck. She was wearing a red bathrobe, and Tom smiled and waved frantically. He swore to me that she opened her robe and flashed her breasts at him before she gunned her accelerator and left us behind.

"Bullshit," I said.

"You miss everything, Mikey," Tom said. "I swear, she winked and then gave me a show."

The snow had stopped, the sun reflected off the white fields, and we found a classic rock station out of Champaign-Urbana. We had Zeppelin playing. Tom lit a cigarette when he finished his cheeseburgers. If you passed us—the van could barely get up to sixty-five—you might have thought we were on our way to a hunting lodge up north or something. You wouldn't have guessed about the cargo we were hauling back home.

Sometime around the Indiana border, Tom said, "Did you see the rocks he had with him? The bag of dirt?"

"Yeah, what about them?" I said.

"Moon dust," Tom said. "Rocks from the moon."

"Tom," I said.

"It is," he said. "Moon rocks."

"You could take them to the university," I said. "I bet you could have a professor there look at them. Somebody could tell you for sure what kind of rocks they are."

"No way," Tom said. "I'm not trusting some professor with this stuff."

"Tom," I said.

"I believe it, Mikey, and that's that."

We didn't say anything again until we hit Michigan, where the lake effect snow started up and made the air heavy and foggy.

"I can't believe that's my dad back there," Tom said.

"He's not back there," I said, "That's just a body. He's with God now."

"God?" Tom said. "What have you seen to make you believe in that?"

The windshield was dense with mist and outside the snow rushed across the road in a blur. Tom fiddled with the heat and defrost buttons for a minute, which made the windshield fog up even worse.

"Do something," Tom said. "I can't see."

WHEN WE GOT BACK to Detroit, the snow was falling in great blinding walls and we skidded onto Livernois and fishtailed the van into the parking lot of Salowich and Stevens Funeral Home. Mr. Stevens was waiting for us in a suit at the entrance, his face sober. Some of his assistants helped us get the casket out of the van, and Mr. Stevens assured us the body would be ready for the funeral procession and Mass the next day.

Tom and I headed up Michigan Avenue back to Maple Rock. The streets were still snowy, and that meant Nick was not home. Tom dropped me off at my door. I asked him if he wanted to come in, but he said he'd better go check on Tanya and the kids and his mother.

"Thanks," he said. "For doing this."

"You'd have done it for me," I said.

"That's what you think," he said.

"Fucking Polack," I said, and shut the door of the van.

It was after midnight, but Ella was still awake. I held her, and she buried her face in my neck and started to cry. She was not a crier, and I worried that something bad had happened while we were gone.

"What is it?" I said.

"I'm just glad that you're home."

"Any word from Nick?" I said.

"None," she said.

"How's Sunny?"

"Not good. Your mother and Maria are over there with her."

"Huh," I said.

"Michael, you don't know where he is, do you?"

"No," I said. I had an idea, sure, a great fear of where he might have gone, but it seemed too ridiculous and painful to say it.

We went into Rusty's room and watched him sleeping in his bed, his covers kicked off, his arms wrapped around Lucky the Dog, who looked up at us and thumped his tail on the bed. It still sometimes was odd to me to see another young boy in what used to be Kolya's room. I'd see Rusty in there, and I'd feel like I was a teenager again, looking at my kid brother.

Ella and I went into our room, and watched Nina sleeping in the crib next to our bed. A mobile hung above her bed, and I watched the blue-and-green light it cast rotate on Nina's tiny face. She sighed in her sleep, kicked one foot and then the other, and was still again. At that moment, with Ella's small frame slumped against my body, it was almost impossible for me to imagine the feeling that my father or Bunny Slowinski or Nick had in their hearts on the nights they slipped away.

———

THE NEXT MORNING we arrived at the funeral home in our dark suits and overcoats, me and Tom and two of Tom's uncles from Toronto and Pete Stolowitz and J. J. Dempsey. In the chapel, we hoisted up the casket and loaded it into the hearse. We followed the hearse in our old Fords down the snowy streets, past the alleys full of garbage and the abandoned cars and the boarded-up and burned-out houses. We turned on to Clippert and passed a family of Mexicans bundled up against the cold, and they stopped and bowed their heads and made the sign of the cross. We drove across the potholes, and our cars shook and our hearts rattled like there was gravel in our chests.

When we got out of our cars, we could hear the crying of the women already, my mother and Aunt Maria and Mrs. Slowinski dressed in black and headed up the slick concrete steps of the old church. They wept when they saw us stepping out of our cars into the cold morning, wept with a decade's worth of despair, as if whatever was happy in their present lives had disappeared that morning.

The domes of St. John's looked flat and cold in the sky above us, and the red brick of the church was the color of rust. In our dress shoes, we slipped and struggled to hold our footing, the heavy casket pulling on our arms and shaking because Tom could not stop shaking. In the church, the light was dim and the smell of candles and incense and damp wood and cough drops made us dizzy. We walked down the red carpet to the altar, the priest in his robes ahead of us, the tired gold of the icons shining in front of us. The choir began to sing, "Lord have mercy, Lord have mercy." We set the casket at the front of the church, and Mr. Stevens, walking behind us, opened the top half of it, and I saw for the first time, for the first time in almost thirteen years, the face of Valentine "Bunny" Slowinski.

The choir droned from the balcony, and the seraphim and cherubim swirled around the head of Jesus above us. Ella and Rusty and Nina sat in the pew next to me and my mother and Mack, and Aunt Maria sat behind us, holding her Rosary, with Sunny and the kids next to her. It was hard to look at any of them, and I started to feel light and my head spun and I thought maybe I would black out and start to float up along with the blue smoke of incense to the icon of Jesus in the Jordan River

The priest sang in Ukrainian, in the relentless and pleading voice of the divine liturgy: "With the just spirits who have reached their end, give repose to the souls of Your servants, O Savior, keeping them in the happiness of life in Your presence, O You who love mankind. In Your abode, O Lord, where all Your saints repose, give rest also to the souls of Your servants, for You alone love mankind. Glory be to the Father and to the Son and to the Holy Spirit."

Just as I was about to pass out, I thought I heard Tom's moaning cry, and I stood up and walked out along the side of the church to get some air.

There was still no sun. The snow kept falling, piling up in high drifts along the road, tinted black from the exhaust of passing cars.

The priest sang behind me: "Christ, our true God, who has power over the living and the dead, through the prayers of His immaculate Mother; of the holy, glorious, and all-praiseworthy apostles; of our venerable and godly fathers, and of all the saints, will place the soul of His servant Valentine Slowinski which has departed from us, in the mansions of the just, and will give him rest in the bosom of Abraham, and number him among the just, and will have mercy on us, for He is good and loves mankind."

Behind me, I heard the choir respond with "Amen," and the parishioners and the priest begin singing the Ukrainian funeral hymn "Vichnaya Pamyat," "Eternal Memory," and without even thinking about it, I stood on the steps of the church, looking out at the hopeless neighborhood, and, as if by rote, softly sang the refrain.

Feeling better, I went back inside the church, walked up along the side, and slipped back into my pew between Ella and my mother. Nina was asleep in her carrier, and Ella could not seem to stop looking at her. Rusty crawled on my lap and whispered, "What's wrong?" in my ear. A few minutes later, Tom and his mother and their family came to the front of the church for a final viewing of the body. You could hear Tom whisper to his sons, "That was your grandfather."

And Tanya whispered, "Thomas. No."

Then the casket was closed.

I got up with the other pallbearers and went to the front of the church. Tom and I took the handles in the front. The choir was singing "Vichnaya Pamyat" again. Smoke from the incense floated around our heads. I nodded at Tom, and he tried his best to nod back. The doors of the church opened, letting in the whitewashed light of the December morning. The walls in the back of the church were lined with men in dark overcoats, glum and slouching, and in the corner, beneath the final station of the cross, I thought—for a minute, I was sure—that I saw Nick standing there, watching us. I was so sure of this, that, after we loaded the casket in the hearse, I spent a few minutes darting around the congregation, looking for Nick's bearded face, his blue eyes, listening for his voice. But he wasn't there.

AFTER THE BURIAL, after I had stood at a the side of the grave at St. Hedwig's with my wife and my children, after I visited the graves of my long-dead grandparents, after I shook the hands and clasped the shoulders of so many people I might never see again, I found Tom smoking a cigarette by the maintenance shed. The afternoon was already slipping into the evening. The sky had cleared.

Yes, there was a moon. Yes, it was full.

Perhaps you read this now and think of us as fools, consider us naïve for believing as long as we believed that you had gone to the moon, for believing that some day you'd come home.

But look:

Is there some happiness in Maple Rock?

Of course, there is!

Still, that doesn't change everything. It doesn't change this:

Like an eye, the moon follows us wherever we go.

# acknowledgments

I OWE MANY THINGS to many people. Here goes. First of all, thanks to my editor, Becky Saletan, for her enthusiasm, intelligence, and vision, and to everybody at Harcourt who helped pull this together, including André Bernard, Stacia Decker, Laurie Brown, Jennifer Gilmore, Patty Berg, and Paul Von Drasek.

Also to the good folks at the University of Wisconsin-Madison MFA program, who provided focus, funding, and their amazing instruction in the nick of time: Lorrie Moore, Coach Judy Mitchell, Ron Wallace, Jesse Lee Kercheval, and Amy Quan Barry. Also to the University of Michigan, where these people first gave the go sign: Nick Delbanco, Andrea Beauchamp, Daniel Lyons, Janet Mendler, and especially Charles "Pa" Baxter and Eileen "Ma" Pollack who were never too busy to offer encouragement and advice.

Thanks to my brother-in-law, Jeremiah Chamberlin, and my sister, Natalie Bakopoulos, for their friendship, editorial advice, and good humor. To my mother, Luba Bakopoulos, and my grandparents, Gregory and Eva Smolij, who taught me, above all, to live with a big heart. Many thanks to my father, George Bakopoulos, and his wife, Pat, for their unyielding love and support. Also to Chet and Ginny Okopski for their unflagging belief and friendship and to Rachel Okopski for a cheerful willingness to help. And to Madeleine Thien, our dear friend, who's been there for the wild ride and the long haul.

Thanks to Francis Coppola's *Zoetrope: All-Story* and especially to Adrienne Brodeur, who first said yes, and to Holly Rothman who said, "Keep going." To the wonderful people behind the Sewanee Writers' Conference—Cheri Peters, Wyatt Prunty, and Phil Stephens—and to Richard Bausch and Tony Earley for their helpful pep talks. Big bad love to my Murfreesboro pals: Ben Percy, Lisa Lerner, Kathleen Hughes, and Holiday Reinhorn. Thanks to the Vermont Studio Center for a Pleasant T. Rowland Fellowship, and to Jason Bellipani, who made the month dangerous and fun. Thanks to the staff of the Christine Center in Willard, Wisconsin, for spiritual sustenance and the perfect hermitage for a writer.

Also to these fine friends for many gifts: Martin and Melissa Scanlan, Steve Myck, Mike and Molly Strigel, Mark Benno, Greg and Connie Parker, Jim and Maria Duncan, Denise Miller and Raul Mendez, Stephen Bunker and Dena Wortzel, Becky Mitchell and Jim Thoreson, and Herbert Hill. And to my Madison writing group: Heather Lee Schroeder, Guy Thorvaldsen, Andrew McQuaig, Heather Skyler, Ron Kuka, and especially Tenaya Darlington, who made me send in this book. Thanks to Trudy Barash of Canterbury Booksellers for giving me a job buying books, and thanks to all of my fellow booksellers. To teachers Ron

Quick and Jane O'Brien and coach Doug Buckler for their profound influence. To Mike Gravina, Alex Goecke, and the rest of the crew: Stibbs, Noone, Brent P., Freeborn, Petey, Norm, Tough Pig, Gordo, and Brain for so much material and also thanks to the gentlemen of 300 E. Jefferson.

Finally, to four people who have made all the difference: Elwood Reid, who showed me the light over and over again and taught me what work is; Mark Gates, sales rep extraordinaire, for generosity and friendship above and beyond the call; my agent and pal, Amy Williams, for her tenacity, wisdom, and patience; and finally to my wife, Amanda Okopski, for bringing creativity, wonder, passion, and joy to me on a daily basis.